Constance Santego

Language of a Soul

Constance Santego has been practicing and teaching *The Nine Spiritual Gifts, Granted From Spirit,* for over twenty-three years. She lives in British Columbia, Canada, with her husband.

www.constancesantego.ca

ALSO BY CONSTANCE SANTEGO

FICTION
The Nine Spiritual Gifts Series
Journey of a Soul – (Vol. I Michael)

NON-FICTION
The Intuitive Life, The Gift of Prophecy, Third Edition
Fairy Tales, Dreams and Reality… Where Are You On Your Path? Second Edition
Your Persona… The Mask You Wear
Angelic Lifestyle, A Vibrant Lifestyle
Angelic Lifestyle 42-Day Energy Cleanse
Archangel Michael's Soul Retrieval Guide
SECRETS OF A HEALER, SERIES:
Magic of Aromatherapy (Vol. I)
Magic of Reflexology (Vol. II)
Magic of The Gifts (Vol. III)
Magic of Muscle Testing (Vol. IV)
Magic of Iridology (Vol. V)
Magic of Massage (Vol. VI)
Magic of Hypnotherapy (Vol. VII)
Magic of Reiki (Vol. VIII)
Magic of Advanced Aromatherapy (Vol. IX)
Magic of Esthetics (Vol. X)

FOR CHILDREN
I am big tonight. I don't need the light!

Language of a Soul
The Gift of Tongues

A Novel
2nd in the series, The Nine Spiritual Gifts
"The Gift of Tongues"

Constance Santego

Vol. 2

LANGUAGE OF A SOUL
Copyright © 2021 by Constance Santego.
All rights reserved. No part of this publication may
be reproduced, distributed, or transmitted in any form
or by any means, including photocopying, recording,
or other electronic or mechanical methods, without
the prior written permission of the publisher, except
in the case of brief quotations embodied in critical
reviews and certain other non-commercial uses
permitted by copyright law. For permission requests,
write to the publisher, addressed "Attention:
Permissions Coordinator," at the address below.

Published by
Editor: Ana Joldes
Interior Layout: Constance Santego
Book Layout: ©2017 BookDesignTemplates.com
Cover Design: Jennifer Louie
Soft Cover ISBN: 978-1-990062-03-2
eBook ISBN: 978-1-990062-04-9
Created and published in Canada. Printed and bound
in the United States of America
Ordering Information: csantego@gmail.com

Dedicated

to Nefertiti, my first

encounter

with a channeled soul!

Language of a Soul

The Nine Spiritual Gifts

In the New Testament, my favorite story is "The Gifts."
Corinthians 1, Chapter 12, Verse 4-11
(It may be a little differently worded
depending on which Bible you have).

The variety and the unity of gifts
There are many different gifts, but it is always
the same Spirit; there are many different ways of
serving, but it is always the same Lord. There
are many different forms of activity, but it is the
same God who is at work in them all in
everybody. The particular manifestation of the
Spirit granted to each one is to be used for the
general good.
To one is given from the Spirit the gift of
utterance expressing **wisdom**; to another the gift
of utterance expressing **knowledge**; in
accordance with the same spirit to another, **faith**,
from the same Spirit; and to another, the gifts of
healing, through the same Spirit; to another, the
working of **miracles**; to another **prophecy**; to
another, the power of **distinguishing spirits**; to
one, the gift of **different tongues** and to another,
the **interpretation of tongues**. But at work in all
these is one and the same Spirit, distributing
them at will to each individual.
The New Jerusalem Bible

Awaken to the spirit world, for there lie your gifts granted by Spirit.

Constance Santego

Fact:

All biblical references, science, and Tamara's (Constance's) teaching matter is real *(slightly changed to fit the characters).*

Most locations and characters are fictional.

This novel was written as a story inspired by Spirit to give you, the reader, a new perspective, a new way to learn the nine spiritual gifts, and an opportunity to empower your life.

Prologue

The first novel in this "The Nine Spiritual Gifts" series was about learning to "Distinguish Spirits." How to tell spirits apart, how to test them, and what happens to a soul when it dies. Archangel Michael is the angel that you can pray to to help you get rid of evil spirits or help lost souls go home.

Tamara was sitting at her desk, deciding what to type.

Her next lecture was coming up soon, and she had to finish the description so that she could send out the emails and post the event on her website.

I have talked about one of the nine spiritual gifts granted by spirit, "Distinguishing Spirits." In my first set of lectures, I spoke about the spirit world being real.

She decided to start by creating a checklist to review what she had already taught.

- ✓ I talked about the journey of a soul and the two most important aspects a person needs to remember before they die.
  - o To believe in love-light energy.
  - o To have led a virtuous life.
- ✓ I talked about ghosts and the importance of not becoming one.
- ✓ I talked about dark entities and the importance of testing a spirit.
- ✓ I talked about removing an entity or attachment from a person.
- ✓ I talked about reincarnation and past lives.
- ✓ I talked about virtue and sin.
- ✓ I talked about how to pass through the pearly gates.

What difference does it make if a person believes that a soul has an afterlife or that ghosts are real?

The real question should be, how can I help? My clients come to me to talk to their beloved ones, the people they loved that have left this earthly plane. What if I could teach them how to do it themselves?

That's it. That's my next lecture. I will talk about the gift of tongues and how to speak and interpret the spirit world's divine language.

With this new inspiration, Tamara started to type her next lecture's advertisement.

No matter how much time goes by, there will always be days where you will miss and think of your loved ones that passed. Days that you wish more than anything that you could hear her voice, see his smile, or feel the warmth of their embrace.

How many times have you wanted to phone and tell them something special, then remember they are not available to take your call? How many days, weeks, months, or years has it been since you could connect with them?

What if you could have one more moment with them? What if you knew how to communicate in the sacred language of the spirit world?

Come and learn the Language of the Soul.

In this second book of the series, "Language of a Soul," the focus is on "Tongues," how to communicate with a spirit and how spirit tries to communicate with us. Archangel Gabriel is the angel to pray to to help deliver God's messages to you and for inspiration and creativity.

Chapter 1

The blue spotlight was on her, and the color from the light inspired Isabella to take a breath and play her role.

She had beautiful regal blue eyes, painted to look like a goddess. Her hair was as dark as night and reached her shoulders, with bangs that accented those sexy eyes. Her head was adorned with a web of jewels that sparkled in the light as she moved. Barely five-foot-five, she elegantly wore a floor-length gown that seemed enchanted, so silky smooth, with a sash tied gently around her slim waist. The softest leather sandals cradled her feet.

Many called her "majesty," some "braved Queen," but very few ever called her by her new name, Cleopatra, Queen of the Nile. She was born into an era that required strength and hope.

"We desire riches, fame, and success, but in life, most of us desire love," she said in her bed-chamber as she looked out into the night's sky.

Thirty-five-year-old Isabella Jackson was the actress playing the part of Cleopatra and knew that to excel in this movie, she needed the audience to believe that she was Cleopatra.

Her confidence and inner beauty shone through in all that she said, how she moved, what she wore, but it was her inner knowing of a Goddess that guided her to play her part so magnificently.

After filming a few hours of the dailies, as the film business likes to call the unedited footage shots for the movie, Isabella went back to her dressing room. Her living quarters had been in a very extravagant recreational vehicle for the last few months, with air conditioning and all the bells and whistles. Not that Isabella even noticed the temperature in Egypt these days.

I don't think I can go on like this… not without him.

It had been a couple of years since that first day she set eyes on him. She intuitively knew that she had met the man of her dreams. As corny as it sounds, it was love at first sight. Of all the places in the world that it could have happened, it was during a short impromptu mid-January vacation on Red Mountain in Aspen, Colorado.

He was forty-five, tall, with dirty blond hair, extremely handsome, originally from Sweden, and a named partner in a big corporate law firm based out of Switzerland.

She had boldly asked him out on the first date. Lucky for her, his English was limited, and with his busy schedule, he didn't have time to follow the media and rarely went out to the movies. He didn't know how famous she was.

The instant chemistry was like bees to a flower, sweet and succulent. It only took a few days of being in his company that she knew that he would become her one true love.

He had told her that one of the things he loved about her, other than her beauty, was that he didn't feel guilty about not having enough time for her. It was actually the other way around.

She loved that she could always be herself around him, not feeling like he would judge her or love her just for her beauty and money. How rare it was to find a man that she could let down the invisible shield that she had put up so many years ago to protect herself from the fans and the crazies—the people who didn't respect her privacy.

She loved it when they both had time to meet up in Aspen. The mountain held such good memories. The resort they stayed in was extremely selective as to who could book a suite. Only the rich and famous could afford this caliber of a luxurious ski-in-ski-out establishment. A place where she knew she could take shelter from the paparazzi while sipping drinks and recouping in his arms. Isabella had all the privacy that she needed, that they needed.

It was a fairy tale: Two people who met and fell madly in love. She was about to go public with the relationship when it happened.

After not seeing each other for months, their lovemaking seemed epic. Isabella felt like her soul had left her body and was floating in a bath of ecstasy. He made her feel like she was the only living soul on the planet.

As the gentle snow fell outside, christening the tree branches with its grace, lying there in front of the fireplace, she snuggled closer to him on the sheepskin rug. The heat of the fire just added to the afterglow feeling. Isabella lay there mesmerized, watching the flames as if they came alive, seducing each other in their sacred dance. *I could lie here just like this forever.*

As he pulled her in closer, kissing her on the forehead, he said, "Come on, let's go for a romantic midnight ski in the moonlight." He had convinced the staff at the ski resort to open a lift and allow them to ride to the top and ski down.

The night was magical. The moonbeams filled the night sky, illuminating the snow so brightly that no lights were needed.

In the silence of the night, you could hear yourself breathe. As the ski lift went higher and higher, the ice crystals sparkled like diamonds on the branches.

As they descended off the chair, their skis made fresh tracks through the powdery drifts. Isabella could feel the wind as it blew through her hair as she cascaded down the slope. She imagined that he was relishing in the moment of this one last ski before going home tomorrow because she was.

She saw his sexy smile as he looked over and sped past her. He looked like a pro as he raced down the hill. A moment later, he disappeared from her view as the ski run curved around some trees.

Knowing that he had won their imaginary race, she slowed down and enjoyed the silence of the moonlit night as she skied toward their lodging. Expecting him to be there gloating, she put on her best smile. He was not at his usual spot along the snowy path waiting for her.

Using her ski poles to help maneuver closer toward the luxurious hotel, she still did not see him. A moment of panic fluttered through her system. *What if...*

Hurrying now, clicking out of her skis, she ran clumsily through the front entrance. She scanned everywhere, but he was not there.

Isabella's heart started to pound so hard that she thought it would burst right out of her chest. She ran back outside to see if maybe he had gone for a second run. She was anxiously waiting for his return while looking at the clock on her phone every few seconds. *He should be here by now.* She dialed his phone, no answer. Worry instantly turned into fear.

Isabella heard voices coming her way and smiled, thinking that it might be him. Instead, it was the two ski attendants that let them ride the lift. Running over to them, she asked if they had seen him, but they hadn't.

Frantic now, she ran back inside directly to the front desk and called up to their room, no answer. Her only option left was to report him missing to the ski-patrol office.

With the light of dawn, they found his body. Her worse nightmare had happened. He had hit a tree and broke his neck. The coroner said that he would have died immediately and probably didn't even see the tree due to the shadows of the night.

Hans, I need you! How am I going to live life without you?

Chapter 2

Hans couldn't remember how he got back to their hotel room. As the entrance door opened, he saw Isabella come in. Coming closer to her, he said jokingly, "I guess that means I won the race."

Isabella walked right by him and sat on the leather chair in front of the fireplace.

"Okay, I'll let you win next time." Not even a smirk from her. "Hey, what's up? I'm only joking."

Still ignoring him, Isabella brought her knees up and rested her elbows on them. As she brought her hands up to her face, tears started to flow down her cheeks.

Feeling like a jerk now for not noticing that she was really upset about something, he said, "Iss, what's wrong?"

Isabella started to sob uncontrollably.

Hans came around and knelt beside her. "Iss, tell me what's wrong. Did you hurt yourself?" He looked for bruises or blood. Nothing. "Please, Iss. Tell me what's wrong."

He put a hand on her knee to comfort her, but his hand went right through her body. *What the?*

A moment later, he saw a bright light and realized that he was dead. He felt his body start to vibrate as if he were a washing machine. It felt as if each cell was separating from one another, becoming vaporous. Panicking, with all the human ability he had left, he grabbed onto the arm of the chair. An invisible force started to pull him in the opposite direction. His legs were now floating higher than his head. His fingers couldn't hold onto the chair any longer. The invisible force had won.

No. I'm not leaving her!

Trying to hold on to anything that could keep him here on Earth, he envisioned a random memory of when he was young—he remembered a painting.

It illustrated a story that his grandfather had shared many times with him and his cousins. His stories always started with the words, *"This tale has been passed down from generation to generation… my grandfather used to tell it to me. Listen carefully, my little ones, because it's not folklore."*

Chapter 3

Instantly coming out of her dream, Lexi replayed her sister's question. *Have you found out what unfinished business Hans has?*

Although she was exhausted, she decided not to wait the remaining fourteen minutes before the alarm went off to get out of bed. The only thing stopping her was the thought of a strange man in her apartment, even if he was only a ghost. It scared the hell out of her.

Lexi didn't understand how or why her sister, Susannah, could communicate with her, but she had to admit that it was great having a big sister become one of her guardian angels.

"Hans, are you there?" she whispered, peeking over the covers and looking nervously around her bedroom.

Hans nodded as he looked over to the person calling his name.

She didn't hear a reply. Adrenaline started rushing through her veins as she bravely put her feet on the floor. Quickly, she got out of bed and grabbed her robe, covering herself… just in case he was watching.

The thought of a new ghost in her apartment brought back memories of her sister being tormented by dark entities in the afterlife.

Lexi thought to herself, *What if Hans is dark?*

After awkwardly getting dressed, her cell phone rang just as she was about to run out the door.

"Hello."

"Hi Alexandra, it's Edward. I was wondering how you've been… and if you wanted to go out for dinner. Are you busy Friday night?" Edward felt like he was back in high school as his knees went weak, nervously waiting for her response.

"Hi Edward, sure, that would be nice, but I am just dashing off to work. Do you mind texting me the time and place? Oh ya, and what I should wear, will it be formal, semi-formal, or casual? You know, a girl has to know these things."

Edward gave an acknowledging chuckle. *Phew, she said yes.* "Great. I will text you all the information. Enjoy your day, Alexandra."

"You too, Edward."

She had been so busy at work at the 5th Ave Manhattan designing studio, creating the new spring and fall fashions that she didn't have time for much else these days. Though, Reverend Hawthorne had slipped into her mind a few times since Christmas dinner at her mom's.

Hmm, a date is it. Maybe mom was right. No matter, it will be so enjoyable to talk to someone I have something in common with, Susannah. A tear started to form as she grabbed her coat and purse before going out the door. *I still miss her so much.*

Just as she did, Hans went to stop her by blocking her way.

As Lexi stepped through the doorway into the common hallway of her apartment building, a chill ran through her.

He tried to chase after her, but the door became a barrier, and Hans could not follow the lady who had earlier called out his name. It was as if he had reached the end of a chain that bound him, and his body was jolted back into the room.

Testing his theory, he walked around the apartment. He could go freely into any of the rooms, but as soon as he went through the exit door, he encountered an invisible force that pulled him back.

Sitting on the couch, he looked up and noticed a painting. It was an excellent replica of "The Wild Hunt of Odin" by Peter Nicolai Arbo. Of all the stories his grandfather would tell, this was his favorite.

Leaning back into the couch, he stared at the hunting party of airborne horsemen moving across a darkened sky. It was as if he could hear his grandfather's voice come alive.

Odin is the god associated with wisdom, healing, death, royalty, the gallows, knowledge, war, battle, victory, sorcery, poetry, frenzy, and the runic alphabet.

Hans was used to his grandfather being a bit wordy as he told his version of the Nordic pagan folklore.

The leader of the "noisy riders" is no other than Odin, and accompanying him on the wild chase is a horde of elves, fairies, and the dead.

Hans squinted to look at the horsemen. His grandfather was right. They were elves, fairies, and the dead.

He heard his grandfather's voice as he said, *All living souls that these horsemen pass must avert their eyes so that they too are not abducted into the underworld or the fairy kingdom.*

Hans knew what his grandfather's next words would be.

Children, say your prayers before you sleep so that your soul is not taken from your bed to join Odin's army. Better yet, pray that it is Thor leading the hunt, the god of thunder and the strongest son of Odin. Pray that it is he who will protect you and will come to help you defeat your battles and torments.

Hans just sat there, staring at the painting, trying to remember the old customs.

Chapter 4

Tamara had booked her next lecture at one of
the most amazing performing arts college
theaters in New York City. It was a dream come
true.

"Welcome back. I hope everyone's holiday
season was magical. Isn't this a fairy-tale
theater?" she said as she moved her hands in a
motion to display the grandeur of the space.

The stage curved out into the audience, with
beautiful red crushed velvet curtains hanging
from the ceiling to the floor, creating a regal
feeling. The lighting and sound were manned by
the students learning how to use the theatrical
stage systems.

Tamara was looking into an amphitheater-
style of seating. She knew the theater could hold
five hundred people, and the place was nearly
full. "I believe that a soul continues its journey

into the afterlife once it has left Earth. I believe
the reason we are living on Earth is to evolve
our soul for the advancement in Heaven, with
the ultimate goal being Nirvana.

"In my last lecture, I finished off by saying
that a better question might be, what if this was
your last lifetime? You were never coming back
down to Earth, ever again."

Tamara took a moment to pause and let what
she'd just said sink in. "What would you do
differently?"

Slowly walking the stage, she said, "What if I
could tell you that there is a celestial 'Siri' of
sorts to gain the answers to the questions you
have? An intelligent assistant that offers a faster,
easier way to get things done."

Giving another pause, Tamara could see in the
audience that her lectures were gaining the
attention of some noteworthy people in the
media.

As she turned her head, she saw a face in the
audience that she was not expecting.

Sitting in the third row was one of her first
students, Isabella Jackson. Tamara was so
excited to see her. It had been almost ten years
since she had seen Isabella in person, but it was
hard to forget her. Isabella was everywhere:
Instagram, Facebook, TV, radio, any media you
turned to.

The first time Tamara met Isabella was in one
of her spiritual classes. Back then, Isabella was a

young and beautiful girl who was on a personal quest to find her true calling.

It was one of the first courses Tamara ever taught. It was called "Your Persona… The Mask You Wear." The training revealed the four personality channels of audio, knower, visual, and feeler.

Tamara smiled to herself. *Interesting that she is here tonight since I am talking on the same subject but referring to it now as the language of the spirit world, the celestial language. The language used to communicate with angelic spirits. Ah, that explains all the media in the audience; they're here for Isabella. And here I thought it was because of my lectures.*

Smiling a genuine smile to Isabella, Tamara continued by saying, "We live in the era of information where computers and artificial intelligence, micro and nano, quantum, and space travel are part of our everyday lives. It only makes sense that there is a 'Siri' in the spirit world that you can ask a question and receive an answer. I find it fascinating that the word 'Siri' is spelled with four of the six letters in 'Spirit.'"

Tamara walked over to her stool, and before she took a seat, she took a sip of water from the bottle sitting on top of it, thus giving her a moment to collect her thoughts. Like all her other lectures, she knew her topic for the evening but not always how it would play out.

Listening to her intuition, she sat down on the stool and looked directly at Isabella. "Tonight, we have a special guest in the audience. Isabella, will you please be so kind as to join me up here on the stage?"

Isabella was used to being in the limelight. It was her soul's purpose in this lifetime, being a famous actress. Isabella stood up, and as she walked to the stage, her aura emanated the essence of a goddess.

Tamara signaled for a second stool to be brought up on stage.

The hug that Isabella gave Tamara was the sincerest embrace of love and gratitude that a successful student would gift a teacher. The ultimate acknowledgment anyone could give.

Tamara had to wait before she could continue talking until the standing ovation, lights flashing from all the cameras, the sound of the cheering, and applause coming from the audience quieted down.

"Thank you, Isabella, for coming up here and joining me. Everyone, I am sure you already know who Isabella Jackson is, but you probably don't know how I know her. Isabella, would you mind sharing your story with us?"

"Tamara, I would love to. Thank you."

Chapter 5

"*I*was nineteen and had just moved to New York City. I had been accepted into one of the most prestigious and promising acting schools in the nation. But … I didn't just dream of becoming a star. I actually dreamed of becoming a star. Meaning I had a dream that was so lucid, I could see myself as a famous actress." Isabella smiled and said, "Yes, for years, I was a struggling actress with dreams of making it big on Broadway."

Seeing Isabella on stage brought tears to Tamara's eyes. She was so proud of her journey.

Turning to Tamara, Isabella continued, "I struggled on my path for so many years, and if it wasn't for you, Tamara, I am not sure where I would be right now." Isabella leaned over and gave Tamara another hug. Releasing Tamara, Isabella took a deep breath and closed her eyes.

She was recently voted one of the most beautiful people in the world by a very reputable magazine. Tamara knew she was a beauty on the inside as much as she was on the outside.

"My story is simple. Thanks to Tamara, I believe in an all-knowing entity, an entity that is pure love and light. This energy guides me in everything that I do, say, see, and know. My riches, fame, and success are all because of my ability to communicate with these celestial beings. I call them my guides and angels.

"Don't get me wrong, I pray to God, but he is so busy. Instead of talking to me directly, he delivers his messages through Archangel Gabriel's team of celestial beings."

There were mixed reactions from the audience. Some people were clapping and cheering. Some couldn't believe their ears, but the media was eating it up like candy, recording every word.

As she looked over to Tamara, she said, "It is this beautiful soul, my Earth angel, who taught me how to communicate with the Holy, the celestial guides and angels who help deliver God's messages to me. I pray every morning and receive the answers to my prayers through meditation. Tamara teaches that prayer is asking, and meditation is listening. Listen carefully to what she has to say, for she is gifting you the wisdom and knowledge of the spiritual gifts granted by spirit."

With that said, Isabella leaned over and kissed Tamara on the cheek, got up, and left the stage. Instead of going back to her seat, she picked up her stool and walked toward the side of the stage, just behind the curtains. That way, she could listen to the rest of the lecture without the commotion that comes with being famous.

Chapter 6

Tamara clapped her hands in gratitude as Isabella left the stage.

Continuing with the lecture, Tamara said, "There are nine spiritual gifts. As many of you know, the last set of lectures that I did before Christmas was based on 'distinguishing spirits.' Tonight's focus is on the gift of tongues, the celestial language of a soul, which in the Bible is a two-part gift: the gift of tongues and the interpretation of tongues. What comes to mind when you hear the gift of tongues?" Tamara waited a moment before continuing.

"Many Christians believe that being able to speak in tongues is a sign of being filled with the Holy Spirit. Some of you are probably familiar with the term 'Holy Rollers.' These are parishioners who roll in the aisle as they are overtaken by Spirit and babble in some language that almost no one can understand, including themselves.

"Some religions indeed promote that kind of behavior. It is called Glossolalia.

"I disagree with it.

"DID THE PERSON TEST THE SPIRIT FIRST, before they let it enter their body? Hey, just because you are in a church doesn't mean a lower-energy spirit cannot access your body.

"Think about it. What does the word 'fill' mean? You fill something up, right? In this case, you are filling your body. What is it being filled with? The Holy Spirit? Well, I would agree it is a spirit. Holy, I am not sure. DID THEY TEST THE SPIRIT before they let it enter their body?

"Don't get me wrong, I believe in tongues, just not in the unsafe way it might be performed.

"What if you didn't test the spirit, and now you are speaking a spell or a curse?

"How do you know that you aren't?

"In the New Jerusalem Bible, Corinthians 1, chapter 14, verse 13 it reads, 'That is why anyone who speaks in tongues prays that he may be given the interpretation.'

"When you go home this evening, read online or in any Christian Bible these two scriptures, Corinthians 1, chapters 12–15 and Acts, chapters 2–3.

"Tonight, I am going to explain the proper procedure of tongues and back it up by using science."

That got the journalists to have a seat and stick around.

"Imagine turning on a radio and adjusting it to a channel where your favorite music is being played.

"The sound of music is broadcast over an AM or FM frequency. The music or voices you hear are being transmitted by invisible radio waves through the air to an antenna or cell phone."

Tamara went over to her stool and grabbed her cell phone. She held it up for everyone to see. "Each radio station uses a different frequency or channel. Your cell phone works as a receiver when you play music, read a text message or answer a call. When it sends out your message, it becomes a transmitter."

She put the phone back down and continued talking. "Your body is similar to a cell phone, in that you have a transmitter and receiver built right into your brain.

"I imagine all of you have heard of extrasensory perception, also known as ESP, or your sixth sense?" Tamara could see many heads nodding in the audience.

"Speaking in tongues is a celestial language and uses an invisible frequency of energy that your brain can naturally transmit, receive, and comprehend. And just like all languages, speaking in tongues is learnable.

"'Tongues' is the native language of your celestial soul. I believe the language is stored in your consciousness, and all you need to do is access it.

"Let me give you an example. How many of you have learned a language other than English as a child?"

Many hands went up in the audience.

"How many of you as a child were brought up learning one language and then moved to another city, country, or school and were given no other choice but to learn the new language?"

Again, many hands went up in the audience.

"How many of you over the years, due to the lack of practice, forgot how to read, write, speak, or understand your native tongue?"

Again, many hands went up in the audience.

"The fascinating thing is, as an adult, if you were to return to your original community where you could only speak your native tongue, you would remember very quickly how to speak and interpret that language again."

Tamara took a breath and then said, "Now, let's go back to the concept of speaking in tongues, a language unbeknownst to the person speaking it. When a person speaks in tongues, it can only be two things: They remember their native language or an entity has possessed their body.

"I know what you are thinking, 'Tamara, you channel spirits.' True, but I do not allow them to enter my body. I only interpret what they are saying.

"To speak in tongues is meant to speak in God's language, and all you need to do is learn or remember the language … You do not have to roll on the floor or have an entity possess your body to contact a spirit and communicate with it."

Tamara wanted the audience to ponder on what she had just said. "We will be taking a twenty-minute intermission, and when we come back, I will be giving a demonstration."

Chapter 7

Tamara went over to where Isabella was sitting.

"Isabella, it is so nice to see you." Tamara gave her another hug.

"You too, Tamara. It's been a few years, and so much has happened since then. I've been following you through all your published books."

"Ah, that is so sweet of you. I have watched all your movies and have been following you through the media. You've done very well for yourself, but… right now, my Spidey senses say that something is up, that you are not here just by chance."

"Yes, you haven't lost your touch. I am hoping that you will have time to meet with me privately."

"Sure. When are you thinking?"

"Would tomorrow or the next day work?"

"For you, I'll make it work. Just text me when and where?"

As Isabella hugged her, she said, "You're the best!"

Tamara gave Isabella her cell number, another hug, and said, "See you soon."

After taking a quick restroom break, Tamara walked back onto the stage, sat down on her stool, took a breath, and said, "Please, find your seats."

She then continued with her lecture by saying, "The Bible, written over two-thousand years ago, needed to be translated into English from other languages: Hebrew, Greek, and Aramaic. In the Bible, there is a story written to the church at Corinth to pray for an interpreter, 1 Corinthians 14:27.

"Today, many governments, businesses, and people have used an interpreter's expertise to translate for them. It is necessary that we understand what is being spoken or written.

"Imagine that you are at a conference or on a tour in another country and don't speak the language. A translator comes in handy. Maybe you have needed a translator for reading legal or medical documents. I've even used a computer program to translate emails to and from my family that lives in Europe.

"No matter if you have or haven't used a translator, most of you know what Morse code is. This is a perfect example where you would need a translator.

"Morse code is a frequency of energy transmitted in the form of dots and dashes. It is international, and it does not matter if you speak German, English, Mandarin, or any other language. The dots and dashes will need to be interpreted and translated into the letters of the alphabet."

Tamara drew some dots and dashes on a whiteboard that had been brought up on stage. "The most famous Morse code used is... ---... The English translation is SOS. You could send this code out as many times as you wanted to, but unless someone knew how to decipher it, your message would never be understood. Do you know what SOS in English stands for? Save our souls.

"Another modality that sends out messages by using the same symbolic coding is a telegraph machine.

"Sign language is another great example of communicating without speaking that anyone can learn. You can move your fingers any way you like, but unless you know the exact combination of manual articulations, you are just moving your fingers.

"Even as far back as 400BC, beacon fires and drumbeats were used to send messages."

Tamara took a moment to look at the audience, making sure everyone was following what she was saying, which they seemed to be.

"To interpret any language, the interpreter must listen carefully. This is also true to safely communicate with Spirit … it is done best to sense the entire phrase and then interpret the message."

Tamara excitedly said, "Get ready. We are about to do just that, learn how to interpret Spirit's words, Spirit's celestial language."

The sound of applause and a couple of woot-woot shouts could be heard from the audience.

Smiling from the reaction, Tamara continued, "Spirit communicates using a celestial language, but it needs to be deciphered. This code of communication that Spirit uses is transmitted through specific frequencies of energy that only your sixth sense can interpret.

"There are four channels or frequencies a person can choose from to decode any divine message. I call these channels Audio, Knower Visual, and Feeler. Think of these four channels similar to a radio station sending out a frequency. An example would be FM 99.9. Each frequency or channel has its unique wavelength.

"If you want to hear another radio station, you will need to change the channel to a new frequency. This is the same action required to sense another Celestial Channel. You will need to switch to a new frequency.

"The Audio channel is a frequency of energy, and like Morse code, this energy needs to be deciphered. This energy comes in the form of words that you can hear out loud, in your head, or written.

"The Knower channel uses thought energy, as in telepathy. The Visual channel uses images or dreams. The Feeler channel uses energy that you can feel emotionally.

"My point is that there are many ways to communicate other than using words, but most importantly, the celestial language is learnable.

"The first step in learning how to decipher the celestial language is to know where the four celestial sensory transmitters and receivers are in your body.

"Let's have some fun. Ready to learn where they are located?"

The audience went wild with cheers and applause.

"To start with, I am going to have you lightly press on each location. I want you to learn how to kinesthetically activate the signal and learn how to focus on that particular frequency of energy."

Tamara put a finger just behind her ear.

"To activate the Audio channel, lightly place your pointer finger behind your ear, near the top, and find the indent on your skull. You do not have to press hard. If you haven't already, go ahead now and touch the spot behind your ear. By the way, it can be either ear or even both at the same time."

Tamara watched as most people tried it out.

"To activate the Knower channel, put your hand on top of your head, the baby soft spot."

After a moment, she then put a couple of her fingertips to her forehead, between her brows, and said, "Next, to activate the Visual channel, put two or three fingers here, between your brows."

She waited a few moments before continuing.

Tamara put her hand on her stomach. "Lastly, to activate the Feeler channel, put your hand on your tummy. Anywhere near or over your belly button is fine. Again, lightly, you do not have to press hard to activate it."

She demonstrated it all again, saying, "Behind the ears is for the Audio channel, on top of your head is for the Knower channel, between the brows is for the Visual channel, and on your tummy is for the Feeler channel."

Bringing her hands back down, she said, "I have taught this technique to activate the channels for many years now, and once you understand the sensation of each channel, you do not have to touch the spot to activate it. Instead, you can just think of the spot.

"Each person is born with a primary channel that they mostly use. It will always be one of these four channels: Audio, Knower, Visual, or Feeler. This is important to know and understand because a ghost or a once-human spirit can only contact you through the primary channel they used while alive on Earth, but a demon or angelic spirit can contact you using any of the four channels.

"I do not have time tonight to teach you how to find your main channel or how to develop the others, but I do teach that in a course called 'Your Persona… The Mask You Wear.'

"Tonight's focus is on the gift of tongues… 'how' to communicate with the spirit world. I am ready for a volunteer. Who would like to come up?"

Chapter 8

*M*any hands went up in the audience.

Tamara chose a young girl who looked like she was in her late teens, maybe early twenties.

"Hi, what is your name?" Tamara asked the girl once she was standing beside her on the stage.

"Astrid."

"Do I detect a Swedish accent?"

"Yes, I am originally from Stockholm."

"Astrid, have you ever spoken in the celestial language of tongues before?"

"No, I do not believe so."

"I am going to have you demonstrate speaking in a different language for me. Please say, 'Hi, I am Astrid,' in your native Swedish tongue."

"Hej jag är Astrid."

"Thank you. Okay, now tell us a little bit about where you lived, but tell us in Swedish."

"*Jag är född i Sverige och växte upp i Stockholm men som vuxen flyttade jag till New Jersey.*"

Tamara looked at the audience and asked, "How many of you understood what she just said?"

A few hands went up in the audience.

"Astrid, please translate into English what you just said."

"I was born in Sweden and grew up in Stockholm, then moved to New Jersey as an adult."

Tamara looked at the audience again. "The four aspects of language, how to speak, read, write, and comprehend are all processed in four different parts of the brain."

Tamara looked back at Astrid. "How long did it take you to learn English?"

"Oh, goodness. I learned a bit in high school and have been practicing while living here in the United States. To be honest, my English is not very good."

"Astrid, your English is great. Don't kid yourself." Turning back to the audience, Tamara said, "I guess that she means that she can speak it, but with an accent. She can comprehend what others are saying and probably at first only if they spoke slowly. Her reading was probably better than her writing of the English language."

Turning to Astrid, she waited to have her acknowledge what she had just said.

"It is true, when I came to the United States, I could understand people but was afraid to talk in case I said something wrong and would look stupid. I could read a menu and road signs and ask where a restroom was. The basics. It took a few months to get comfortable with speaking the language."

Tamara spoke to the audience again, "The celestial language is no different. With practice, you will become better and better.

"Astrid, would you like to know what your main celestial channel of communication is?"

"Oh, yes, I would."

Tamara stood there with her eyes closed for a moment, then said, "Visual."

"Ah, and how do you know that?" Astrid asked.

"I muscle-tested which celestial language was your main channel."

"You found that out by closing your eyes?"

"No, I found that out from moving forward and backward. Muscle-testing is a technique using body-movement feedback to get a yes or no answer. I just used my body as a tool to get the answer. Thank you for volunteering to be on stage with me. You were wonderful. I am so grateful that Spirit always helps me choose who to bring up on stage."

Tamara hugged Astrid just before she left the stage.

Turning to face the audience, Tamara said, "I will be offering a four-day course to teach you how to communicate with your angels, guides, God, Jesus, and your loved ones who have passed on.

"In this course, I will be teaching two of the four parts of the celestial language. You will be learning how to speak and interpret tongues.

"You will also learn how to muscle-test your primary channel and how to decode each channel.

"You will gain the knowledge needed to be able to receive and transmit a frequency of energy that you can use to communicate with the spirit world."

Tamara walked over to the whiteboard, picked up a marker, and wrote "Audio," "Knower," "Visual," and "Feeler."

"These are the four different channels that God, the Holy Spirit, or anyone in the spirit world uses to communicate with us.

"For those interested in taking the course, please refer to the program sheet you were given when you entered the theater."

Tamara bowed to the audience, then said, "Night, everyone. Remember to go online and sign up if you wish to receive my newsletter and be informed of my next lecture and workshop dates."

Chapter 9

*I*sabella, not wasting any time, texted Tamara the following day. *How do you tell someone that life is not worth living anymore?*

Hi Tamara, it's Isabella.
Would you have time to meet for a coffee?
I need your help.
My schedule is a little flexible right now because my next movie hasn't started filming yet :)

Isabella was grateful that Tamara had instantly texted back…

Hi Isabella, I have time this Wednesday, but it will have to be later in the evening, around 7:30. Can we meet at our favorite little coffee shop, you know, the one where we used to go after class?

———

*I*sabella grabbed a cappuccino and sat in the quietest part of the café.

Moments later, as Tamara walked into the café, she instantly recognized Isabella even though she was wearing dark glasses and a wig. "Nice costume. What name am I supposed to call you, 007?" Tamara said, smiling as she sat down and took off her coat.

"Funny. Honestly, Tamara, if I don't, we will never get a chance to talk."

Tamara looked around the café as the waitress set a beverage down in front of her. "Thank you," Tamara said, a bit surprised.

"I ordered you a drink when I came in. I hope Chai tea is still your favorite?"

Tamara took a moment to smell the exotic scent and savor the blend of spices that flowed over her tongue as she took a sip before she said, "It is. Especially this tiger spice flavor… So, what's on your mind, Isabella?"

Taking a breath as tears started to flow down her cheeks, Isabella said, "I don't know where to start."

Sitting up and leaning closer to her, Tamara whispered, "Oh, dear me. What is it?"

"I lost…" Sniffling and taking a tissue from her purse to wipe her nose, Isabella continued, "I lost him a few weeks ago in Aspen."

"Who?"

"The love of my life. He died…" Taking a moment to wipe the tears flowing from her eyes, Isabella continued, "Tamara, I just need to talk to him."

While Isabella regained her composure, Tamara sat back in her chair and said, "I see." Tamara silently took a breath and asked up for help. The answer that came was, *"Have her come to your course."*

"Umm, okay, this is what we are going to do. Spirit says for you to come to my celestial language course. And, since you are who you are, I will make sure the class is small, about five people that I trust."

"What, are you crazy? A class?" Isabella wasn't sure if she wanted to be with other people. This was a private matter.

"No, and actually, it is a course with a few classes, four to be exact."

"Really, a class? You can't just do your magic and talk to him for me?"

"Nope, not this time. The way you are acting, he was no ordinary man. One conversation is not going to fix how you are feeling."

"No, he was the love of my life. I guess you're right. One conversation is not going to fix this."

"Exactly. You are going to have to learn how to talk to him yourself."

Taking a deep breath and sitting back in her chair, Isabella said, "Okay, if I agree to do this, when are you thinking of starting the classes? Because I only have about a month before I start shooting my next movie, and this time, it's in Peru."

"Give me a day or two to figure out a plan and gather everyone together."

"Don't get me wrong, Tamara, I am grateful, but it's not quite what I was thinking. I am going to have to trust my guides that this is the best thing for me right now."

"When have your guides ever been wrong?"

Chapter 10

Tamara was used to Spirit changing her course schedules and knew there was always a good reason for the surprise. She decided it was probably a blessing in disguise since the originally planned course had about a hundred people attending. It would be great to do this smaller class first for the practice.

After bringing an extra chair into the living room for tonight's class, Tamara went into the kitchen to make some tea. She started thinking to herself. *I'm happy with my plan to have the workshop here at my home. Especially since there will only be Isabella, Lexi, and four other ladies, I won't have to worry about the paparazzi bugging us.*

She heard a knock at the front door and went over to open it. She was surprised to see that one of the new students, Jane, had brought a friend with her.

"Tamara, this is my friend Tammy." Pleadingly she said, "I hope it will be okay that she can stay. She lost her son a few months ago, and the pain is tearing her family apart."

Tamara looked up into the night's sky and slightly shook her head, saying, "Obviously, Spirit wants her to be here. Hi, Tammy. Nice to meet you." Tamara held out her hand to greet her.

"Thank you for letting me stay, Tamara. I really need to be here. I feel like it's my only hope."

Tamara showed them into the living room and offered them tea.

Next to show up was Lexi and another surprise guest. *What is it tonight? Bring-a-friend night?*

"Well, hi, you two. Reverend, I mean, Edward, what are you doing here?"

"Hi, Tamara. I know I am not invited, but I am praying you will let me stay. Alexandra told me about your new class. It's been a couple of days, and I still couldn't get it out of my head. I insisted that I drive her over here, hoping that you will let me stay and participate."

"Well, this should be interesting," Tamara said as she let them in.

Betty, Karla, and Kate all showed up on time and with no other unexpected guests.

Once everyone was settled comfortably in the living room, Tamara had everyone introduce themselves.

"Hi, I am Betty," the petite redhead said. "I have known Tamara for a few years now and have taken a couple of her other courses. When she called to ask me if I would switch to this group instead of waiting for the other one, I jumped at the opportunity of being in a smaller class size."

"Betty, tell us why you want to learn how to communicate in tongues?" Tamara said.

"Well, I lost my husband after twenty-five years of marriage to stomach cancer a year ago, and it was devastating. I miss him dearly. I have dreams about him and wake up in tears because I can never talk to him. I am hoping this course will fix that."

"Thank you, Betty, for sharing that. Yes, if you practice everything that I am about to teach you in this course, you will be able to communicate with him. That is if he wants to talk to you. There is always a chance that the spirit is busy or has reincarnated and can't speak with you."

Tamara noticed Edward's subtle change in body language as she was finishing speaking to Betty. *This should be a fascinating group with you here, Reverend.* Tamara turned her head and looked at the next student.

A tall brunette said, "Hi, I am Tammy. Jane was an angel and brought me here tonight. When she told me that she was coming, I had this weird sensation all over my body. I just knew I had to be here too." Tears started to form as she said, "I lost my six-year-old son a few months ago to leukemia. His twin brother wakes up screaming, saying that he sees Tommy in his sleep. I am desperate to find the answers I need that can help my situation. I am so appreciative of you, Tamara, for letting me stay."

"Thank you, Tammy. I am sure you will find what you learn here very beneficial."

Tamara looked at the next student. She resembled a librarian type that you'd see on TV.

"Hi, I am Jane. I am here because my mom had a fatal heart attack, and I would like to talk to her."

"Thank you for sharing that, Jane." Tamara noticed that one of the other students, Kate, the youngest of the group, had crossed her legs and arms at hearing Jane's introduction.

"Kate, tell me why you are here." Tamara turned to her instead of the next student in the circle.

A little startled, Kate said, "I am here because I have ghosts that haunt me. It doesn't matter where I am or what I am doing. I can be on a date having a nice dinner in a restaurant, and suddenly a ghost insists that I go over and talk to a person that I have never met before. It is starting to become a real problem in my life."

"Thank you," Tamara said, now understanding why the girl had crossed her arms and legs while speaking; she was guarding herself against ghosts.

"Karla, how about you? Why are you here?" Tamara was looking at a cute Barbie-type blonde.

"To be honest, I am not sure. I just know that I am supposed to be here. I can't tell you why I know this. I just do."

Tamara turned to Lexi, whom she got to know very well over the last few months.

"Hi everyone, I am Alexandra, but please call me Lexi. I recently lost my sister, Susannah. Tamara and Reverend Hawthorne helped me retrieve her from the Void. It was an incredible experience and the first time that I had ever communicated with a ghost. I am here tonight because my sister came to me again in a dream and asked if I knew why this man was in my apartment. I tried speaking to him, but no one answered. I need to learn how to talk to this ghost."

"Thank you." After nodding to Lexi in acknowledgment, Tamara looked at the Reverend. *This should be interesting.*

"Hi, I am Edward. As a Reverend, I deal with death all the time. I need to know how to help others with similar issues that you all are having. If I can learn anything that can help me assist them, then I believe this is why God led me here tonight."

At that moment, Isabella, who was listening from another room, walked in and sat down in the empty chair beside Tamara.

The surprise of seeing a celebrity so close created new energy in the room. The other students became more aware of their composure, and a couple of them were star-struck.

"I would like you all to meet Isabella. She is the reason you are here tonight. With Spirit's help, you all were chosen to form this unique group."

"Isabella, please tell everyone why you are here."

"Hi, everyone. I recently lost the love of my life and need to talk to him. I asked Tamara to talk to him, and instead, she created this class and said I needed to learn how to do it myself."

Chapter 11

After all the introductions, Tamara addressed the group, "It doesn't matter if you are rich or poor, healthy or sick, young or old, the celestial language is programmed into your DNA.

"When a baby is born, this innocent soul must learn how to do everything: eat, talk, walk, read, write, and even love. Learning something is easier with a teacher than learning it on your own. In tonight's class, I am going to teach you the four channels of the celestial language. As you know, I call them Audio, Knower, Visual, and Feeler."

Tamara looked at everyone in the group. "If you want to connect with a person who is dead, it is much easier if you know what their main channel was when they lived here on Earth.

"The easiest way for me to share this knowledge is by explaining each channel's personality traits. Let's start with the Audio channel." Tamara gave each person a handout.

"As you read each channel, you will notice that each has specific characteristics that describe a person's personality traits.

"Some of you may have seen these before if you took my course or read my book, 'Your Persona… The Mask You Wear.'"

Lexi hadn't, so she looked down at the papers.

Audio Channel:
Oral and Written Language
Clairaudience (French for clear hearing)
The specific personality traits for the people with Clairaudience as their main channel are:
- Words are very important
- Love to listen to music
- Hear and understand the lyrics to a song
- Enjoy typing or writing with a pen
- Are very literal, blunt
- Need detailed and factual information
- Love information in a printed format
- Need to have everything in writing so there is no miscommunication
- Can seem arrogant
- Can be loud
- Childhood toys: Play telephones, any type of computer, bang-on pots, anything that makes noise

- Adult toys: Computer, iPod, stereos, communication, cell phone, webcam, karaoke
- A cell phone is their lifeline to the world. They cannot live without a cell phone and probably have more than one
- Will not turn off their phone(s) unless made to!
- Cannot miss a call (even when sleeping— will answer it at any hour)
- Listen to the radio
- Are extremely good at spelling, grammar and punctuation
- Love languages, probably speak more than one
- If a Poker player, they use textbook rules
- Can be verbally bullying
- Need to hear it, or read it, to believe it
- Their handwriting is long and literal
- Will read the instructions on how something works
- For travel / driving directions, they use street names, left or right, miles or kilometers
- Need everything very clear and precise; it is either correct or wrong
- May have done graffiti as a kid
- Love to talk (in person, on the phone and in letters, Facebook, chat rooms)
- Love to have money in the bank, RSPs, stocks, etc. (Numbers are facts!)

- If they have an addiction, it is only because someone said it was cool

In the shopping mall:
- Will only buy brand-name items
- Items must be on sale or a great deal!
- Will stop and talk to everyone they know
- Will bring a friend for their feedback
- Will buy online (eBay)
- Purchase for fashion and trends
- Automobile will be new or a classic (great stereo and a great deal)
- Their house will be focused around their sound system and computer
- If they have a tattoo, most likely it will have words and sayings on it

Knower Channel:
Knowledge / Thought
Claircognisance (French for clear knowing) also spelled claircognizance with a "z"
The specific personality traits for the people with Claircognizance as their main channel are:
- Overanalyze / consider all the alternatives, think about all possible scenarios
- Research everything, even a simple purchase
- Usually take days to decide what to do about a decision, idea, or problem
- Are very cautious

- When they know a subject, they can give instant recall of the information without blinking an eye
- Can usually sense things ahead (read a situation / intuitive)
- Seem to be calm and have inner peace unless pushed to respond
- Are aware of consequences
- Are quiet and soft-spoken *(unless second language is Audio*, then they are a bit of a know-it-all)
- Become self-sufficient and hate to ask for help
- Notice any spelling, grammar, and punctuation errors
- Are usually loners (do not need others)
- Childhood toys: Brain stimulant, Rubik's cube, one-person games
- Adult toys: Scrabble, Sudoku, crossword puzzles, science, books, library, Google, bridge
- If a Poker player would not play in person until they know the game inside and out
- Play the odds / calculation of percentages
- Very patient
- With age, can be very self-confident
- Usually, lets others go first while they are watching, listening, and getting a sense if they should also do it
- Handwriting is very clear and readable

- When they know something, they know it
- Always second-guessing themselves out of doing most things
- If he / she says "think" *(they do not know it yet)*. If he / she says "know" *(they do know the info)*
- Listen to the news or read about current events
- Only have a cell phone for emergencies or to access the internet
- If they have an addiction, it is only because they need to shut out other people

In the shopping mall:
- Go only if they have to; they hate crowds
- Purchase for need and purpose
- Will go to every store to compare items and then go home and think about it
- Would try on everything a few times and still need time to decide
- Their automobile will be useful
- House will be either dirty or extremely clean, definitely functional
- They would not usually have a tattoo

Visual Channel:
Pictorial / Symbols
Clairvoyance (French for clear seeing)
The specific personality traits for the people with Clairvoyance as their main channel are:
- Love TV and movies

- Likes art, to draw, and paint / color
- Need to see how something works to understand it
- Need to see it to believe it
- Every item in the house has a special place
- When speaking, usually tell stories
- Very materialistic and love nice things, ADOS (attention deficit… *oh, shiny*)
- Travel or driving directions: Draws you a map, tells you the colors of the surrounding buildings
- Childhood toys: Light bright, dress-up, Barbies, art, beautiful dolls, fireworks, movies
- Adult games: Would rather not play, but do like DVDs, movies, Pictionary, any non-competitive game that everyone wins at
- If a Poker player can see and read subtle body language
- Love the psychology of the game
- With a good hand, gets excited and makes quick decisions
- Needs eye contact. Likes to look you in the eyes when talking to you
- Talk very quickly, so they do not lose their train of thought
- Talk on more than one subject at a time
- Do not totally finish their sentences, but it will make sense by the end of the conversation

- Hate talking for very long periods of time on the telephone, need to see the person
- Handwriting is usually neat and can be pretty
- Need to spell-check everything on the computer or have someone else edit
- Love sticky notes for reminders
- Only have a cell phone for necessity (usually business)
- Love to buy things. Need to see the dollar value
- Trust what they can "see" as valuable
- Notice themselves in pictures, mirrors, or windows
- If they have an addiction, it is to escape into another world / story or to look cool

In the shopping mall:
- Window displays and store ambiance is very important
- Notice even the slightest changes from the last visit
- The floors in a change room must be clean to try on clothes
- Usually will not buy anything they cannot see in real life
- Notice the clothes on mannequins. *Oh, that looks cute.*
- If it looks good, they may spend over budget. Price is not important

- Their automobile will be good-looking, shiny, clean, with good visibility
- House will be big or showy, looks clean, everything has a place, all rooms have a theme
- Has fine furniture
- Lots of ornaments
- Tattoos would be beautiful and colorful

Feeler Channel:
Kinesthetic / Touch
Clairsentience (French for clear feeling)
The specific personality traits for the people with Clairsentience as their main channel are:

- Are always busy… go, go, go… can't sit still
- Are great at getting the job done—and quickly
- Are very spontaneous and will try anything once
- Go by their gut feeling
- Love to play sports and be active
- Are very competitive
- Need to use their hands / Love to touch things
- Tell stories with lots of emotion
- Are a bit moody or emotional
- Are very sensitive to taste and texture
- Talk with their hands (even when driving) and are very touchy when they talk

- Can be very sensitive to the energy of others, bad or good
- Need to feel it to believe it
- Love the beat of a song (tap along)
- Only have a cell phone for work, to keep in touch with family and friends, or to play games
- Need <u>real</u> money in their pocket
- Are very creative with their hands, wood carving, pottery, models
- Childhood toys: Lego, stuffed animals, forts, cars, anything fast, action figures
- Adult toys: Video games, fast anything, sports / fitness, board games, playing cards
- Their handwriting is fast and usually messy
- If a Poker player love to play for fun or on the internet
- Hate to lose in public
- Go by gut feelings, luck, or the odds are against them
- May not play many hands if not sure they can win
- Do not like to lose
- Are forgetful, cannot find things easily
- Take a long time to calm down after having an issue
- May sleepwalk or act out in their sleep
- If they have an addiction, it is only because it feels good or to not feel at all

In the shopping mall:

- Will only notice what they are going in for
- Do not like waiting while someone else shops
- Quick in and out of all stores unless just to walk around *(good exercise)*
- The food court is the best place
- Usually will not buy anything they cannot touch first
- Purchase for fit and durability
- Their automobile will be fast, big, and can go off-road
- Their house will be spacious, comfortable, temperature-controlled, inviting, with enough room for all the toys, not always clean
- Tattoos would have a deep meaning and would probably be about another person

Chapter 12

After a quick break, and once everyone was settled back in their seats, Tamara continued, "Your ability to communicate with the spirit world all depends on your first contact.

"Did you hear them? Did you just know they were there? Did the spirit come to you as a vision? Or did you feel them?

"These four channels, Audio, Knower, Visual, and Feeler, are frequencies of energy. They are waves of energy being transmitted invisibly through the air."

Tamara was about to continue when Edward asked, "How do you know if you are talking to a loved one or a bad spirit?"

"Good question. You are a little ahead of us, but it is a good question. You might not know at first, so that is why you need to test the spirit. That doesn't mean you can't talk to it. The spirit world is not much different from meeting people here on Earth. Before deciding on trusting a stranger you've just met on an airplane, waiting in a doctor's office, or online, you would get to know them better. Same with meeting a spirit for the first time; you are going to get to know it better before you trust it with your life or heart."

Edward nodded.

Tamara continued with what she was originally talking about, "I can tell a person's main channel by how they talk. There are keywords that people use. A person whose main channel is Audio would say things like: 'Dinner sure *sounds* good right now,' 'I *hear* you,' '*Listen* to that,' 'I don't think we are *talking* the same language.'

"A person whose main channel is Knower would say things like: 'I *know* I am hungry for dinner,' or 'You *know* what I like to eat, so you decide,' 'I *knew* that,' 'I am thinking,' 'I don't *understand* what you are saying.'

"A person whose main channel is Visual would say things like: 'Dinner would sure *look* good right now,' 'I can *see* that,' 'See ya later,' 'We don't *see* eye to eye.'

"And a Feeler would say things like: 'My tummy *feels* hungry right now,' 'That food has a weird *texture*,' 'Let's *go* for a *walk*,' 'I don't think we are on the same *path*.'"

Edward interrupted again by asking, "So, you are telling me that if I listen to a ghost, I can tell what their main channel is?"

"No. Actually, 'listen' is a word that an Audio would use. That is your main channel, Edward. You are an Audio. Naturally, if you are an Audio, you would expect everyone else to be as well."

"I'm an Audio. How do you know that?" Edward challenged Tamara.

Tamara smiled. "Edward, I have taught for a lot of years now. Only Audios talk in class without being asked. This is especially true in the first couple of days around a new group.

"Here is what I can tell you. Tammy is a Feeler. When she introduced herself, she said, 'a weird sensation came all over my body.' Those are Feeler words. Betty said that she dreamed about her husband. That makes her a Visual. Kate is all four channels. She never used any one word to describe her situation. Jane is an Audio. She said she talked with her mom. Karla is a Knower. She said she just knew. As you might have figured out on your own, Lexi is a Visual like Betty. She gets dreams.

"The reason Lexi cannot communicate with the ghost in her apartment is that she is not using the correct frequency or channel. She did not change the radio station's dial, so to speak, and find a new channel. She is using her frequency of Visual, and the ghost is not a Visual. If she is going to communicate with him, she will have to learn what his frequency is and change channels."

"I see. Please continue," Edward said, a little bit embarrassed, sitting back in his chair, deciding to try and not interrupt her again.

"All right, everyone, I think that is enough for tonight. I have told you all what your main channel is, so go home and study all the handouts. Each channel's information is important to understand.

"Isabella, you are mostly a Visual, but you are like Kate. You use all four channels."

Isabella nodded.

Tamara piped up, "Now, I am assuming that you all know that what happens in class and who is in class is confidential. It is okay if you want to talk to your friends and family about what happens to you in the class, BUT do not talk about anyone else who is here!"

Chapter 13

"Thanks again for letting me go with you, Alexandra," Edward said to her as she was getting out of his SUV.

"I am glad you came. It's nice having someone I know in the class. Do you want to come up?"

"Ah. Sure. Let me park, and then I will meet you inside." Nervous and excited now, Edward hurried to the front entrance after parking.

Lexi met him at the door and let him in. As they waited for the elevator, she said, "Good because now you can meet Hans."

Edward stopped in his tracks and said, "If I knew you had company, I wouldn't have come in."

"I don't."

"Then, who is Hans?"

"I don't know exactly. He is the ghost in my apartment that Susannah asked about."

"Alexandra, you talked to Susannah. I thought you said you dreamed of her," he said as she unlocked and opened the door to her 5th Avenue apartment.

"Yes, she came to me in a dream again and asked me if I knew what his unfinished business was."

"And do you?"

"No. I am not sure he's even real. He doesn't talk to me."

Looking around the apartment, Edward made the sign of the cross and sat down on the couch.

Lexi poured him a glass of wine and sat cross-legged on the other end of the couch while taking a sip from her glass. "I know. It's stupid to think that a ghost is in my apartment. I even had a hard time getting dressed this morning. I was worried about a man watching me."

Concerned for Alexandra's safety, he said, "Do you think you are safe here?"

"Oh. Great. I didn't think of that," Lexi said as she looked around her living room. "Edward, do you think you could bless the apartment and get rid of the ghost for me?"

"That might be a good idea." Edward stood up and pulled out a crucifix from his coat pocket. Holding the cross up in the air, he said, "Lord, banish this spirit from Alexandra's home."

Lexi screamed, jumped up, and grabbed Edward's arm as a painting hanging on her living room wall tilted slightly.

"Demon be gone," he demanded.

The painting moved again. Lexi held on tighter. "Oh, my God. Edward, I think you are getting the ghost mad. I am going to call Tamara."

"It's pretty late. You might be waking her up."

"Then what do you suggest? Because I am not living here with a ghost."

"You could talk to Susannah. So, why can't you talk to this one?" Edward asked.

"I don't know."

"How do you talk to Susannah?"

"I always dream about her. She is a vision in my mind, but Hans does not appear in my dreams. And I have tried talking to him, and that doesn't work either."

"Okay, what did we learn in class tonight? What did Tamara say the four channels were?"

"Audio, but he is not talking, so that can't be it. Visual, but he doesn't appear in my dreams, so that can't be it. What's left?"

"Knower and Feeler."

"I wish Tamara had taught more. I don't know how to talk to Hans. Edward, you made him mad trying to banish him, so what ideas do you have now?"

"None. I don't know how to communicate with a ghost. That is why I am taking the class with you."

"You believe in ghosts?" Lexi asked.

"I don't know what I believe. I know you believe that Susannah became a ghost. I know that many of my clients talk about their loved ones visiting them after they have died. I wish there would be more concrete evidence one way or the other if ghosts were real."

The picture moved again. "Edward, I can't sleep here tonight. I am going to go to my mom's."

"Don't you think it is too late to be waking her up? Come to my place. It is a big place with lots of guest rooms that never get used."

The picture moved again. "Yep. Okay. Let me get a few things." Lexi went into her bedroom and grabbed a small suitcase, and quickly threw a few things in it.

Chapter 14

The next morning Lexi awoke quite abruptly to tapping at the door. *Where am I?* Instantly sitting up and looking around, it took her a moment to remember that she had slept over at Edward's. *Right, the ghost is in my apartment.*

Lexi went over to the door and peeked her head around as she opened it.

"I am making breakfast and coffee. Want some?" Edward asked.

"That is so sweet. I will be down in a moment."

Before going downstairs, she quickly dressed and texted Tamara that it was vital that she speak with her.

An "out-of-office" reply came back that she was away on business. The date of her return was the following week.

Oh, my God, how am I going to wait for a whole week? I am not living with a ghost.

Once downstairs, Lexi found Edward sitting in the kitchen at a small coffee table. She sat down opposite him, smiling, as she said, "This is very charming."

Edward looked around briefly and said, "I don't like making my staff do work that I am capable of doing, and this is quick and easy for me."

"Wow, someone who cares about their staff. Rare."

"Without them, I can't do all this," he replied sincerely.

"Without you, they don't have jobs," Lexi said as she took a drink of her morning coffee. *Rare might be an understatement in this dog-eat-dog world.*

Changing the subject, Edward asked, "Have you thought about what you are going to do about your guest?"

"Well, I prayed that you could get rid of him, but that didn't work."

"To be fair, I have only done one exorcism, and that was back when I was still at seminary school."

"You could have told me."

"You didn't ask."

"Right, you're an Audio. I'll try to be more literal next time."

"Have you tried getting a hold of Tamara?"

"Yes, I just did, but she is out of town on business until our next class."

Without looking up from his coffee cup, he said, "You could stay here."

"I can't impose on you like that." *Could I?*

"We can stop by your place and pick up a few more—"

She stopped him before he could finish. "Ah, no way! I'm not going back to that haunted painting!"

"I would say that you are over-reacting, but with everything we've been through together, I am not sure anymore."

"I'll just go buy some more clothes. I haven't been on a shopping spree for a while anyway."

Edward stood up from the table and hastily put the cups and plates into the dishwasher. "Sounds like fun. Let's go." Looking at the surprised look on Alexandra's face, he smiled. *One point for team Edward.*

Chapter 15

Stuck in Lexi's apartment, Hans found himself staring at the painting he was bound to. The next thing he knew, his ghostly spirit was teleported back in time, and he was sitting on the floor in his Grandfather's living room. He and his cousins were listening to their *farfar*, his dad's dad, tell one of his legendary stories in his native tongue, Swedish.

Deciding to tell an ancient Nordic myth, Olof started by asking his grandchildren, "Have I told you the story about the dwarves?"

The children cheered. They liked that one.

"How about the trolls?"

The children booed. They didn't like that one.

"How about the one with the elves? Did you like that one?"

The children cheered again.

"*Farfar*, just pick one. We like them all," said Hilde, Hans's cousin. She was nine, a year younger than Hans, and he hated it when she acted like she was in charge.

Pushing his glasses back up from sliding down his nose, Olof started to speak in a deeper voice than usual. "Way back at the beginning of time, Adam and Eve had many children. One day as Eve was bathing the children, God came and surprised her with a visit. For fear of being judged, she quickly hid those that were dirty."

"Ah, *farfar*, we hate taking baths," said Hans's younger cousin, Gustav. He was six.

"God asked, 'Are there no more children?' When Eve said no, God said, 'Then let all that is hidden, remain hidden.'

"Do you know what dirty children become?"

The younger children screamed and grabbed on tight to the older cousins.

"*De underjordiske*, the ones living underground, lost souls who have to live under the surface of the earth, in the dirt."

"Ah, *farfar*, that is ridiculous," said Hilde as she crossed her arms in disbelief.

He looked lovingly at his granddaughter and said, "Ah *nej*, Hilde, this story is as old as the Nordic Sea. This legend is passed down from generation to generation. You will be telling your grandchildren this story one day."

Continuing with the story, he said, "One of Eve's children, named Huldra, though some called her Tallemaja, was one of the children

Eve had hidden. Though, for some mysterious reason, Huldra remained above the ground. She was a beautiful and flirtatious child who was neither good nor evil. While she was living in the woods, she became troll-like, wild, with a long cow-tail which she had to hide behind her back upon meeting any human, for she scared them. She was very lonely."

The youngest of the cousins hopped right onto Hans's lap, telling him, "She scares me."

Hans's grandfather pointed a finger at the children. "Now, children, what is the moral of this story?"

"To take your bath," Hilde blurted out.

"*Nej*, but that is a good one."

"God loves clean children, said Nora, another of Hans's younger cousins.

"*Nej*."

"Come on, *farfar*, what is it?" little Erik, sitting in Hans's lap, called out.

Olof spoke slowly while looking at all his grandchildren, "Not to lie."

"What, how do you get that from the story?" Hans piped up.

Olof looked over the rims of his glasses to Hans. "Hans, how did the story begin?"

"With Eve washing her children."

"*Ja*, but what did she do?"

"Hid her unwashed children."

"*Ja*, and did she lie to God when he asked, 'Are there no more children?'"

"Ah, yes, she did. How did I miss that point? I will be more attentive next time, *farfar*."

"Hans, as long as you seek the truth, you will always find the answer to the question."

At that moment, Hans's grandmother called out from the other room, "Alright, children, time for dinner,"

"Aw, *farfar*, tell her not yet. We want another story," little Erik pleaded.

Olaf loved telling his grandchildren the old Norse folklore. The words in the stories related to real-life lessons. He loved how they subtly taught morals and virtue. "Next time, I will tell you about the Vette."

Hans was instantly back in Lexi's apartment, staring at the painting. This particular story was what guided him always to seek the truth throughout his law career.

Chapter 16

$\mathcal{I}$t was later the next day, and Isabella would be leaving their alpine hotel room in about an hour. She had barely slept a wink since the ski patrol had confirmed that Hans had died.

Life won't be the same without him. Sitting on the couch with her knees up, drinking a cup of coffee, and staring out of the window while she waited for her ride, she drifted in and out of reality.

It was springtime, and they had only known each other for a few weeks, when she decided to make a surprise visit to Switzerland. He was at work at his Geneva law firm when she entered the office. His secretary smiled, recognizing her at once. Not only for her being famous but also because Hans had excitedly shown her a picture of his new girlfriend when he returned from Aspen.

Isabella was excited that he could take the rest of the day off and drive them to a small town called Lauterbrunnen.

The town reminded her of "Heidi." The story also had a valley nestled deep between the alpine mountains.

After a short sightseeing tour of the town, they rode a cable car up to Grutschalp, where he hugged her closely. Feeling safe in his arms, she was in awe of the beauty of the valley as they moved higher and higher up the mountain. It was so surreal.

After getting out of the cable car, they instantly walked over to another and rode it up to Murren.

Their journey continued with a walk along a narrow mountain path to Gimmelwald. High above the world, she strolled along the trail, holding his hand. She noticed that spring had started to show by the fresh green grass growing on each side of the path, but even higher up, she could see the snow-covered peaks of Eiger, Monch, and Jungfrau, reminding her that winter wasn't over yet.

Being in Switzerland with Hans was enchanting, and as she breathed in the crisp mountain air, she pinched herself to make sure she wasn't a character in one of her movies.

When they finally arrived in the Swiss village of Gimmelwald, it was like going back in time. The old-style log cottages had shutters on the windows, with cascading spring blooms of red and white flowers flowing out from the windowsills.

As they continued walking through the village, she smiled at the performance of a man dressed in lederhosen. She loved seeing the traditional shorts held up by suspenders. He was playing an alpenhorn. Isabella couldn't believe how incredibly long the horn was, guessing at least eight feet. They watched as the man playing it held the smaller end to his mouth, and the other end rested on the ground, with the hollow base turned up to the sky. The deep harmonic sound that came out when he blew echoed not only through the mountainous valley but also through her.

Before evening, they took a train back down the mountain to Lauterbrunnen, ending their journey at his place with a romantic night of lovemaking.

Coming back to the present moment, she started to sob again. *I never thought I could love someone as much as I love you.*

Isabella's mind drifted off again. Things didn't change much, living in the historic town of New Castle, Delaware. Many outsiders called it a hidden gem and said that if you blinked while driving through it, you'd miss it.

Isabella was a ten-year-old child who was suddenly growing up with a grieving single mom with no close family nearby. Her dad, at the age of thirty-eight, died of what the doctor reported as natural causes. Her mother never questioned the doctor and took the large sum of money the chemical company he worked for had given her, saying it was grievance pay.

Isabella kept her family life separate from school, never bringing home any friends. Her only salvation was the theater. She could wholeheartedly imagine that she "was" the character in each play, living vicariously through their exciting lives. Drama class became her new reality.

Her memory fast-forwarded to senior year. She was dating the football quarterback, Dirk. His family had a long history of living in New Castle, and his great, great, great grandfather was one of the original Dutch merchants that had settled into the area. His family was rich and ruled New Castle. She also remembered that in Dutch, Dirk's name meant "ruler of the people." Isabella was a beauty and knew Dirk grew up expecting the best things in life, which now included her.

She had the lead part in the school's upcoming play and had been putting in quite a lot of extra rehearsal time. She was on her way home and decided to cut through the school's football field when she spotted Dirk.

As she started to run toward him, she stopped dead in her tracks as she saw Susie Hasselman, the school's prom queen, come up to Dirk and plant a kiss on him that would have melted an iceberg. Worse yet, she watched as Dirk wrapped his arms around Susie and pulled her in closer for an even more dramatic kiss.

Dumbfounded, Isabella just stood there, out of his view. A piece of her heart shattered as she watched Susie slip her arm through Dirk's and walk off the field together.

Isabella didn't see it coming.

Wiping her tears away, she swore to herself that she would never fall in love ever again, and from that moment on, she dedicated her love to the theater… until Hans.

Chapter 17

It had been one of the best weeks of her life. Lexi had loved staying at Edward's. He was kind, caring, thoughtful, and full of surprises.

That Saturday morning, she had come down for her usual breakfast coffee to find a handwritten note on the table.

Alexandra, I am in the morgue, taking care of one of my clients. It will be a few hours, so feel free to make yourself comfortable.

From last year's visit to the Brooklyn funeral home, she knew the morgue was in the basement. She was so proud of Edward for caring for his family's estate and business. Lexi decided that it was high time that she braved something new and went to find Edward.

Expecting to find a door that led down to a dungeon, she was surprised to see a grand open stairway leading down to the morgue. As she descended the last step, she looked upon what resembled a hospital. There were a few rooms on the outskirts of the main auditorium, which at the moment was filled with medical students from the university. Edward was leading a class and nodded at her as if to say, "Take a seat." She sat down in one of the unoccupied chairs and listened in on the class.

"As I am sure by now, many of you are used to seeing a cadaver. It is our job in the morgue to work with pathologists, and when they are finished determining the cause of death, we prepare the body for viewing," Edward said as he pointed to his "client" on the table before him.

Lexi wasn't sure what she was expecting, but she was not ready for what had happened. It wasn't the dead body with peeled skin that freaked her out. It wasn't the smell. It was the fact that her saliva glands started to activate at the sight of what looked like beef jerky. *Oh, my God, how could this be happening to me? Gross! Stay professional Lexi, don't let the others know you are having a problem with this.*

Edward looked toward Alexandra and smiled, he thought she would have high-tailed it right out of there as soon as she saw the dead body, but no, she was still sitting there. A little green, but still there. "As a mortician, it is our job to create the illusion of the deceased person to look as though they are lying there resting."

One of the medical students raised a hand. "What if you can't? What then?"

"It is usually up to the family if there will be an open viewing of the body or not. Though, sometimes an open casket is the last request of the departed soul, to make sure his or her family has closure."

"Won't it be traumatic for the family to see a loved one who's been in a devastating accident?" another student asked.

"There is always a way to make the deceased look better if someone wants to pay extra for the time," Edward said.

Another student piped up, "You're telling me that this man lying here can be transformed into a version that his family can accept?"

"Yes. That is exactly what I am saying and the reason you all are here today."

"Really?" the same student replied.

Edward looked at the medical student and said, "Yes. Let me introduce you to Jackie. She is a talented make-up artist who has been trained in special effects artistry and has worked on some of your favorite actors and actresses."

Jackie came up front, introduced herself, and started to explain how she could transform the deceased's face using make-up.

Edward went to the back of the room where Lexi was sitting. "Good morning, Alexandra. I am flattered that you missed me so much this morning that you ventured down here," Edward said half-jokingly.

"I didn't know that you taught?" Lexi questioned back as she smiled at Edward. *Oh, my. I did miss him.*

"A couple of times a year, the university sends over their medical students for various reasons. My dad used to do the teaching, and when he died, I took over."

"You are quite good at it."

"You say that like you are surprised."

"Actually, I am." *More than you know.*

"I am almost finished for the day. How about we go for a picnic?"

"Don't you think it is a little cold for a picnic? It's late January."

"It is never too cold for a picnic. Especially where I'm taking you."

"Sounds intriguing. I'll go check my emails while I wait for you." Lexi gave Edward a quick kiss on the cheek and left.

Stunned, Edward stood there for a moment after she left. *She kissed me.*

Chapter 18

Taking a short holiday with Greg for a week at a secluded mountain cabin, and being out of reach of any technology, created a backlog of texts and emails. Tamara saw Lexi's text about needing her help ASAP. Knowing that Lexi didn't usually exaggerate, Tamara read it first. Tamara texted her back.

Hi Lexi, sorry I've been away, and this is the first chance I've had to reply to you. What's up?

An instant reply came back from Lexi.

Hi Tamara, there is a demon living in my apartment. It has been too scary to live there, so I have been staying at Edward's.

Tamara texted back.

What?

Tamara, the ghost, is a demon. A picture in my living room moved when Edward tried to do an exorcism.

Tamara was impressed and texted back.
Wow, he tried doing an exorcism?!

Lexi's phone rang, and she answered it. "Lexi, what are you talking about? You did an exorcism?" Tamara asked.

"We tried. It failed. Instead, we just got it mad."

Thinking quickly, Tamara said, "Change of plans for tonight's class. We are going to do it at your place."

"Do you think that is wise? Won't we be putting ourselves into harm's way?"

"Lexi, the chances of you having a demon living in your apartment are as high as you flying to the moon. It will be okay. I will bring everyone over together. What's your address?"

"Okay, if you say so, Tamara. I'll text you my address. Edward and I will meet you all downstairs in the lobby."

"Sounds good. See you tonight, Lexi." *What were they thinking? Man, I sure hope they haven't ticked the ghost off too badly. Trying to calm a ghost down is not easy. What will I need for tonight?*

Tamara went into a semi-meditative state to talk to her angels and guides on the best action needed for tonight's class.

Chapter 19

Lexi and Edward were waiting for the group at the front entrance of her apartment building. She watched as young Sam, the valet, opened the door to a limousine and out poured Tamara, Isabella, and all her other classmates.

Lexi held the door open to her apartment building and said, "Now, that's arriving in style!"

Tamara looked at her, laughed, and said, "Well, it helps to have friends in high places," as she patted Isabella's shoulder.

"Come on, everyone. Follow me." Lexi escorted the group up to her apartment.

In the elevator, Tamara whispered to Lexi, "I haven't told everyone why we are having the class at your place. I will give them the details once I know what is really going on."

"Well, I am sure you know best," Lexi whispered back as the elevator doors opened.

Nervously, Lexi unlocked her apartment door and turned on the lights.

Tamara went in first. "Please, everyone, come and have a seat in the living room."

Edward grabbed some extra chairs from the dining room.

"Before we start, I would like everyone to hold hands. I am going to create a protective bubble for us and the ghost."

"What, there is a ghost in here?" Karla said as she jumped up to run.

Tamara gently took Karla's hand and guided her back to her seat, then said, "Everyone, hold hands, thumbs pointing left. That way, the energy will flow properly. You will receive the energy through your left hand and give the energy through your right hand.

"Dear God and all the angels in Heaven who help me, please send whoever we need to make sure tonight's class is protected, taught, and understood. Also, please send whoever is needed to help the ghost in this apartment."

Tamara felt a shiver run through her body and knew the ghost was trying to communicate. At first, it was hard for her to understand the ghost's communication channel, but this would give her a perfect opportunity to demonstrate how to communicate with a ghost.

Scared, Kate said as she tried to control her breathing, trying not to hyperventilate, "Tamara, a man is standing by Isabella. He is crying." No matter how often she sensed a ghost, it still freaked her out.

Isabella jumped.

Tightening her grip on Isabella's hand for assurance, Tamara said, "Thank you, Kate. Tell me what he looks like? Everyone, hold hands and breathe. He's not going to hurt you."

Kate took a breath and told the group what she sensed. "He is very tall, with blond hair. I can hear him, but I can't understand him. His accent is too strong."

Jane blurted out, "He keeps repeating 'Iss.' I can hear him." *Wow, I can hear him.*

Betty asked, "Tamara, why can't I see the ghost?".

"I can't feel anything," Tammy said.

"Let's think about this for a moment. Tammy, you can't feel him, and Betty, you can't see him. Is that correct?"

"Yes," they both said at the same time.

"Jane, you can hear him, and Kate, you can… what?"

"I can feel, hear, and see him."

"Class, our ghost is a Feeler and an Audio. No matter what your main channel is, you will have to shift your frequency if you want to connect."

Lexi said, "Oh. That is why Edward and I couldn't talk to him. Our main channel is not a Feeler."

"Actually, Lexi, Edward should have been able to."

"I can't feel or hear him," Edward said.

"That is because you don't want to hear him. You don't believe you can, and so you won't." Tamara looked over to Edward as she shrugged as if to say, "Only you can choose to communicate with the spirit world."

Betty asked, "Why can Kate see the ghost?"

"Good question. That is because Kate felt him first. She made contact using his first channel. For anyone to communicate with a ghost or spirit, they must start the conversation in the ghost's celestial channel. That is why most people will never know that a ghost or spirit even exists. They can't sense the frequency of energy."

Betty said, "I misunderstood that part. I thought you meant you could only communicate using the ghost's channel."

"Sorry, Betty, if I have caused any confusion. Let me give you an example of how I communicate with a ghost. When I make the first contact, I have to wait and sense how they will respond. I'm waiting to react to the first sensation of a channel. Am I going to hear the ghost, feel the ghost, see the ghost, or think the ghost? Once I have made the initial connection and sensed the ghost, I can then switch and communicate with them through my preferred channel. But remember that the ghost always contacts you or replies using 'their' main channel. I am just translating their communication channel into my channel, as you would Spanish into English."

Betty asked, "So, I might not be able to communicate with a ghost because I do not know how to shift from the seeing frequency to any of the other three channels yet?"

"Yes, Betty, that is why most people can't communicate with ghosts. However, you will learn how to shift in these classes, so don't worry if it isn't easy the first time. You'll get the hang of it," Tamara said to reassure Betty. "That is also why Lexi and Edward saw the painting move but didn't understand the ghost was trying to communicate with them."

Isabella started to freak out again and got up to move away from the ghost.

"Isabella, you'll be okay." Tamara squeezed her hand again for reassurance. Spirit had already warned her that there was a good reason to sit beside Isabella tonight.

"Tamara, I can't do this. I don't want to play games," Isabella said as she started to cry but did sit back down in her chair.

"Isabella, who is here with us? Who is tall, blond, and has an accent?"

"Hans!" She put her face down and started to sob uncontrollably into her hands.

A surge of energy was felt within the room.

Lexi stood up. "Hans. That is who Susannah said was in my apartment. Oh, my God. She was right! Edward, she was right! Susannah sent me another message. I am not going crazy!" Lexi jumped up for joy and then remembered Isabella and quietly sat back down.

"Isabella, is this the man you were telling me about? The love of your life?" Tamara asked.

"Yes."

Lexi passed a box of tissues to Tamara, who set it down on the floor beside Isabella.

"Okay, everyone, take a breath. Hans is not a demon, but we must test the ghost."

"But! We know who it is," Tammy exclaimed.

"It doesn't matter. We want proof," Tamara replied.

"Tamara, I tried to get rid of the ghost, and it just got mad," Lexi said.

Tamara turned to Edward and said, "I heard you tried to banish it."

He nodded.

"That is not going to work on a ghost that has a mission and is attached to something in your apartment," Tamara said as she looked around the room.

"The painting moved, the day Edward tried to banish it," Lexi said.

"Right, I forgot you said that." Looking at the painting that Lexi was pointing to, Tamara asked, "Where did this painting come from?"

"Susannah, she gave it to me. Something about an estate sale in Sweden during one of her business trips. I guess, when they were appraising a painting, hidden behind was this one. It's a replica of 'The Wild Hunt of Odin,' so her boss allowed her to have it as a bonus for all the hard work she had been doing.

"She knew I loved reading Nordic legends and mythology, so she gave it to me as a housewarming gift."

Tamara said, "Okay, I understand now. Now, let's test the spirit. Everyone, send love-light energy from your eyes and heart to his eyes and heart. Good. Now, up the love-light energy ten times."

Tamara was satisfied with testing Hans and said, "Alright, everyone, thank you. Take a breath and let go of the energy. It is a good spirit. We will take a quick break, and when we come back, we will figure this all out," Tamara said as she stood up.

Betty and Tammy went over to Tamara and asked, "We don't sense anything, Tamara. What are we doing wrong?"

"Remember that a ghost can only communicate in their first celestial channel and that a ghost does not have a brain to think, contemplate, or reason with—only memories. So, it is up to you to change."

"How do we do that?" Tammy asked.

"Good question. I will share that answer with everyone in the group. I'll be back in a moment."

Chapter 20

When Tamara came back, she said, "Okay, everyone, come and have a seat. Tammy and Betty asked a good question at the break. How can we communicate with Hans?

"For me, my main channel is visual, like you, Betty, and when I first started to develop my celestial language, all I could see was a line. I had to guess the shape. At first, it was an outline of a mountain top. Then as I practiced, the black and white line became a color. Then I could imagine a green line. Then it became trees. Later, as I developed this visual channel, I changed the perspective, and I could see a full mountain. Then I started to play with the image, and I could change the size and make it bigger or smaller. Later, it became even better than watching TV. My other senses added to the reality. I could smell the fresh air and feel the breeze on my skin. After that, I could pop myself into the scene as if I were there. Realize that this took months of practice."

"We want to be able to do it tonight with you guys," Tammy pleaded.

"The natural way for you, Tammy, being a Feeler, is to sense a shiver or tingles. Hans is also a Feeler, and so the contact should be easy. Concentrate on sensing the sensation, no matter what that is. Even the slightest of tingles would count. Then concentrate on where you felt the feeling on your body. You can also shift your intent to sense his emotions or pain, heartbeat, pulse, or what he likes to do. Any of these sensations would allow you to connect with him."

"So, what do I have to do to sense an Audio?" Edward asked. "You said his second channel is Audio, and you said I am an Audio."

"Yes, that is true, and a person could contact a spirit if the spirit used two of the channels, which Hans did.

"Back when I started to practice the channel of Audio, I would get one letter. Literally, one letter from the alphabet, as if it were written on an imaginary whiteboard. As each letter was added to the whiteboard, it would spell a word. Later, I started to hear a whisper and had to guess the word. I was not always correct with my guess. Then, afterward, I could hear a couple of words spoken, and then it became louder like someone was talking to me, like in a dream state. As this Audio channel developed, I could make out accents and knew the person spoke in another language. Then it was like having a conversation through a walkie-talkie, where only one person could talk at a time. Then it was as if we were in the same room."

"Is that why I can't contact him, Tamara, because I am not an Audio?" Isabella asked.

"No, Isabella, you already have the ability of all four channels equally, but he is a ghost attached to a painting in a stranger's home. That is why you could not contact him. I keep emphasizing that becoming a ghost and being stuck here on Earth is a bad idea."

"Can I contact him now?" Isabella asked.

"We don't have to contact him. He is already here. Regardless of whether you can communicate or not, what is the first rule to contact a spirit?"

The group looked at each other. No one could remember if Tamara said it yet.

"Let's find out if it is Isabella's Hans."

Tamara had everyone sit down and hold hands again and take a deep breath to connect their energies. "Okay, everyone, I am going to ask Hans some questions."

Tamara said a prayer before continuing, *Archangel Michael, please be ready if the need arises, and thank you, Archangel Gabriel, for the ability of effortless communication.*

Kate yelled out, "He is kneeling beside Isabella, pleading for her to hear him."

"That is okay. Hans, please focus your attention on my voice. I am here to help you. If you are the real Hans, you will be patient enough to let us test you. Isabella, please send love-light energy from your heart and eyes to Hans's heart and eyes. Just imagine him as he was. Tell me what happens."

"Nothing. Tamara, I can't sense him."

"He flickered, but he is still there," Kate said.

"Good job. Everyone just breathe and let go. Don't try to do anything. Just be," Tamara told everyone. "Isabella, try one more time. Think of Hans and send him ten times the love-light energy that you've just sent him."

Isabella did as Tamara asked.

Kate got excited. "He started to glow."

"Perfect. Isabella, please hold that energy. We are almost there." Tamara was imagining bringing down love-light energy through her crown chakra and down her right arm, sending the energy to the hand she was holding on her right, imagining the celestial energy channeling from one person's hands to the next, around the circle, and then coming back to her through her left hand.

"Okay, Isabella, one more time. This time send him one hundred times the energy that you did last time."

Again, Isabella did, as Tamara asked.

"He is gone! He disappeared!" Kate yelled.

Isabella broke the circle, let go, and started to cry again.

"Take a breath, you guys. He's not gone. He is a ghost bound to the painting. He is still here. Isabella, take my hand." Tamara held out her hand for Isabella to take.

Reluctantly, Isabella took Tamara's hand.

"Is it always this hard to talk to a ghost?" Edward asked.

Tamara looked over to him and said, "It is not hard. Kate has been able to do it since she walked into the room. Karla knows he's here, and Jane can hear him. It is only hard if you are not tuned into his channel. I am demonstrating what to do so that all of you can tune into his channel."

Edward nodded, as if he was about to say something else, then decided it was best to keep silent.

"He held his energy. It was Isabella who let go." Tamara looked at Isabella.

"I can't feel him, Tamara. You talk to him for me," Isabella said through her tears. "Tamara, I can't. I just can't talk to him right now. I need time."

Tamara turned her head to look at Lexi. "Lexi, it's your house. Let's have you try talking to him."

"Oh, my God, Tamara. I'm afraid of ghosts. Do I have to?"

"No, but that is what this course is all about, to learn how to communicate with spirits."

"Right, I forgot that part." Lexi nodded as she remembered they were in a course and not doing an exorcism. Though she prayed for the exorcism, ghosts freaked her out. Closing her eyes, she prayed again. Opening her eyes, she said to Tamara, "I can't. I am too scared of him."

"Fine, it's been a long night. We can try again some other time. Alright, everyone, join hands again. Take a breath and thank the spirit world for helping us. Thank Hans for letting us meet him. Hans, I will help you soon, when Isabella is ready."

Isabella looked at Lexi with pleading eyes. "Lexi, can I please stay here tonight? I would greatly appreciate it."

Lexi looked at Tamara as if to ask her permission.

Tamara nodded. "It should be okay, Lexi. Hans won't hurt Isabella."

"Sure, then it's okay with me. You can stay in the guest bedroom. Let me grab a few things first."

"Tamara, my limo will take you all back to your house," Isabella said as she hugged her. "Thank you."

Tamara said good night to Isabella, promised her that she would call her in the morning, and left the apartment with the other girls.

Edward waited by the door for Lexi to come back with her stuff.

Lexi looked around to see if she wanted anything else, then said, "Isabella, here is my cell number in case you need to contact me. I will tell the staff downstairs that you will be staying overnight."

"Thank you, Lexi. I appreciate this. It's a lot to take in. I can't believe that Hans is here at your place. How coincidental. Funny, how I was praying to talk to him, and God brought me to you. How crazy life can be, our paths crossing and bringing us together like this?"

Lexi hugged Isabella. "Make yourself at home. If you get hungry or thirsty, help yourself to anything in the kitchen."

"Thanks. I'll be fine. I just need some alone time with Hans."

Lexi and Edward left the apartment and took the elevator down to the parking garage, where Edward had left his SUV. They were almost at the car when Lexi said, "Edward, stop, we have to go back. I forgot the papers that I need for work tomorrow."

Chapter 21

$\mathcal{L}$exi ran back to the elevator. *Where did I put them?* As she unlocked her apartment, she yelled, "Isabella, I forgot some papers." Lexi ran over to her computer desk to grab what she needed. "Isabella?" Lexi could see that the guest bedroom door was closed. Knocking on the door, she said, "Isabella, I just needed…" The door slowly creaked open, and on the floor lay Isabella.

Lexi ran over to her. "Isabella! Isabella!" Lexi shouted as she shook her shoulders. Putting her ear down closer to Isabella's mouth, she couldn't hear her breathing. She grabbed her cell phone from her pocket and dialed 911.

"911, what's your emergency?"

"Oh my God, she is not breathing!"

"Stay calm, ma'am. Do you know how to do CPR?"

"Yes, right. CPR." Lexi came out of her original shock and did as the lady on the phone had instructed. All the while, she was praying that Isabella would be okay.

"Hey, did you two just decide to forget a guy in a parking garage?" Edward said as he came back into the apartment.

"In here!" Lexi yelled.

With the tone of Lexi's voice, Edward ran to where he had heard her call out. Seeing Lexi doing CPR on Isabella, he jumped in to take a turn. "I don't understand. We were only gone for a few minutes. What could have happened?"

There was a knock on the door, and Lexi went to let the ambulance drivers in. "She's in here. Follow me."

They took over from Edward and used a defibrillator on her chest to start her heart. A moment later, Isabella began to breathe again but didn't regain consciousness. They were taking her to the nearest hospital.

As they followed the paramedics to the door, a police officer started to ask Lexi and Edward a lot of questions.

Confused for a moment, since Lexi had not seen the officer come into her apartment, she hesitantly started to answer his questions.

"Her name you said is Isabella Jackson, the actress?" Officer Bennet said.

"Yes," Edward answered.

"You two are?"

"I am Reverend Edward Hawthorne, and this is Alexandra Constantine."

"So, this apartment is registered to you, Miss Constantine?"

"Yes."

"Why was Miss Jackson here?"

Lexi didn't know how to answer that question honestly, so she said, "We were here tonight, taking a class together."

"What type of class?"

"A course that teaches you about Audio, Knower, Visual, and Feeler personality traits," she said, trying not to lie.

"Where is everyone else?"

"They left minutes before we did."

"You left?"

"Ah… yes. Isabella asked if she could stay the night in my apartment, and I left with Edward."

Looking at Edward, Officer Bennet asked, "You two are a couple?"

Edward grabbed Lexi's hand and said, "Yes. That is not a crime, Officer."

"Hey, pal. I am not judging. My job is to get the facts. That is what I am doing."

"Officer, can we go now and see Isabella at the hospital?" Lexi asked.

"Are you family, Miss…" He had to look at the paper to remember her name. "Miss Constantine?"

"No. Just classmates."

"Then probably not. The hospital staff will not let you in to see her unless you are immediate family. Not to mention that she is one of the most famous actresses in the world."

Lexi and Edward finished giving the officer the information he needed and were asked to leave the crime scene.

On their way back to Edward's, while Lexi was texting Tamara about Isabella, she asked him, "What do you think happened, Edward?"

"It's a mystery, alright," Edward replied.

"What a crazy night. Why does my life have to be so complicated? What did I do to deserve all this? I used to be normal, you know. I used to go to work, eat, and sleep. Nothing crazy used to happen."

Looking over to Lexi, he said, "I am asking myself that same question," he said half-jokingly. "Hey, don't look at me that way. Until your sister's soul retrieval, my life was normal too."

"So, you're saying it's Susannah's fault?"

"No, but now that you mention it. Maybe."

Lexi smacked Edward on the shoulder. "Hey, be nice. That's my sister you are talking about."

Chapter 22

Hans was alone again in Lexi's apartment, with no way out. Being a lawyer before his death, and even though he had no brain to think with, he could still access his memory of asking questions. He replayed the night's events by asking himself… *What happened? The two people from the other night came back with more people. Then what happened? I saw Isabella, and nothing else mattered.*

He had tried desperately to remember the rest, but all he could do was remember the moment that for a split-second, Isabella was in his arms again, and then just like that, an invisible source of energy was pulling her soul from him into what seemed like a dark tornado.

He remembered grabbing onto her, desperately trying to keep her with him, but his soul was not allowed to follow her. His soul was bound to this apartment, to the painting.

The next thing he knew, he was sitting on the floor with his cousins, listening to his grandfather tell another story.

"Vette is a female mare who gives people bad dreams at night by sitting on them in their sleep. In our native tongue, we call her *Mareritt*, which translates to Mare-ride or Mare-dream," Olof said to his grandchildren.

Little Erik popped back onto Hans's lap. "I am scared of Vette," he whispered.

"If you boys and girls are bad, Vette will come and take you on a ride filled with bad dreams," Olof said as he looked at all his grandchildren.

"Is she from the underworld, *farfar*?" Hans's cousin, Ian, asked. He was a couple of years younger than Hans and was not usually at the family get-togethers. He lived in Denmark.

"*Ja*, that is correct, Ian."

"I was told that if you catch her, you can ride her," Ian said to get a reaction from the old man.

"Ian, that is a secret that little people are not supposed to know." Olof gave his second eldest grandson a stern look.

That's it. That is how I can reach Isabella— through Vette, Hans thought as his memory returned to the present. *I demand Vette, the mare of the night, to come to me now.*

Out of nowhere, a shadow started to appear from the corner of the room. It got bigger and bigger. Hans tried to jump onto the shadow's back and succeeded.

He demanded that Vette take him to Isabella. The shadow disappeared into the night, leaving him on his butt as he fell off the horse.

What, I can't even leave on Vette? I am stuck here forever!!! Hans's temper got the better of him. He started to stomp around the apartment, and as he passed a vase on Lexi's table, it fell onto the ground and shattered into many pieces.

Frustrated, he vanished into thin air.

Chapter 23

The next morning Lexi and Edward went to the hospital. Just as the officer had said, they were not permitted to see Isabella.

Tamara turned the corner in the hospital and saw them pleading with the nurse. As she got closer and heard what they were saying, she came up to them and said, "Nurse Conway," looking at her name tag, "Reverend Hawthorne is Isabella's spiritual counselor. He has legal permission to be present."

"Is this true, Reverend?"

Looking at Tamara, Edward said, "Yes."

"Why, didn't you say so? I will need to see your ID."

Edward produced the required documents from his wallet and was escorted into Isabella's room.

Sitting beside her, he lightly took Isabella's free hand and gently held it. She was plugged into all kinds of machines, and an intravenous IV was attached to her other arm.

Edward made the sign of the cross and started to pray for Isabella. While he was praying, a doctor came into the room to check her vitals.

Edward overheard him talking to the nurse. "Come and get me if she comes out of the coma. If not, I will come back to check on her tomorrow."

Edward finished his prayer and left the room, going back to where he had left Lexi and Tamara. He told them what he had learned, "She is in a coma."

"What? Oh, my God," gasped Lexi.

"Did they say what happened, Edward?" Tamara asked.

"No."

"How is she?" Tamara inquired.

"Not good. Isabella is not breathing on her own."

"What can we do, Tamara?" Lexi asked.

"Hmm, Lexi, can we go back to your place?"

"Sure. Let me call work to tell them I am not coming in today. We'll meet you there shortly, Tamara."

#

Sam, the young valet at the apartment, saw Lexi and said, "Miss Constantine, your apartment is blocked off. It is sealed with that yellow crime-scene tape. You are not allowed into your apartment. You will find that there is a guard posted outside your door."

"What! It's my place."

Looking at Edward, she said, "Do they have the right to do that?"

"I believe they do."

Tamara quickly pulled Lexi and Edward aside and said, "Lexi, we need to be close to your apartment. Do you know your neighbors?"

"Not really. I mean, I do, but not to ask them for something like this."

"We need to go somewhere close."

"The gym is right below my apartment. Would that be close enough?"

"That should work."

Lexi led the way to the gym and used her key to gain access.

Tamara asked her to show her where her apartment should be located.

Lexi walked her to the approximate area.

"I need it to look like we are doing something like mediation. I need to talk to Hans. I will be right back." Sitting down and leaning against one of the big exercise machines, Tamara shut her eyes.

Edward sat on the equipment she was leaning on. Lexi noticed Nick, her neighbor, was coming over. Jumping up, she went over to him before he could disturb Tamara.

"Hi, Lexi, what's your friend doing? It looks kind of weird."

"Hi, Nick. She's meditating." Trying to change the subject, she said, "How've you been?"

"Good. Hey, where have you been? I've missed seeing you around."

"I've been staying with a friend." She smiled as she thought about where she'd been staying.

"What happened at your apartment? The rumor is that a person died. You are the main conversation around here."

"No one died. A friend had a heart attack, I think. I am not sure; they won't tell us."

"Is the person going to live?

"To be honest, I am not sure. She is on life support right now."

"Man, that sucks. Was she very old?"

"No. I think that is why they have my apartment blocked off. She is only in her thirties."

"I heard someone say that they are not sure if it was a suicide or foul play," Nick said, shaking his head.

"Really, foul play? That's crazy."

"Right. Like you would kill anyone, Lexi."

Tamara got up at that moment, grabbed Edward, and walked over to Lexi, and said, "We're ready to go, Lexi."

"Yep. Nice seeing you, Nick. Gotta go."

Edward nonchalantly put his fingers into Lexi's so they could walk out of the gym hand in hand.

"Jealous much?" Lexi asked.

"Hmm, nope. Just making a statement." Edward smiled.

"Men."

"Come on, you two love birds. We have more important things to do," Tamara said jokingly.

The three of them went over to the coffee shop located next to Lexi's apartment.

After getting coffee and sitting down, Tamara said, "It's worse than I thought. Hans said that he, for a brief second, was able to see Isabella, and then she was sucked up by some negative energy. He tried to follow her but couldn't."

With concern in her voice, Lexi replied, "What do we do now? How do we save Isabella?"

"Hans remembered something from his childhood, but he couldn't leave the apartment to do it."

"Don't tell me. We have to go and tether another soul?" Edward said teasingly.

"No, Edward, this time, you will help me by riding a night mare."

"I was kidding, Tamara. Are you crazy?" Looking at Lexi, he said, "She's crazy."

"Crazy or not, we need to save Isabella's soul, and the only way to do that is by you riding a night mare."

Nervously and unsure if she really wanted to know, Lexi asked, "Where is she, Tamara?"

"Hans says she is in the underworld."

"Where exactly in the underworld?" Edward said with attitude.

"You remember seeing the painting in Lexi's apartment on her living-room wall?"

"The one that Hans is attached to?" Lexi asked.

"Yes. It is a painting of entities, elves, fairies, the dead, humans, and many restless souls, also of a god—I am not sure if it is Odin or Thor that are all riding together above the Earth. It is believed that the hunt is for catching souls that are unaware and easy prey."

"How does Isabella fall into that category?" Lexi said, concerned even more now for Isabella's soul.

"Hans said that he saw her swallow something before she went into the guest bedroom."

"So, Nick was right. She attempted to commit suicide, and if I hadn't happened to come back, she would have died?"

"So, you're telling us that Hans said she tried to kill herself?" Edward knew that suicide was a forbidden sin and was now afraid for Isabella's soul. "You don't think they believe we tried to kill her, do you?" Edward said, getting out of his chair, afraid that the rumors Nick talked about might be what the police were thinking.

"Edward, don't get yourself riled up. If the police believed that you or Lexi tried killing her, you guys would be in jail right now," Tamara said factually.

"True. That is true. We would be, and we are not," he reasoned. "So, she tried to commit suicide?"

"That I don't know, but I do know that she is in trouble and doesn't deserve to be where she is. Edward, we are going to need your place again."

"Wow. I didn't sign up for this part of the course," Edward said as he shook his head.

"You signed up for this way before any of my courses, Edward. You signed up when you decided to save souls as a minister. It is part of your job description. For some reason, God chose to place you on my life path again. I believe it is our destiny to save souls, Edward."

Shaking his head, he asked, "Where do we have to go this time? Hell?" Edward prayed that the answer was no.

"No, actually this time, we need to go to the level of Elementals."

Lexi asked uneasily, "What exactly is an Elemental, Tamara? Do you mean like an Elf, Troll, or Fairy?

"Yep. We are going to the level of mythical creatures."

"Oh, bogus, you're joking?" Edward laughed.

"No joke," Tamara said as she got up to leave. "I have a few things I have to do beforehand, but I will pop over around eight tonight."

"You're serious. We're going to do this?" Edward said as he stood up, following Tamara to the door.

"See you tonight," Tamara said as she waved to them and left the café.

"Alexandra, do you believe in fairies?"

"No matter how weird it sounds, Edward, we need to help Isabella."

Putting his jacket back on, he said, "I guess." Still not quite believing what was about to happen tonight at his place, he followed Lexi back to the parking garage in her apartment.

Chapter 24

*T*amara made sure that she had her beautiful wood-carved box full of goodies before driving over to the funeral home. Looking inside, she made sure she had a bit of everything: Vibhuti, Satya Sai Baba, Nag Champa incense sticks, bell and dorje, sage herbs, feathers, seashells, gemstones… *What else might I need? Oh, I might as well put a couple of white candles in there.*

Eight o'clock came faster than she expected, and Tamara was running a little late. Quickly walking up to the front entrance of the funeral home, Tamara said a silent prayer. *Dear God and Angels of Light, I require your assistance this evening. Protect us during this hunt. Protect us from the unknown. Protect us from the dark energy and grant us the power to save another soul. Amen.*

Knowing that Lexi would be waiting, Tamara didn't use the bell. Instead, she tapped on the door by using the brass lion head knocker.

"Hi, Tamara, come in. Edward is waiting for us in the waiting room," Lexi said as she led the way.

Just like last time, the incredible paintings instantly mesmerized her. The old master's stunning art seemed to take her back in time as if she was there watching them paint. Tamara had to shake her head to focus on the task at hand. "Let's get right to it, shall we?" Tamara said without saying hi.

Edward tried to discourage Tamara from tonight's plan by saying, "This destination or, as you call it, the level of Elementals, you really believe it is real?"

Tamara matter-of-factly replied, "Fairy tales come from somewhere. People don't just make the stories up. Usually, it has some bearing on their true life experiences. No matter what I believe, someone out there believes it is real, and so it is. Did you take psychology courses in seminary school, Edward?"

"Yes."

"Then you already know that the mind does not know the difference between real and imaginary. So, tonight we are going to use that to our advantage."

Edward was frustrated that she always had a logical answer. He was even more frustrated with himself for not believing that there is any truth in the science of metaphysics.

Tamara reminded the reverend why he was helping. "Isabella needs our help. I cannot let the underworld take another innocent soul."

"Is that what happens to a suicide victim? Their soul is taken?" Lexi asked.

"Not just suicides. Also, the people who are under the influence of drugs and alcohol. Their soul becomes foggy and loses control of their thoughts, creating a way for the beings participating in the wild hunt to catch the 'beast of the chase,' in this case, their human soul."

"Does a soul who is captured always go to the destination called Elementals?" Lexi asked to further her understanding.

"No. A soul can be taken to any of the underworld destinations. It all depends on who captured it."

"Are these the same destinations that you and Susannah passed on her way to the pearly gates?"

"Yes, Lexi. When you helped me at Limbo's train station, Susannah and I did pass all the other destination stations."

Lexi needed more clarification. "Are those levels considered the underworld because they are under heaven?"

"Yes, but we are also considered to be living in the underworld here on Earth. We are under Heaven, as are the destinations or levels of Hell, Held, Non-Believers, and Elementals."

"How do you know that Isabella is in the level of Elementals?" Edward asked.

"I asked Hans what happened and where they took her soul."

"Tell us, Tamara, how do the participants of the hunt find the souls?" Lexi was so curious.

"By using the old-fashioned style of a fox hunt. The lead horse is white. One light mare is visible to lead the way through the darkened night, so all the other dark mares, called night mares in the underworld, can easily follow. As you might already know, following not too far behind, there is always a master who sets the hounds free during the hunt. In the case of the wild hunt, the master is usually considered Odin, and instead of hounds, he has black Ravens that search for shiny glimmering souls. You might remember the scene from the painting of the 'Wild Hunt' in your apartment, Lexi."

"I do. I wondered about that."

"I don't know how you do it, Tamara, but somehow you can make a fairy tale seem logical," Edward piped up, shaking his head, trying not to get too caught up in her old wives' tales.

"Edward, how is it possible that you can believe in a God, whom you cannot see, feel, hear, or know to be real, but yet you judge?" Tamara questioned.

Not sure how to answer that, he asked, "What do you need me to do?"

Chapter 25

*A*s he sat down on the semi-circle sofa in the center of the room, Edward said, "I can't wait to find out why you think I know how to ride a night mare, I should say nightmare, because that is what you are asking me to do, be in a terrifying dream."

Listening to Edward ramble on, Tamara brought the same small end-table that she had used the last time closer to where she was going to sit. "Edward, you are going to have to loosen up and relax. Trust me. I have a plan."

"This should be good," Edward said as he crossed his arms in disbelief.

"All three of us are going to astral-travel to Hans, in Lexi's apartment. Then I will get him to call the night mare for you to ride. Lexi, I want you to distract the horse by feeding it a celestial apple so that Edward can mount it."

"Fascinating. I love horses. Can I pet it?" Lexi giggled.

"Sure. Whatever you would do in real life, you can do while you are in the astral state." Tamara smiled back, trying not to be disappointed in their childish questions. "Seriously though, this is not a game. We are here tonight to save a soul, Isabella's soul. Keep focused," Tamara reminded them.

"Sorry, Tamara, we do want to help Isabella," Lexi said.

Taking out the bell and dorje, Tamara reminded them what it was for. "I will ring the bell twice when I have finished the meditation so that your souls can astral-travel back here to your body, and then I will remind you to wiggle your toes."

Tamara lit the white candles and placed them far enough away from all of them, making sure there was no way to cause a fire. She stuck the incense into one of the candle edges, lit it, and then quickly blew it out so the smoke would work its magic. Lastly, she took a small amount of Vibhuti on the pad of her middle finger and rubbed some of the ash on all of their foreheads.

"May I say a quick prayer, Tamara?" Edward asked.

"Of course. That would be appreciated."

"God in Heaven. Please bless our souls for what we are going to attempt tonight. Your daughter, Isabella, is in a coma, and her soul needs your help in saving it. Please guide us with your love and show us the way. Amen." Edward ended by making the sign of the cross in the air.

"Thank you, Edward." Tamara took hold of their hands. "Now that we are ready, make yourself comfortable on the sofa. Take a few deep breaths and relax. With every breath you take, you will relax even deeper.

"Breathing in and out.

"Deep breaths.

"Relax.

"In a moment, you will become the size of a pea in the center of your mind. Together, on the count of three, we will teleport from the crown chakra on top of your head to Lexi's apartment, where Hans is waiting for us.

"One, you are the size of a pea.

"Two, with ease and grace, your soul knows exactly where to travel.

"Three, take a breath and imagine yourself teleported to Lexi's living room."

Tamara was the first to arrive at Lexi's. Next was Lexi, and following behind, coming through the astral dimension, a little wobbly, was Edward, still holding onto Lexi's hand.

Hans appeared as all three astral-travelers came into Lexi's living room.

Tamara introduced herself again to Hans, "I'm Tamara, and this is Edward and Lexi. Lexi owns the apartment and the painting that you are in."

"Ah *ja*, the guy who called me a demon and tried to banish me. Dude, that was harsh," Hans said to Edward.

"Ah, sorry. You were a ghost, a stranger in Alexandra's apartment. You would have done it for the person you love," Edward said, trying to justify his actions.

"You love me?" Lexi said as she took a deep breath.

Edward, not realizing what he'd just said, looked at Alexandra and said, "Yes."

Keeping the focus, Tamara said, "Thank you, Hans, for helping us help Isabella. We need you now to call the night mare here."

Hans closed his eyes and demanded a night mare to come to him.

A moment later, one of the most beautiful black mares Lexi had ever seen appeared in her apartment. She couldn't have stopped herself if she tried. Her soul was attracted to the horse. Walking over, soothing it with her voice, she imagined an apple. One appeared in her hand from the celestial world. While feeding the beautiful creature, her instinct was to stroke the mare's head, so she did.

Tamara motioned for Edward to mount the horse.

He was intrigued by the realism of this dream. As he came closer to the mare, he could smell the horse as if it was real. He could hear it breathe and chew as it ate the apple. *Amazing!*

He imagined his leg going over the horse and sitting on its back. As he believed, it became a reality. He was now seated securely on the mare's back.

Tamara kept her focus on saving Isabella by saying, "Edward, you need to ride this mare to the hospital where Isabella is. From her hospital bed, I require you to follow her AKA cord into the underworld to retrieve her soul. Once you find her, please bring her back to the hospital room and place her soul back into her body. Then leave her there and ride the night mare back to us here in Lexi's apartment. In the worst-case scenario, astral-travel back to your body at your funeral home. And no matter what, if you hear the bell ring twice, no matter where you are or what you are doing, the second ring's sound will bring you back to your human body. Do you understand, Edward?" Tamara asked.

"Yes." And with that said, he vanished into thin air.

Chapter 26

It was pitch-black, and Edward could not see a thing. The warmth from the mare between his legs kept him focused. *To Isabella's body in the hospital,* he thought. *Follow Isabella's scent.* Edward decided that he had come this far in the dream, he might as well play along. So, he imagined that the mare had just come from a hunt. He sent a thought to the horse. *Follow Isabella's scent back to where you came from.*

Instantly he was teleported into a mass herd of night mares, carrying all types of entities. He was traveling fast with the herd through the dimensions of the underworld.

If he didn't believe he was in a dream, he would have soiled his pants from fear. Riding beside him was what looked like a warrior, from the days of the Vikings, with his sword raised. As he looked from side to side, he saw mythical creatures riding as if the devil was after their tail. No story he ever heard as a child could have prepared him for what he was witnessing now. Trolls, goblins, elves, fairies, and not the cute and innocent bedtime stories characters he remembered. No, these creatures weren't just after blood and treasures. These creatures were after the life-force essence of the human soul.

He started to pray. *Heavenly Father, please help me save Isabella's soul from the realms of this underworld.*

A moment later, his mare reared up and teleported the two of them into a new dimension, or as Tamara would call it, a new level or destination.

Looking around, he had to wonder where they were.

The mare was still galloping at lightning speed, and Edward hoped it was heading toward Isabella.

As the mare slowed its pace, it descended onto what resembled land.

Edward sat silently on the horse as she slowed down and completely stopped. He was not sure what to do next, and one thing he knew for sure was that he was not getting off this horse. Tamara never told him if he could or couldn't get off, and he wasn't going to leave his only ride home. Edward started to turn his head in all directions, looking around for Isabella.

Waiting for something to happen, Edward decided to call out to Isabella, "Isabella, it's Edward. Are you there?"

He didn't hear an answer.

"Isabella, please answer me. I know you are here."

Still, no answer came.

"Isabella, I demand that you answer me."

"I am here," came a faint voice in the distance.

Edward clicked his heels lightly into the mare's ribs to nudge her to go in the direction of the sound.

"Isabella, it's me, Edward, from class. Alexandra's boyfriend."

"I know who you are. Why are you here?"

Edward was frantically looking around to see Isabella. He could hear her, so why couldn't he see her? "Isabella, where are you? Come out so I can see you."

A hand appeared from out of the air and started to pet the mare's nose. "Edward, I do not want to live without Hans."

"So, you've decided that living here is better?" Edward looked around at this foreign land.

"I had no idea that I would end up here. I thought that if I died, I would be with Hans."

"Isabella, I am here to take you home, back to your body. Get on behind me."

"No."

"What do you mean, no? You would rather live here than on Earth?"

"I don't want to live anywhere without him."

Getting worried that his time was running out, he prayed to God again, *Dear God, give me the words to convince Isabella to return to her body.*

"Isabella Jackson! I have found you, and I claim the right to demand your soul to get on this horse." Instantly, Isabella was sitting behind Edward on the night mare.

The sound of the first ring of the bell was heard. Edward had a split-second to make it back to the hospital room. Knowing only one being that could perform miracles, he said, "Dear God, teleport us to Isabella's hospital room, destination Earth."

Just before the second ring sounded, Edward threw Isabella's soul into her body and teleported back to the funeral home.

Chapter 27

Lexi's body twitched, and instantly she opened her eyes. "Did we do it? Did it work?"

Tamara let go of both hands as she felt Edward stir. Sitting up, she waited patiently for Edward to come back into consciousness.

"So, did it work?' Lexi asked again.

Opening his eyes and quickly closing them again due to the bright light of the candle flame, Edward tried to sit straighter on the sofa. Trying again, he opened his eyes. This time the light was not so bright.

"Take your time, Edward. There is no rush. Wiggle your toes and come back fully into your body," Tamara reminded him.

Edward felt like he was drunk. His body felt like it didn't belong to him. As his blood started to flow faster in his veins, he became more coherent, and logic was flooding back into his mind.

"Tamara, what kind of drugs are you burning? This hallucination was worse than a suspense horror movie," Edward said. He was trying to determine what had just happened—rubbing his head, attempting to decipher what was real and what was imaginary.

"Edward, I am dying to find out. What happened? Did you do it? Is Isabella back in her body?" Lexi said for the third time.

"I am not sure. I think so."

"Edward, what do you know?" Tamara asked.

Looking at the two girls, he shook his head. "I know that I am not volunteering to help you again, Tamara."

"You would have wanted me to let Lexi go instead?"

"Okay, you made your point. No. All that I remember is that I only had enough time to throw Isabella's soul at her body. I don't know if it landed there."

"You did what?" Lexi yelled.

"Hey, it was that or nothing. I ran out of time. Next time, you ride through the underworld and save a soul."

"I did. Remember?"

"Right. I almost forgot. I guess it was my turn. Well, it's not easy."

"That I can agree on." Lexi nodded.
"Okay, you two. There is nothing more we can do tonight. In the morning, Edward, go to

Isabella in the hospital and make sure that she is okay." Tamara packed up her belongings and started to leave.

"That's it? Are you not going to ask me what happened or what I saw?" Edward asked Tamara.

"Why? You don't believe what you saw." Tamara smiled back.

"Well, I want to know?" Lexi said.

"Night, you two," Tamara said as she let herself out of the building.

"You do know that she is only burning incense, right?" Lexi asked Edward.

"Well, it better be."

"Was it scary for you too? I was scared when I had to go into the Void to save Susannah, and I had my dad with me. You must have been afraid all by yourself."

"I prayed to God a couple of times during the experience. It always gives me strength. How do you think Tamara does it?" Edward asked Lexi.

"What do you mean?"

"I mean, how does she stay sane with all that she knows about the celestial world?"

"Ah, now that is a good question. She believes that what she is doing is for the good of humanity. She believes that all souls deserve to be in Heaven. I guess that is enough to shield her from the judgment of others."

"Alexandra, how does she distinguish between reality and the imaginary?"

"What do you mean?"

"I mean, when I was in the dream, it felt real. I could even smell the horse and feel the heat from her body. How does a person stay sane when they know the truth about celestial beings?"

As she snuggled up to him, Lexi said what she thought, "I guess it's because she believes her soul has a purpose on Earth and that she has to fulfill her destiny."

Leaning his head onto her, he said, "I meant what I said."

"That you love me."

"Yes." He turned her chin softly toward his and leaned in with the tenderest of kisses.

Chapter 28

Waking to the voices of his staff, Edward quickly had a shower and made his way downstairs.

Casandra, the funeral home office assistant for the last fifteen years, met him in his office. "Alexandra asked me to remind you to go to the hospital as soon as possible. I didn't see it on your schedule, so I penciled in the time at 10:15. That should give you enough time to be back here for the viewing of Mrs. Webster."

"Thanks, Casandra. That will be fine."

"I like her."

"Who?"

"Alexandra. She isn't like your last girlfriend, who freaked out and ran when she saw her first dead body."

Turning his head away from the daily files, he said, "I think she is the one."

"I hope so, Edward. You deserve to be happy."

"Hey, I'm happy."

"You know what I mean."

Nodding and drifting into last night's kiss, he replied, "Ya, I know what you mean."

"Who are you visiting at the hospital?"

Bringing him out of his heart's desire, "Ah, a classmate of Alexandra's." Trying not to lie.

"I can pray for her if you tell me her name."

"Thanks, Casandra, I wish I could, but I promised to keep it confidential."

"Really. A celebrity then."

"I didn't say that."

"You didn't have to. I know the drill all too well." Smiling at Edward, she turned and walked out of the office.

#

It didn't take Edward long to drive to the hospital. Checking in at the nurse's station to report his arrival, he was escorted by two bodyguards into Isabella's room.

Surprised to see her sitting up in bed, as she looked his way, he made the sign of the cross. "Reverend Hawthorne, so nice of you to come and check in on me." She made a gesture with her hand to shoo away the guards. "Come and have a seat. We have much to talk about."

"How are you feeling, Isabella?"

"Like I was ripped away from the underworld on a horse."

"What, you remember that?" Edward moved closer to her and sat on the edge of the bed.

"Damn right, I do."

"I didn't even tell Alexandra about what really happened. I thought I made it all up in my head."

"By the way, the next time you throw a soul, use a little less force."

Shaking his head in disbelief, Edward asked, "What? You know… how? Dang it, you mean I'm going to have to start praying to God now about saving the souls in the underworld too?"

"Okay, so, what is the plan now, Edward?"

"Plan now? No one told me about a new plan. My job was to get you back into your body."

"Well, I am back, and I still don't want to live life without Hans."

"Isabella, don't say that too loud. You do not want me to have to tell the authorities what you just said. I am a man of the cloth. There are laws I must follow."

"Edward, get me out of this place."

"I will try my best, but Isabella, you tried to commit suicide. That doesn't go over too well with the doctors."

"Edward, the pain is unbearable. I can't go on like this."

"Isabella, let's pray. Please, God, give Isabella the strength to find the peace she is searching for. Give her the ability to continue her life's journey. Grant her the ability to speak with Hans, the love of her life, so that she can ease her pain."

Patting Isabella's hand, Edward said, "I will be back tonight. I'll figure something out."

Chapter 29

Edward stopped quickly at the hospital on his and Lexi's way to tonight's class at Tamara's. He had been popping up to see Isabella every day since she came out of the coma. The doctors called it a miracle.

"How is my favorite live client?" Edward joked.

"What? You have someone dead that you like better?" Isabella laughed back.

"I hear a rumor that you are getting out of here in a couple of days," Edward said.

"Well, you know how rumors go. They can be exaggerated. Hey, say hi to everyone in tonight's class. I wish I could be there."

"You'll be there soon enough."

"I feel great. I don't know why my doctor is keeping me here."

"I am sure they are just taking precautions. You are a celebrity, you know."

"Edward, what are the rumors of why I'm in here?"

"The tabloids are making a killing on you right now," he joked, smiling a huge smile to make her buy it.

"No, really. What does it say?"

"A bit of the truth. That you have a broken heart."

"And… the not so true?"

"That you tried to commit suicide."

"Ah, Edward, that part is true as well."

"I was trying to soften the blow, Isabella. You did learn the lesson that taking your own life is not the answer, right?"

"I learned that in taking my own life, I don't get to be with Hans if that's what you mean?"

"That too, but the really good news is that we think we have a plan for you."

"Really? One where I can be with Hans?"

"Kinda like that."

"When do I get to know about this plan?"

"Soon. Tamara and Alexandra are trying to figure it all out. I will tell you as soon as I know more. Now get some rest."

"Ah… yes. That is all I get to do here. I am sick of resting."

Edward smirked. "Hang in there, Isabella. The worst is almost over."

"Thanks, Edward, for coming. I really appreciate what you have done for me."

"Okay, I didn't sign up for all the metaphysical stuff, but I did sign up to save souls, and yours is worth saving."

#

As Edward got into the driver's seat, he leaned over and kissed Alexandra. "Thank you for being so patient. I am sorry the guards won't let you in to see her."

"Not a problem. Rules are rules."

"Shall we venture over to our next class and find out what Tamara has in store for us all?"

"I can't wait. She always has something interesting to say."

Chapter 30

Tamara opened the door to let Edward and Lexi into her home. "Glad you two could make it. It means a lot to me to finish what I started, and the remaining ladies deserve to learn what they are here for."

Edward found a seat next to Karla, and Lexi sat beside Tammy.

"Thank you, everyone, for helping to communicate with Hans."

"Is Isabella not joining us tonight, Tamara?" Betty asked, noticing she was not in the group.

"No, not tonight."

"Is it true what we are reading in the tabloids about her trying to commit suicide?" asked Kate.

Tamara decided there was no sense in lying to them and said, "It is."

"Is it because she couldn't speak to Hans?" Jane asked.

"I am not sure of that part." Tamara started the class before anyone else could ask more questions about Isabella. "You all have lost someone dear to you. Every person deals with death differently. Sometimes their death happens in an instant, and for others, they wished it had. I believe losing a child is one of the hardest losses to handle. So, tonight, we are going to help Tammy."

It took Tammy a second after hearing her name to comprehend what was about to happen. "Oh, Tamara, that would be… I don't have the words to express my loss."

"Not that you have to, but if you would like, please share your story with us," Tamara said to Tammy.

"He died when he was six years old, my Bobby. When he was born, he was tiny compared to his twin brother, Jack. He had to stay in the hospital in an incubator for weeks after Jack came home.

"I visited every day. I wasn't allowed to bring Jack to see his brother because the doctor was worried about germs. It killed me to be away from him for so many hours at a time, fearing every time I left the hospital that I would get a phone call telling me that he had died. They never did, and he fought to survive. After months in the hospital, he was finally allowed to come home.

"He was so small compared to Jack. He seemed so frail. As the boys aged, I could tell that Bobby would never catch up to his brother in size. By the time they were four, they looked like they were two years apart.

"Bobby's condition was not diagnosed for another year. He was five when they told me he had cancer, leukemia. He never came out of the hospital, and again I had to wait until my husband came home from work to see him. This time, I had to take turns with Rob, my husband, because he also needed to see his son.

"I resented the time my husband spent with him. I felt like he was taking away the precious time I had left with him. I know that was selfish, that, of course, Rob deserved to see his son, but it was my baby. I wanted all the time I could have with him before…" Tammy started to sob uncontrollably.

One of the other ladies got up and went over to pat her on the back to comfort her.

Tamara stopped her by saying, "No, Karla. Please, sit back down. It is okay to let her cry and let her feel whatever it is that she needs to. Letting the tears flow so that she can heal from this."

"Can I at least give her a tissue?" Karla asked, reaching for one.

"No."

"What, really?" Karla stared at Tamara, not believing what she had just heard.

"Karla, if you pat her on the back or give her a tissue, you are telling her to shut up."

"I am not. I am just being kind."

"When we are young, we are brought up to stop crying by our parents by giving us a hug or a kiss on the booboo," Tamara explained.

Lexi blurted out, "Or if you were like me, my dad used to say, 'Be a big girl and suck it up, buttercup.'"

"The point is that an excellent counselor knows to state that there is tissue available if the client needs it. You wouldn't believe how many people have a box of tissues sitting in front of them, and instead, will use their sleeve to wipe their nose." Tamara took the box of tissue from Karla. She set it down beside Tammy's feet, saying, "Continue when you are ready, Tammy."

"I need to know that he is okay. I need to know that Bobby is being taken care of."

"Would you like to do that now?" Tamara asked Tammy.

"Yes."

"Tammy, make yourself comfortable, and in a moment, I will ask that you take a few deep breaths.

"I am going to take you to your son. Is that alright with you?"

"Yes," Tammy said as she leaned back into the chair and let her head fall forward as she closed her eyes.

"Take a deep breath, and as you exhale, allow it to take with it any tension in your body.

"Breathing in and out.

"In a moment, you will notice a staircase. I would like you to start climbing the stairs now. With each step you take, you will go deeper and deeper into a trance. Fully aware of my voice and your surroundings, but still very, very relaxed." Tamara paused for a moment to allow Tammy to walk up some of the stairs in her mind's eye.

"In a moment, you will be at the top of the stairs, and at the top of the stairs is a door. Open the door and go inside." Tamara and the group were watching Tammy's subtle facial expressions. You could tell that she'd just opened the door by the way she took a breath.

"Great. Go inside. What do you see?"

"It is a room like a waiting room."

"Can you have a seat?"

"Yes."

"Good. Have a seat. If you need to, take a number or something. Go ahead and do that now."

Tammy slowly shook her head.

"What is happening now, Tammy?"

"Nothing, I am just waiting."

"In a moment, someone will come up to you to take you in to see your son. Are you okay with that?"

"Yes."

"Tell me when someone comes."

A few moments passed, and then Tammy nodded.

"A man's coming over to me and asks me to follow him."

"Good. Follow him."

Tammy nodded again.

"Tell me what happens next."

"I feel like we are going into a bright room of love."

"Great. Now, what happens?"

"The man is telling me that my son, Bobby, is okay." Tears started to run down Tammy's face.

"He says that because Bobby was so young when he died, a guardian angel has been looking after him."

"Awesome. Ask if you can see Bobby."

Tears started to roll down Tammy's face, even though a smile began to form on her lips.

Shivers ran through Tamara's body, and she knew that Tammy was able to communicate with Bobby. She did not know what was happening, but she knew that a lot could be communicated within a few seconds. It might be a few moments in our reality, but in the celestial world, it could be hours.

Tamara gave them a few moments together before she said softly, "When you are ready, say thank you to the angel for looking after Bobby, and then take a breath and wiggle your toes coming back into your body. Opening your eyes, knowing that you can go back and visit your son any time that you wish to."

Tamara sat up straighter and looked at the other students, and gave a smile. A few moments later, Tammy opened her eyes and immediately took a tissue to wipe her nose. "That was incredible, Tamara. Thank you!"

"You're welcome."

Edward asked, "But I don't understand. How did she communicate with Spirit?"

Tamara looked over to Edward. "Tammy's first and main channel is 'Feeler.' To communicate with the spirit, she needs to feel. The best way to do that is through meditation."

"How do you feel, Tammy?" Tamara asked.

"Incredible! For the first time since Bobby was born, I feel that he is okay. Actually, he is better than okay. I don't have to worry about him anymore."

Edward being so curious, asked, "Did you get to see him?"

"Yes, and he was beautiful. He wasn't sick anymore. He was healthy, beautiful, and well looked after. He was happy to see me, and he gave me the biggest hug ever. I can rest assured that he is okay.

"He told me to start to live my life and that Jack was going to grow up to be a football star. Can you imagine that all he cared about was that we were going to be okay?" Tears started to roll down her cheeks again.

"Thank you, Tammy, for letting us witness your story," Tamara said as she got up and gave her a hug. "We will take a short break, and then we will have time for a couple more."

Chapter 31

Lexi went over to Edward. "Do you think she is okay?"

"Who?"

"Isabella?"

"I have been praying for her. I think she learned her lesson and will not try to commit suicide again if that is what you are asking."

"No. I am asking if you think she can get over Hans."

"Hmm. I don't know about that part. She seems to have lost herself in her grief, and now that she knows he is in your apartment, I don't think she will be moving on too soon."

"Oh. I didn't think about that. What am I going to do? I can't have her stay with me, and I can't stay at your place forever."

Edward was taken aback by her comment. *Why couldn't she stay at my place forever?*

At that moment, a text came in on Lexi's phone. Clicking on it, she said, "Speaking of the Devil."

Hi Lexi,
I hope you are enjoying the class. Say hi to everyone for me.
Can I ask a favor of you?
They are releasing me from the hospital tonight, and I was hoping you would let me stay at your place?
Please!
Forever in your debt, Isabella.

"That is weird. We were just talking about this. She wants to stay at my place. Edward, what do I do?"

"Well, you did say that you are not staying at your place while there is a ghost living there, so I don't see the harm in letting her stay. She is not going to forget Hans, and I am assuming that she will not go too far from him now either. Plus, I like you staying at my place."

Lexi smiled at Edward's last words. "You are so kind to let me stay there. I have enjoyed my time there more than I thought I ever would."
Way more than I thought I ever would.

"So, what are you going to tell her?"

"I guess you're right. There's no harm in her staying at my place."

Lexi texted Isabella back.

Hi Iss,
You are missing a very interesting class.
Tamara is demonstrating how to
communicate with our beloved ones in
Heaven.
I guess that since Hans is here on Earth, you
might not need to know this part anyways.

You are welcome to stay at my place. I will
ask Sam to let you in. Just tell him that you
are my cousin, Lily. Visiting from… just tell
him your hometown, New Castle.
See you soon, Lexi

Looking up to Edward, Lexi said, "Okay, that's done. Guess I am staying at your place tonight."

"Oh, darn." *Oh, yay!*

Just then, Tamara asked everyone to come back to their seats.

Chapter 32

Tamara asked Jane to share her story next.

"Hi, everyone. As you know, I am Jane. My mother died of a heart attack, and I talk to her all the time, almost every day."

"How do you know it is her, Jane?" Tamara asked.

"Because I see a sign from her while I am sitting in the park."

"What sign do you see?" Tamara was now very interested since a woman in her late fifties talked to her right now, begging for Jane to let her go.

"Her favorite color, red."

"Jane, explain to me in more detail. Tell me exactly what happens when you see her." The spirit hovering around Tamara was getting antsy, saying over and over again, *"Let me go."*

"Well, okay. I sit on my mother's special bench at the park. I start talking to her. I know she is there because I keep seeing her favorite color as the people pass by."

"Jane, are you telling me you see people pass by wearing red? Is that correct?"

"Yes."

Tamara could hear the spirit pleading to have her ask Jane how long this has been going on. "Jane, what makes this bench special?"

"It is a memorial bench that I paid for in her honor."

"That was nice of you to do that," Tamara said as the spirit said again, *"Ask her how long."* "How long have you been sitting on that special bench?"

"Twenty-five years."

Tamara sat back in her chair. It was starting to make sense. The spirit was held to Earth by Jane and wanted to be freed. The question now was how to go about this tactfully.

Kate looked at Tamara and said, "Aren't you going to help her? She is asking you to set her free."

Everyone looked at Kate and then at Tamara, not sure what was going on.

Tamara looked at Kate and then at Jane and said, "Jane, your mother is here right now and is asking to be freed. Do you know what that means?"

Jane shook her head.

"It means that twenty-five years is a very long time to be held to Earth, and she wants to go home to Heaven now."

"What? That is crazy. She's in Heaven. I know she's in Heaven. She was a good person. What would be holding her to Earth?"

Kate stammered out, "You are, and she is begging Tamara to set her free."

Jane was instantly in tears upon hearing Kate's blunt words.

Tamara intercepted by saying, "Kate, you are correct, but part of why you are here is to learn tactful ways of communicating with a client, in this case, Jane. There is a kinder way of doing this. Watch and learn."

"Jane, Kate is right. Your mother is here, and yes, she is asking to be set free. Do you know why she is asking to be set free?"

"No."

"You love your mother so much that for over twenty-five years, you have visited her almost every day by sitting on your favorite bench in the park, talking to her. Waiting to see her color go by. Jane, do you know that is actually a Visual trait, not an Audio trait?"

"No. I thought you said I was an Audio."

"At first, I thought you were. But as you described your encounter with your mom, those are all Visual traits."

"But I talk to her."

"Yes, but you cannot understand when she talks back to you. She is definitely an Audio. That is how I am communicating with her right now."

"I don't understand." Jane was wiping her face from all the tears.

"You bought a bench, which is materialistic, a Visual trait. You placed it in the park for everyone to see, again a Visual trait. You see her color as you sit on the bench, a Visual trait. Also, you cannot hear her, which if you could, you would be using an Audio trait, but you can't."

"So, I am a Visual?"

"Yes, that is your main channel," Tamara said with a slight smile.

"Now, would you like to learn how to communicate so you can understand your mom?"

"Yes," Jane said, sitting up a bit straighter and wiping away more tears.

"Great, let's do that now, shall we?

"Everyone, hold hands again, please. Thumbs left. Take a deep breath. Archangel Gabriel, please come to our assistance and have your angels deliver this message to Heaven and tell them that Jane's mom… Jane, what is your mom's full name?"

"Teresa Jane Lancaster."

"That Teresa Jane Lancaster is coming home. Thank you, Archangel Gabriel, for taking care of this important message."

Tamara addressed the spirit, "Teresa, thank you for being so patient and loving your daughter so much.

"Jane, it is time to let your mother continue her ascension to Heaven. In a moment, you are going to take a deep breath, and when you exhale, you will be releasing all ties to your mother so that she can rise to the glory of God. Knowing that once she is in Heaven, you will be able to communicate with her."

Jane took a deep breath and let it out slowly. *I love you, mom! I pray that I will be able to speak to you and hear you speak back to me.*

Kate squealed with glee. "You did it, she left. Good job!"

Jane looked at Kate and started to cry.

"Why are you crying? She left. That's a good thing." Kate couldn't understand the problem.

"Kate, you have to understand that Jane has been holding her mom here for over twenty-five years. That is a long time. Now she does not know how to communicate with her. We have to show her how to do that so that she will feel the love of her mother and know that she did the right thing."

Kate nodded but didn't understand. It was so easy for her to see, hear, feel, and know when a spirit was near. *How could anyone not know that the best thing for a ghost or spirit is to be in Heaven? Where they are free.*

"Jane, are you ready to communicate with your mom now?" Tamara asked.

Jane nodded.

"Great. Take a deep breath and wiggle your toes, relaxing in your chair and releasing any tension in your body.

"Breathe in and out, relaxing. Knowing you will be communicating with your mom very shortly.

"Good. Take a deep breath in and out.

"Relaxing.

"In a moment, you will be escorted to the level of love—a level where love is felt and emanates from everyone and everything. As you take your next breath, in your mind's eye, you will be teleported to the level of love."

As Jane took her next breath, Tamara said, "Great. Now allow all that beautiful love-light energy to fill your body. Just let the energy flow in you and around you."

Tamara could see Jane's facial expressions change from a stressed, teary look to a calm and peaceful look.

"Jane, in a second, I am going to ask Archangel Gabriel to appear. You might see a lady, or you might see a man. Gabriel appears as both. I personally sense Archangel Gabriel as a man, but many say this angel appears to them as a woman. No matter, you can trust who appears. I am here to make sure you are safe. Tell me when you see someone."

Jane nodded. "I see someone, but I can't tell if it is female or male. I do see the most amazing golden coppery white glow. I can hear its words. It is saying, 'Your mom is waiting for you,' and that it is okay to communicate with her now?"

Tears started to flow out of Jane's eyes as she saw her mom for the first time in twenty-five years. "Mom! Oh, mom, I have missed you so much. I came to visit almost every day. Did you hear me?"

Kate started to cry. She could not believe the emotions and love that were flowing between Jane and her mom.

Tamara told everyone, "We will allow Jane to have a moment with her mom."

A few moments went by, then Tamara said, "Okay, Jane, you have a moment longer, and then I am going to break the connection. I want you to know that you can communicate with your mom anytime you want to by taking a breath and imagining going to the level of love from this moment on. She will always meet you there."

Everyone in the group, even Edward, had a tear in their eye as they witnessed the holy meeting of Jane and her mom.

"Jane, take a deep breath, and say goodbye to your mom, knowing that you can now chat with her anytime you want to."

Jane wiped her eyes, giving a small, forced smile.

Chapter 33

Tamara told everyone to take a quick break and meet back in the living room in ten minutes.

Once everyone was back and sitting down, Tamara said, "Betty, it is your turn to share your story."

All eyes went to Betty.

"As you already heard in the first class, my husband died many, many years ago of liver cancer. I didn't really know how bad it was because he put up a brave front and kept his pain to himself.

"At first, he just didn't have the energy that he used to. Then he had trouble walking upstairs. Soon after that, he had to be on oxygen, trucking his canisters around everywhere he went.

"Then one day, he was in the hospital struggling to breathe. That is when we found out that he had cancer. He came home for almost a week and then ended up back in the hospital. He lasted a few more days, just enough time for the rest of the family to get there.

"I remember feeding him his last meal. It was pudding. I tried to spoon it into his mouth without spilling any, but some kept getting on his lips. After a few bites, he didn't want any more.

"I remember our son was sitting beside him, talking with him when it happened. All of a sudden, he sat up a little further and started to blabber about something. It was incoherent. None of us could understand. Then he laid his head back down on the pillow and shut his eyes for the last time.

"It wasn't until the next day that the tubes were removed, and his organs shut down. That is when the doctor pronounced him dead.

"The part that I remember the most was when he was babbling and then shut his eyes. I knew his soul had left his body. I closed my eyes and tried to tell him to go to the light, but all I could see was his energy going down and down, in a swirl of energy like a tornado. I remember praying to God to help me pull him up into the light. A moment later, I saw his sisters, who had passed years before and were there to get him. To bring him home into the light with them.

"I was so relieved. I don't know what I would have done if I hadn't taken a few of Tamara's courses and learned how to make sure his soul went into the light."

Looking over to Tamara, Betty mouthed, "Thank you."

Tamara nodded and then said, "Do you talk to him?"

"Yes, but it is always in my dreams."

"That is how it can work for some people. Dreaming about him so that it doesn't feel so real or thinking you are going crazy because you can see him. If it works for you, and you are happy with the way you are communicating, then don't worry about trying any other way."

"Yes, I am happy. I love seeing him in my dreams. Sometimes he is the age he died at, and other times, he is younger."

"Do you have any questions for me, Betty? Anything you need from this class?"

"Hmm, no, I think that just being here and hearing everyone's stories helped me to solidify what I am doing is right for me. Thank you, Tamara, for offering this class for us."

Everyone nodded and agreed with Betty by thanking Tamara.

Chapter 34

On the drive home, Edward looked over to Lexi and said, "Hey, a penny for your thoughts," as he grabbed her hand tenderly.

She glanced over sleepily and said, "No, it isn't about the class, even though that was interesting. All those people's stories about talking to their loved ones who have passed over. I am so glad that Susannah talks to me in my dreams and that Tamara taught me how to meditate so that I can communicate with her consciously."

"It is fascinating. I'll say that much," Edward said.

Sitting up straighter in the passenger's seat, Lexi asked, "Edward, can you drive to my apartment, please? I forgot I need a specific outfit tomorrow at work."

"Really, you need a special outfit?"

"I know. It is silly, but I have a special client coming to look at my drawings for the outfit we are creating for her, and she is very flamboyant and expects everyone else to be. Besides, it's fun dressing up."

Edward laughed at the thought of dressing up so outrageously to match Lexi and shook his head to get rid of the notion.

Lexi texted Isabella that they were making a quick stop to pick up some more clothes.

She received a quick reply saying not to worry, that she was out.

Edward came up to help Lexi get whatever funky outfit she was thinking of wearing the next day and was excited to see her in it. One thing about Lexi, she was never boring.

As they entered the apartment, Lexi quickly went into her bedroom and grabbed what she needed. As she came out, she was about to say something but stopped abruptly.

The painting was gone.

The replica of the painting, 'The Wild Hunt of Odin' by Peter Nicolai Arbo, was gone.

Lexi dropped what she was holding and turned on the living-room lights.

It really was gone.

Lexi ran from room to room. All of Isabella's things were gone.

"Edward, what the hell? She stole my painting."

"I see that."

"I can't believe she took it, took him without asking me."

"Lexi, here, look, she left you a note."

> *Lexi, I am genuinely grateful for all that you guys have done for me. I pray that one day you will forgive me for taking the painting.*
> *I couldn't live without him.*
> *My producers called and said that I needed to be on the flight today to Peru. I am so sorry. I couldn't go without him. I know it won't make up for it, but I e-transferred you some money for the painting.*

Lexi took out her phone and entered her bank account code. She sat down on the couch and stared at her phone.

"What, what did the note say?" Edward asked as he took the note from her hand and read it.

Looking at Lexi, he said, "How much did she pay you for the painting? Was it enough?"

Lexi gave him her phone.

He sat down beside her and said, "I would say that was enough."

Lexi tried texting Isabella about the crazy amount of money deposited, but she never returned the message. Then she decided to text, *"I forgive you for stealing my painting. You could have just asked me for it."*

Chapter 35

It was amazing how fast a week went by.

Tonight was the last class on the four channels: Audio, Knower, Visual, and Feeler.

Karla was the last one to walk in. As she sat down, she said to Tamara, "I had the weirdest thing happen to me this week."

Excitedly Tamara replied, "Cool, tell us all about it." She could feel the vibration coming off Karla and knew that whatever she was about to share would be incredible.

"I was at a heavy-metal concert, and the band was playing a song. It was an old song, written back in 1988. It was all about the painting on Lexi's wall. You know, the one that Hans is tied to. I couldn't believe the lyrics and had to look them up after I got home from the concert. I think the lyrics were talking all about inner power, strength, and the eternal battle or struggle we all have. It made me think really hard about what you are teaching here, Tamara.

"I started to search on the internet about Archangel Gabriel, God's messenger. That led me to Israfil, the angel who blows into the trumpet to signal Qiyamah, the day of judgment. Israfil has four wings and is sometimes referred to as the angel of music. I was amazed to find that the angel Israfil is believed to have visited Muhammad before Gabriel did."

Kate piped up and asked, "Who is Muhammad?"

Karla turned to Kate and said, "Muhammad is the final prophet. Archangel Gabriel was sent to deliver a message from God to Muhammad.

"Muhammad wrote the Quran, which is the central religious text of Islam, believed by Muslims to be a revelation from God, Allah, himself. It is the holy writings of their religious belief, equivalent to the Bible for Christians.

"Muslims believe that the Quran was revealed to Muhammad through Archangel Gabriel.

"I also found some Arabic literature, 'the Mi'raj,' translates to 'Muhammad's Night Journey,' and it talks about Muhammad walking from Mecca to Jerusalem and back in one evening. Which is impossible unless you had the help of an angel."

Kate turned to Tamara and asked, "What does all this have to do with our class?"

Tamara smiled, looked at Edward, and said, "Reverend, I believe you have some answers here."

"Me? What do you think I can say about this?" Edward looked surprised and a bit confused.

Tamara kept her smile. "I know that as a man of God, you had to study the Bible."

"Yes, but I didn't study the Quran."

"Edward, where is it written in the Bible about Archangel Gabriel?"

"Oh, well, that I can tell you." Edward pulled out his phone, and a moment later, he said, "First, Gabriel is mentioned in the Old Testament, in the book of Daniel, Introduction to the Prophets, 8:16. It is written…

"*'The angel Gabriel interprets the vision.*
I heard a human voice cry over' the Ulai,
'Gabriel, tell him the meaning of the vision!'

"Then it goes on to talk about what Gabriel said to Daniel.

"Gabriel is also mentioned two more times, but this time in the New Testament. Once to Zechariah in the writing of Luke 1, 11-25. It talks about how Gabriel came to him to tell him that his wife, who was past childbearing days, was about to give birth to a baby, who later became John the Baptist.

"Then again, in Luke 1 26-45. Gabriel came down to deliver a message to the Virgin Mary about the birth of Jesus.

"Is that what you wanted me to talk about, Tamara?"

"Yes, that was perfect. Thank you, Edward and Karla, for sharing such an important part needed for this class.

"Karla, it would make sense that you would be sent a message through music. Archangel Gabriel works in cryptic ways. He or she delivers the message in any form that the receiver may understand. In your case, since you are a Knower, he knew that you would start to research everything about him. That it would lead you on an amazing path of enlightenment."

"It did that, for sure. It opened my mind to a whole new world. Who knew that heavy rock music was singing about something so profound?"

Tamara stood up and said to the group, "God talks to all his children, in many languages, even through music. He has many angels that help him deliver his messages. Archangel Gabriel is a special angel and only comes when it is very important.

"First, let's go back to what an angel is. Angels are messengers of God and help us expand our consciousness. You have many angels that help you along your path of enlightenment.

"All babies are granted a guardian angel at birth. As we age, many different angels come to help us. Some stay with us forever, while others come and go as they are needed.

"Just as in the military or politics, there is a hierarchy of command, similar to the ranks in the angelic world, and each rank has a specific job description."

Tamara wrote them down on a whiteboard that she had taken out from behind the couch.

Hierarchy of Angels

Highest Order
1. Seraphim: "Spirits of Love," the highest level to God.
2. Cherubim: "Spirits of Harmony"
3. Thrones: "Spirits of Will"

Middle Order
4. Kyriotetes: "Spirits of Wisdom
5. Dynamis: "Spirits of Motion"
6. Elohim: "Spirits of Form"

In some writings, it is Dominions, Virtues, and Powers.

Lowest Order
7. Archai: "Spirits of Time" or Principalities
8. Archangels: "Spirits of Fire"
9. Angels: "Spirits of Life"
10. Humans: "Spirits of Love and Freedom"

Tamara continued, "Our world is controlled by the government. We have a President or Prime Minister ruling each country, similar to the highest order. The middle order is similar to the politicians ruling each state or province. The lowest order is like our city officials, running each city or district.

"As humans, we only seem to be exposed to the lowest order, angels and archangels. The difference between an angel and an archangel is that the archangel is higher up in the ranks controlling a specific aspect of human wellbeing.

"In Archangel Gabriel's case, he controls communication and has many angels in his service to help deliver God's messages.

"To be visited by Archangel Gabriel himself is rare. It needs to be for a very important reason, as in the birth of Christ. Thankfully, he has sent his 'team of angels' many times to help me when I am teaching a class.

"Tonight, we are going to finish our class with a prayer that you can say to ask for Archangel Gabriel's help.

"Oh, Blessed Archangel Gabriel, a powerful messenger of God. Please surround me with your white light so that I may see the truth and know what's best for my overall wellbeing. Deliver to me the message of great importance, and help me hear what God has to say to me so that I can follow his guidance and fulfill my life's purpose. Thank you for aiding in God's revelations. Amen."

Tamara ended by saying, "During the four classes, you should have learned how to communicate in all four channels. Tammy's story shared how to communicate using the channel of Feeler. Betty's story shared how to communicate using the channel of Visual. Jane's story shared how to communicate using the channel of Audio, and Karla's story shared how to communicate using the channel of Knower. Kate can communicate in all four. Lexi is also a Visual and sees her sister Susannah. Edward, you are an Audio-Knower, and when you are ready, you will be able to communicate with the spirit world all on your own, not just when you are helping me save souls.

"Please remember that taking a breath shifts your intent and energy to vibrate at a frequency so that you can communicate with Spirit. Remember always to test the spirit before you trust it! Night everyone, and thank you for coming."

As they stood up, Lexi asked Edward to meet her in the car. Standing back and letting everyone else go out first, Lexi then said to Tamara, "Thank you for tonight's class. Hey, I need to ask you something."

"You're welcome, Lexi. It is always a pleasure to have you in my class. What is it that you need to know?"

"What am I supposed to do about the two million dollars?"

Tamara just stood there staring at her. Not much surprised her, but this did. "What two million dollars?"

"It is a long story, and I know you must be tired. I will contact you tomorrow and tell you all about it." Lexi gave Tamara a big hug and left.

After cleaning up from the group's class, Tamara went to bed and prayed to her angels. *Thank you all for the help that you gave me during my classes and lectures. I am so grateful for all your guidance and words. And, what in God's name is going on? How did Lexi end up with two million dollars? Amen.*

Chapter 36

Around her head, she wore a coiled turban of many bright and colorful folds, with a tasseled fringe. Placed upright in it were two feathers of a rare and curious bird, called the caracara, a species from the Falconidae family.

Knowing that textiles represented a form of status and wealth, she never wore the same clothing twice. She was so rich that her clothes were covered with jewels and turquoise pieces, and her body was adorned with gold and gems.

If one didn't recognize her status by her turban, then one jeweled piece, in particular, would show who she was. On her chest, she wore a badge made of hummingbird feathers framed with gold and a royal shield engraved with a picture of the sun god.

She was dreaming that she was the Sapa Inca Huayna Capac, the Inca emperor, the ruler of

the Kingdom of Cuzco, and the son of the
late Topa Inca Yupanqui and Mama Ocllo Coya.

As she looked around in her dream, she saw
polished dry-stone walled structures, hundreds
of man-made terraces, and mountaintops as far
as the eye could see. Intuitively, she knew she
was in the middle of a tropical mountain forest
in the Andes. Far below lay the Amazon basin
with its rich flora and fauna.

In her sleep state, she was instantly inundated
with all the Inca history.

She was a South American Indian from a
small tribe in the southern highlands of Peru.
The native people of this region all addressed
her, the emperor, as "Lover of the Poor," "Chief
Inca," or "Son of the Sun," as the Inca was
believed to be a direct descendant of the sun
god.

During her dream, she even saw her own
death. She was mummified, and her entire
palace became her burial place. According to
their custom, her entire staff would remain in the
palace and look after her if she would ever need
anything in the afterlife. Her people frequently
visited her tomb to be "consulted" on pressing
affairs, even after her death.

Waking up from her dream, Isabella
remembered that she was playing the part of his
princess sister, who was also his primary wife,
Coya Cusirimay. The Inca was polygamous and
had many wives, a common occurrence among

the royalty and the upper class of the fifteenth century. It was also customary for them to marry their siblings. In the movie, her role was the Sapa Inca's most important wife, known as the Coya, which meant Queen. According to history, she was considered his legitimate wife, and only from the legitimate ones would the next crown prince be chosen as Inca.

In the movie, she was playing the part of a Queen, married to her brother, the emperor. She was second in command, and as Queen, she lived in a grandly decorated "separate" palace from him.

As she sat up, she looked at the painting sitting on the couch in her RV. At each set, while shooting the film she was starring in, she received a private trailer or RV to live in. This time it was an RV, resting on a plateau high up in the Andes of Peru.

Getting out of bed, she walked over to the painting and caressed its frame, "Good morning, Hans."

"Morning." Hans sat on the edge of the bed, staring at her caressing the frame. *"Why can't she hear me? I'm right here."*

Isabella heard the knock at her door just before the director's assistant, Dale, said, "Five minutes, Miss Jackson."

Quickly brushing her hair and putting it up in a ponytail, she rushed out of the RV, saying, "See you in a few hours, Hans."

Today's shoot was about her talking with the shaman of the village, trying to convince him to speak to the spirit world about what to do about the Spanish invasion.

Translated into the official language of the times, Quechua, Isabella recited her lines, "As your Queen, I demand that I have a council with the paqo!" Isabella knew that *paqo* meant "masters of the sacred mountains."

"Coya, your wish is my command, but I cannot disturb him at this time," a young Peruvian man said, playing the part of the shaman's apprentice.

"You will!"

"I cannot. He is not here," stammered the young man, scared for his life.

"Where is he? Bring me to him!"

Bowing most graciously, the apprentice replied, "My Coya, I cannot. He is high on the mountaintop seeking council with the Gods. I have no way of knowing where he is. He keeps that a secret, even from me."

Annoyed with his answer, the Coya thought for a moment then said, "Seek me out as soon, and I mean as soon as he returns. Do you understand?"

"Yes, my Coya. As soon as he returns."

Isabella turned and left the set as the cameras followed her exit.

"Perfect! Just perfect!" yelled the director. "Isabella, you never cease to amaze me with how convincing you are in every part you play. Absolutely brilliant. You are worth every penny I pay you.”

Isabella gave him a warm smile and headed back to her RV to be with Hans.

Opening the door to her RV, she said, “Hey hun, I’m back. Sorry I took so long. Today’s shoot is the one where I am about to meet the village’s shaman for the first time. Hans, are you listening?”

Looking around the RV for Hans, Isabella tried to imagine that she could see him, trusting he was with her because of the class at Lexi’s apartment. What was it that Tamara had said? *“When a person’s energy is too wound up or scattered, they cannot sense the spirit world.”* Surprisingly enough, today, she could not feel him in the RV anymore.

“Hans, where are you?” As she went to caress the painting, she screamed.

Moments later, a knock came at her door. “Miss Jackson, are you alright?” Dale asked just before he opened it. Coincidently he was walking past her RV toward his own as he heard her scream.

“It… it… he… is gone,” she said faintly as she sat on a chair.

“Who is gone?”

“Hans”

“Who is Hans?”

“My…”

Others had run up and were standing outside her RV, wondering what all the commotion was about.

"Miss Jackson, are you alright?" Turning to the people outside, Dale yelled, "Someone, get the medic," just as Isabella fainted.

Chapter 37

"Hey Lexi? Lexi, wake up," Susannah was calling to her sister. *"Lexi, Hans needs your help."* Susannah was hovering above Lexi's bed, trying to get her attention.

"What? Who? Susannah, is that you?" Wiping her sleepy eyes, Lexi was trying to wake up from a dream. Looking over to the alarm clock, she could see it was 5:45 AM. Laying her head back down on her pillow, in a dream-state voice, she heard her sister calling to her again.

"Lexi, come on, wake up. Hans is in trouble, and he needs your help!"

Just as Lexi rolled over to her side, her cell phone rang. Groggily she said, "Hello?"

"Lexi, it's me, Isabella. I need your help. Someone stole Hans!"

The phone went dead.

Lexi sat up and looked at the recent calls. There was one from Edward, but he had called the night before. She looked again—nothing from Isabella. She checked her text messages—nothing.

"That's weird. I must have dreamed Isabella was calling me." Getting up to go to the bathroom, she left her phone on the bed.

She heard it beep.

She quickly finished up, so she could see who just texted.

Nobody.

Lying back down and covering herself up, she closed her eyes to go back to sleep.

The smoke alarm in the other room quickly made a buzzing noise and then went silent.

Lying there, Lexi prayed to Archangel Gabriel, "Please help me communicate with whoever is trying to get a message to me. I will listen, I PROMISE. Thank you."

"Lexi, it's me, Susannah."

Lexi almost jumped out of her skin. She wasn't ready to hear her sister's voice. Nervously, Lexi said, "Susannah, is that really you? If it is, what was your favorite toy when you were growing up?"

"Good job, Lexi, for testing me." They'd taught this to her in guardian angel school. *"Lambie."*

Lexi started to tear up. "Oh, my God. It's you, Susannah! I have missed you. How are you doing? What are you doing? I am so nervous."

"It's okay, Lexi. I am one of your guardian angels now, and I have been assigned to inform you that you must buy three plane tickets: one for you, one for Reverend Hawthorne, and one for Tamara. Right away!"

"What? That's crazy. Why?"

"Hans needs your help."

"Hans, Isabella's Hans?"

"Yes."

"He's a ghost. Why would he need our help? He's with Isabella. She took the painting you gave me. The last time I heard from her, she was going to be filming in Peru. Susannah, you must be mistaken."

"Lexi, you need to buy three tickets now. Right now. Don't ask. Just do it."

"I don't even know where she is."

Lexi's phone beeped. Looking at it was a picture of Cuzco, Peru. "I don't believe it. How did you do that?" Getting out of bed, Lexi went over to her computer and bought three tickets to Peru. Looking at the departure time, she had three hours to get to the airport.

While texting Edward and Tamara, she said, "In God I trust."

EMERGENCY!!!
MEET ME at the airport in one hour.
Pack your bags for tropical weather.
I know… but Susannah made me buy three tickets. Hans needs our help.
We are going to Cuzco, Peru!

Your tickets are in the attachment.

Chapter 38

Anxiously waiting for Edward and Tamara at the JFK Airport check-in, Lexi paced back and forth. "What if they don't come?" she said to Susannah.

"They will."

Lexi checked her phone, but no messages. "I don't think they got the message. They're not coming."

"They're coming."

Lexi was extremely nervous. If they didn't come fast, they would miss the flight. Tapping her foot, she tried calling Tamara, but it went to her voice mail. Lexi tried calling Edward, and the same thing—it went to his voice mail.

"Oh, my God, Susannah, this is crazy."

A security guard looked her way.

Silently in her head, she said to Susannah, *"Great, now they think I am nuts, talking to myself."*

"Here they come, Lexi."

Lexi looked up and saw Edward and Tamara running to the gate.

"Oh, my God, you guys. I thought you were never going to get here in time," Lexi said to them as they came toward her.

Rushing now to get through security, Lexi didn't have time to explain. The three of them ran and just made it on the plane and were escorted into the first-class section.

Sitting down, Lexi looked at both of them and said, "Man, you guys are amazing. I am not sure if I would have dropped everything and come running if either of you had called me. Who am I kidding? Of course, I would have. Hey, wait. Why didn't you guys try to call me to find out what was going on?"

Edward answered first, "I tried, but your phone kept going to voice mail."

"Me, too," Tamara said. "It was Susannah that convinced me to come. She visited me this morning and told me an airline ticket was coming, and it was vital that I be on the plane."

"Sure, you get a message from Susannah, and I just had to make sure that Alexandra was okay. There was no way I was going to let her go to Peru without my protection. By the way, where are we going once we get there?" Edward asked.

"That's a good question. Susannah never told me that part," Lexi said as she looked inquisitively at Tamara. "Did you get to find out that part?"

Tamara put her head back and closed her eyes as the plane picked up speed and ascended into the air. Taking a breath, she said, "I am sure sometime within the next eleven hours, Spirit will let us know."

Edward looked over at Tamara. "How can you be so calm?"

Tamara opened an eye. "Hey, you are in first-class flying to Peru. We might as well enjoy it," she said before closing her eyes and reclining further into her chair as the flight attendant passed out blankets and a pillow.

Edward grabbed Lexi's hand and squeezed it. "How are you doing?"

"I could talk to her," Lexi replied.

"Who?"

"Susannah. She was talking to me as if she was right here, and I could understand her. It was still like a dream in my head, but I was fully conscious."

"Really? That's fascinating. That's the first time?"

"Ya, usually, it is only in a dream that I can hear her, but this time I was awake."

Edward squeezed her hand again. "I am not sure what I got myself into this time," he said as he put his head back and shut his eyes.

Chapter 39

Coming to, Isabella yelled hysterically, "My painting, it's been stolen!"

The director's assistant, Dale, calmly said, "Isabella, the medic said you fainted. It would be best if you calmed down. Tell me again, what painting are you talking about?"

Looking at Dale, Isabella said, "Don't talk to me as if I were a child. You would freak out too if the painting you just paid two million dollars for was stolen." She knew money always made people stop and take notice. She needed the attention on the painting, not her.

"You're telling me, Isabella, that you had a painting in your RV worth two million dollars?"

"Yes. It means a lot to me, and I couldn't leave it at home."

Dale just shook his head and said, "I'll go get the security guards."

Isabella couldn't believe that Hans was missing. *They would never understand.*

A few moments later, a tall and husky security guard came into Isabella's RV and asked, "Miss Jackson, can you please describe the painting?"

"It's smaller than the original. It's about 32 inches wide by 48 inches long. It's in a dark wooden frame, and it has men riding horses on it."

"Okay, I will check around. It shouldn't be that hard to find something of that size being moved out of your RV."

As the security guard turned around and walked down the two steps, he added, "I'll be in touch shortly."

"Thank you," Isabella said as she shut her door.

A moment later, she heard a light tap at her door and Dale calling out, "Five minutes, Miss Jackson."

Putting her head down, she brought her hands up to support it. *What do I do now?*

Chapter 40

Getting off the airplane, Lexi, Tamara, and Edward went to find their luggage. As they were waiting for it to come down the carousel, a man came up to them and said, "Miss Constantine, we have a taxi waiting for you."

Surprised, Lexi looked at Edward, then at Tamara, and then back at the man. "Um, I didn't order a taxi. How do you know my name?"

Edward said, "Isabella must have done it."

The taxi driver, in his broken English, with a Spanish accent, said, "Your sister ordered the taxi for you. I think she said her name was Susan."

"Susannah?" Lexi said.

"Yes, that's it."

Lexi stared at the other two. "Freaky."

Getting their luggage, the three of them followed him to his taxi and got in.

Once they were settled and had started traveling on the road, Edward asked, "Where are you taking us?"

"You'll see," replied the taxi driver.

Edward asked again, "I would like to know where we are going?"

The taxi driver turned the music up and said, "Soon, we will be there."

"Are we going to see Isabella?" Edward asked.

The taxi driver just nodded.

#

The terrain had gotten very rocky and steep. They were climbing higher and higher up a mountain, and Edward could see that they were above the clouds. Looking at his watch on his wrist, he noticed it had been a few hours since they left the airport. Asking the taxi driver with a sterner voice than before, he said, "Where in God's name are you taking us?"

Lexi grabbed Edward's hand as the road became a very narrow gravel path. As she looked down, she could see patches of land between the clouds. Scared that the taxi might go off the cliff and they would fall to their death, Lexi shut her eyes.

"Tamara, do something," Edward said.

"What would you like me to do, Edward? Wave my magic wand?"

"Sure, if that would work."

"Funny. You would think that a man of the cloth would trust in God more."

"I trust in God, but I am not sure if I trust in this taxi driver's ability to see through the clouds."

"Almost there," the taxi driver said. "Don't you worry. I'm a good driver. I had only one accident, and they lived."

Edward looked at Tamara and rolled his eyes. Making the sign of the cross, Edward said a silent prayer.

A few moments later, the vehicle turned onto an even narrower dirt road and stopped. The taxi driver quickly got out, opened the back, and removed their luggage, placing it on the ground beside the SUV.

The three passengers had barely gotten out and taken hold of their luggage before the driver was backing up the vehicle.

"Wait!" yelled Edward. "Where are we?"

"You are here," the taxi driver responded.

"What are we supposed to do now?" Edward yelled louder.

The driver put his head out the window and yelled back, "Walk."

"What the! Alexandra, what in God's name did you get us into this time?" Edward said to Lexi as he ran after the taxi driver. "Come back!"

Walking back, a bit out of breath, Edward said to the girls, "He's gone. What do we do now?"

Tamara turned and started to roll her luggage toward a dirt path and said, "Well, I guess we walk. That's what he said to do."

Lexi followed Tamara.

Edward looked back toward the road, praying that the taxi driver would come back. Having no other choice, he started to follow behind the girls. He had to hurry because the path was not wide enough to fit more than one person at a time, and he didn't want to lose them.

Chapter 41

Lexi stopped to rub her feet; the cute pair of sparkly pumps were killing her.

"Here, let me see your shoe," Edward said. He took out a pocketknife and cut off the heel.

"Hey, those are Versace. Do you know how much they cost?" Lexi squealed as her beautiful shoes were ruined.

"With the money you received from Isabella, you can buy another pair," he said as he cut off the other heel. "There, that should be more comfortable."

Lexi put her shoes back on. Well, she couldn't argue with him there. They were much more comfortable to walk in. "I wonder how much farther we have to walk. It is getting dark and really chilly."

"Hey, Rev? Do you have matches or a lighter in your bag?" Tamara asked, half-jokingly, knowing he didn't smoke.

"Yes, as a matter of fact, I do."

"Good to know. We might need them," Tamara said, knowing it was going to get really cold this high up in the mountains at night.

"What, you think that someone is going to let us just stay overnight out here in the jungle?" Edward said, not believing that Isabella would not have thought of sending someone to meet them at the drop-off point.

"Technically, it's not the jungle. That is hundreds of feet below us. No, we are high up in the Andes, and it gets cold up here," Tamara said as she stopped to pull out a second shirt from her luggage. "I wish I had asked Spirit what clothing to bring, but I assumed we would be in tropical weather. My fault for not asking in the first place."

Lexi looked over and said, "I didn't bring anything for this kind of weather."

Edward stopped and opened his bag. He pulled out a long-sleeved shirt and gave it to Lexi. "Tamara, do you want one?"

"Yes, thank you, that would be great. Edward, you didn't bring a flashlight, did you?"

"No, that I didn't think of bringing."

"I think we are going to have to stop and make a fire. I can't see up ahead, and it's getting too dark," Tamara said as she squinted.

"Ya, I think you may be right. I can't see anything either," Edward said as he found a bit of a clearing and let go of his luggage to look around for some firewood.

Lexi and Tamara rolled a couple of tree stumps over to a flat area, and within a few moments, Edward had a fire going.

"Where did you learn how to do that?" Lexi asked.

"Boy Scouts, of course," Edward said as he proudly smiled at her.

"Of course, you were a Boy Scout, silly me." Lexi laughed. "How long do you think we will have to walk tomorrow? How will we know when we arrive?"

"That's a good question," Tamara said. "I think it's time that we say a prayer to our angels and ask for help. Lexi, ask Susannah for help, will you?"

"Good idea. Susannah, please help us now. It is getting really cold. We didn't bring any food, and I have to go to the bathroom. I am not sure what the purpose is for this crazy experience, but we would really appreciate your help right now."

Just as Lexi was about to say something else, a white powder came from nowhere. Before she could even scream, she fell into a deep sleep. They all did.

Chapter 42

*L*exi wiggled her feet. Her hands were tied behind her back. Struggling, she tried to free herself but couldn't. The knot just got tighter. Frantically, she looked around her surroundings. Lying not too far away were Edward and Tamara, who were also tied up and still unconscious.

She kicked Edward's foot. Nothing; he didn't even flinch. He was out cold.

She scuffled over a bit and was able to kick Tamara's foot. Same reaction—nothing.

Panic started to replace the thought of being cold. She was not cold anymore. As she looked down, she was wearing a brightly multicolored native woven wool sweater. Touching it, she knew it wasn't sheep's wool, but was not sure what type of wool it was, maybe *llama* or *alpaca.* On her feet was a blend of leather and fur-type shoes.

Looking at her surroundings, she noticed the three of them were in a type of one-room house made of clay and natural stone, with a roof of hard grass. There was a fire going in a modest fireplace and a small wooden table with a couple of wood chairs. In the corner was a cot-type bed covered with a similar wool blanket as her sweater.

A native man walked in just as Edward started to stir. He was not very tall and was a bit plump. He reminded her of a picture that she once saw of a Canadian Eskimo. He walked right past her and sat down on one of the chairs, staring at the three of them.

"Hello, I am Lexi, and these are my friends. I think there has been some kind of mix-up. Please, untie me."

Nothing, he didn't even blink.

"Sir, do you speak English?" she said, trying again.

Nothing.

Edward started to make a noise as he woke up. Groggily he tried to sit up and noticed his hands were tied as well as his feet. Struggling now, he squirmed on the floor as the man sitting on the chair came over and blew some more white powder into his face. He instantly was out cold.

Lexi was terrified. She didn't know what to do or why they were being held captive.

"Tamara, wake up," she thought in her mind. She was trying to send a message to Tamara psychically. As she tried, the man looked at her and blew some of the white powder in her face, and she went back into a dreamless sleep.

As she came to for the second time, Lexi noticed Tamara was awake and sitting at the table eating something out of a wooden bowl.

"Tamara," Lexi whispered. "What is going on?"

Tamara looked over and said, "It will be okay. Just stay calm, and he will untie you." Tamara nodded at the man. He went over to Lexi and freed her hands.

Lexi got up quickly, ran over to Tamara, and sat down beside her. "Oh, my God, Tamara, what is going on?"

"From what I can make of it, we are in a shaman's home. He has brought us here. Wherever here is."

"Are we safe?"

"Yes, I don't think he intends to hurt us. I think we were tied up for our protection. He was afraid we might do something stupid, like try to run away. We would have surely died in the cold outside."

"I don't think Edward is going to be too pleased when he wakes up."

"I think you're right. Maybe go over and sit by him, so when he does wake up, you can calm him down."

"Good idea. Where is the little girls' room? I really have to pee."

"Tamara laughed and said, "Right outside in the outhouse by the trees."

"What, you're kidding, an outhouse?"

"Yep, and it smells."

"Great, can this adventure get any worse? Susannah, if you are laughing right now, it's not funny." Lexi drew her sweater tighter around her body and ventured outside.

Chapter 43

"I can't believe you all kept me sedated for two days. I'm starving. Where is the outhouse?" Edward said as he stood up. Tamara had undone his ties the first day, knowing he wouldn't wake up for a while.

"How did you know there was an outhouse?" Lexi asked him.

Looking around, he said, "I don't see anything in this primitive hut."

"Oh, good point."

As Edward went outside, Tamara said to Lexi, "Are you going to tell him, or should I?"

"I think I better. No point in him getting mad at both of us," Lexi said with a polite smile.

As Edward came in, Lexi set a bowl of food down and motioned for him to come and sit at the table.

"What is this?" Edward barked, not feeling his usual self. "It smells funny."

"It is mashed potatoes, and I think the meat is llama, or maybe it's alpaca. I'm not sure," Lexi said as calmly as she could. "Hey, it's food, and you said you were hungry. Eat!"

"Yes, ma'am."

"Edward? I have something I need to tell you," Lexi said as she sat on a stool that was near the fire.

Between bites, he said, "Hey, this is actually pretty good. It tastes like chicken. Kidding. It actually tastes like elk or deer meat, but not so gamey." Looking up with a smile, he said, "What's up, buttercup?"

Lexi smiled but wasn't sure where his good humor was coming from. She would have to remember to feed him if he ever got grumpy. "Edward, I'm glad you are sitting down. I am not sure how to tell you this… We are stuck here for a while."

"What do you mean… a while?"

"I mean, I have no idea when we can leave."

"What?"

"Well, we can't speak the language, and the man doesn't seem to speak English."

"We have been trying to communicate but not with much luck," Tamara added to the conversation.

Edward looked from Lexi to Tamara and back again, speechless.

A few moments went by, and Lexi said, "Edward, say something. You're scaring me."

Edward just looked at her, put his fork down, got up, and went outside.

Following him, Lexi said, "Edward, where are you going?"

"To find some answers."

Lexi came back in and said, "Tamara, we've got to stop him. He doesn't know what kind of mess we have really gotten ourselves into."

Chapter 44

"Miss Jackson, we found someone that says they saw your painting being moved out," the security guard said as he found her after her last shoot.

"So, where is it?" Isabella was getting frustrated with everyone around her. Her mood swings had been off the charts in the last couple of days.

"Well, that is the problem. Nobody knows."

"So, who took it?"

"You might not believe this, but the guy says it was a shaman."

"A what?"

"A shaman."

"I heard you the first time." Isabella was shaking her head. *What would a shaman want with my painting?* "If you know who took it, why can't you go get my painting back?"

"Nobody knows where the shaman lives."

"Really? Nobody knows where he lives? That seems impossible. How about a tracker? Hire a tracker to find the shaman."

"No one from the village will go. They fear his voodoo. The natives here are very superstitious people and will not do anything that might displease the Gods."

"What hogwash. Voodoo. I'll show them what voodoo is." Isabella stomped off and went into her RV.

Coming out of her RV, Isabella was dressed in her Coya outfit. Walking over, she jumped into a four-person quad that was parked by her trailer. Following her instincts, she started the engine, pulled away, and drove up into the mountains. She drove as far as the dirt road would let her, then she continued a little further on foot.

Sitting down on a rock, she opened the bag she was carrying and pulled out a small flat leather-covered drum with a wooden stick. She had them because, in her next shoot, she was about to summon the shaman. Figuring that the director would have kept the script true to life, she started to beat the drum.

Allowing her spirit, her inner genie, to subconsciously hit the leather at whatever tempo and rhythm were needed to summon a shaman.

Isabella started to go into a trance-like state as her body swayed to the beat of the drum. As she hit the leather, the deep rhythmic boom echoed through the mountain range. As each vibration traveled through her body, the deeper into the trance she went.

"What do you want?" Isabella heard someone say in her meditative state.

"You have my Hans, and I want him back. In the name of your Coya, I demand you return him to me!"

"No! He is disrupting the energy of the mountain."

"What? How is that possible? He is a ghost."

"Exactly. He is not supposed to be here on Earth."

"He is mine. I want him back now!"

"No!"

"You cannot keep him. You stole him from me. How did you even find him?"

"There was a disturbance, a ripple of negative energy, and I followed it to the problem."

"I need him back. I can't live without him."

"You can."

"No, you don't understand. I can't."

"You don't understand. He is not supposed to be here. He is creating negative energy on our mountain."

"Help me!"

There was no reply.

Isabella came out of her trance state and started to weep.

Chapter 45

As Tamara was coming out of the stone hut, she saw Edward walking over to the shaman.

Opening his eyes from his telepathic communication with Isabella, the shaman stood up, turned, started walking, and waved for them to follow.

Not sure where they were going, Edward, Lexi, and Tamara dropped everything and walked for miles behind the shaman in silence.

The shaman stopped and took a rattle out of his bag. He started to shake it as he looked up to the sun, chanting.

Not sure what to do, the three of them looked on in disbelief.

Tamara whispered, "I watched a documentary on the Inca shamans while we were on the flight over. There are shamans worldwide. Most people think of them as healers, which they are, but they are way more than that. They are actually honored for their ability to communicate with the Gods spiritually."

Edward and Lexi sat down on a tree trunk that had fallen over, listening to Tamara and staring at the man's actions.

Tamara continued, "It is believed that shamans possess metaphysical abilities and are chosen to become students at a very young age. These boys do not learn the craft by verbal instruction. They learn it by practical experiences."

Edward was enchanted by the sound of the man chanting. It was rhythmic and intoxicating.

"The documentary went on to say that a shaman believes in the Eagle, a representation of God, or the universal soul. He believes that the human soul is the light body, swirling around the physical body.

"What I found most extraordinary was that a shaman believes that for one to talk to the universal soul or God source, one must cleanse their negative emotions, judgments, guilt, ego, and self-doubt. A person must cleanse their over-active mind before one can talk to the spirit world."

Lexi asked, "Tamara, do you believe that we must cleanse ourselves before we can communicate with God?"

"I think I do. I know when I am teaching a class that if a student has too many judgments or contradictory beliefs, the student seems to miss the connection."

"What do you mean, 'connection?'" Edward asked.

"Well, what I know to be true is that if someone doesn't believe, then that is what the universe will reflect back, to prove that they are correct, either way. When a student allows even a glimmer of acceptance that metaphysics is possible, the universe reflects the wonders of the universe, and all kinds of possibilities are achievable."

"So, what you are saying is that if a student is open enough to the possibilities, then that is what becomes their reality?" Edward was now very interested in the conversation.

"Tamara, what did the documentary say about how to change your belief if you don't believe, or if you want to but are too stuck in your ways?" Lexi asked, really thinking of her Catholic mother back home in New York City.

"As you know, Lexi, we can't change anybody. All we can do is offer ideas or suggestions that he or she can try. The documentary mentioned that the Inca shaman uses the power of undoings."

"The power of what?" Edward asked, not sure if he'd heard her right.

"The power of change. Like with a seesaw, only one person can be in control at a time.

"Your mind only knows right from wrong, or yes and no. Maybe is not an answer. Your past influences your future. Your habits, beliefs, and upbringing all affect your everyday decisions. You react to your memories, and your subconscious mind controls these memories, which influences your daily actions."

"Oh, my goodness, Tamara. How in the world do you expect us to change our memories?" Lexi asked, wishing that she could be more trusting in all this metaphysical, spiritual mumbo jumbo.

"Lexi, it is not as hard as you think. I really liked what the documentary had to say about that. It explained that the shaman has you do things backward."

"Backward?" astonished, Edward repeated what Tamara had just said.

Tamara nodded. "One suggestion was to walk backward for forty-five to sixty minutes."

"You've got to be kidding me. Who could do that for an hour?" Edward said, not believing that anyone could do that.

"They said that the opposite action to what you subconsciously do would change or reset your memory. Your body will not know what to do naturally, so you can reprogram your belief at that time."

"Really? That is fascinating," Lexi said as she imagined walking backward.

"Is there an easier way than walking backward?" Edward asked, not sure if he could do that.

"To change your body's memories, the documentary also mentioned putting your clothes on opposite to your normal way. If you put your right arm into your sleeve first, instead put your left arm in. You could also try wearing two different colored shoes or eating with your opposite hand. Even changing the direction in which you sleep can shift your memories and allow new neuron pathways to be created."

"Fascinating ideas, Tamara," Lexi said just as the shaman finished his chanting.

The three watched as the shaman put away his rattle, swooped down, and grabbed a guinea pig that happened to run by at that instant. Within moments, the shaman had sliced its throat, cleaned it, and had it on a stick roasting over an open fire. They did not go hungry that night.

Before sleep, the shaman started to chant again as he blessed the ground and looked up to thank the stars. He put more wood on the fire, curled up on some leaves beside the heat, and fell asleep.

The three of them decided to do the same. Out loud, Edward said a grateful prayer for them all before he fell asleep.

Lexi and Tamara both said, "Amen," and closed their eyes.

Chapter 46

In the morning, Lexi awoke to the shaman's chanting, and the smell of chicken, which she found out later, was a wild goose.

"The shaman prays out loud to Mother Earth, known to them as *Pachamama*, in their ancient Quechua language," Tamara said as she walked over to put more wood on the fire.

Lexi watched in awe as the shaman produced yet another small packet from his bag. When he unwrapped the paper, inside were coca leaves, incense, nuts, dried Amazonian flowers, brown sugar, and a bit of vicuña wool. Lexi watched as he poured some red wine on the items.

Tamara explained to Lexi, "Shamans believe that you must give back something to Mother Earth in exchange for whatever you take."

"Oh, I see," Lexi said as she watched the shaman rewrap the packet, place it to his lips, and whisper something.

He then motioned for them to get down on their knees and proceeded to lightly press the packet to their heads, hands, back, and feet as he chanted more words.

Tamara clarified what he was doing, "I believe he is thanking the spirit world and asking them to protect us on our journey."

Edward was intrigued by the morning ritual as the shaman placed the packet into the fire. It was so quiet; all you could hear was the crackle of the contents burning. The aroma of the incense seemed to bless their bodies as it rose with the smoke of the fire.

The three watched as the shaman carefully selected three coca leaves out of his bag and fanned them out with each stem facing down toward the ground.

Tamara whispered, "This is called the *K'intus*—a 'bouquet,' representing the coming together of prayer or offering, with the tips of the leaves reaching up to Inti Tayta, the Sun and Sky, and the stems reaching down to Mother Earth."

The four of them sat eating coca leaves, wild bird meat, and drinking a bit of sweet wine.

Tamara said, "Make sure you spit the last mouthful of wine down at the ground for *Pachamama*."

Edward looked at her in disbelief but obeyed her wishes. No sense in taking a chance to upset Mother Earth.

After putting out the fire, the shaman motioned for all of them to follow him again.

The rough terrain they were walking was wild, and the path they were following offered some of the most breath-taking scenery one could ever see, with green mountains and snow-topped glaciers. They had been walking for two days. So far, they had seen volcanic rock, a desert below, lakes, grassland, and forests.

At lunch, they had reached an ancient ruin. The shaman allowed them to look inside. It seemed to be a religious or ceremonial site. It had a mammoth granite monolith at the entrance and various sculptures and carvings along the remaining walls.

"Alexandra, did you know that the monolith was created from a glacier activity more than a million years ago?" Edward asked.

"No. That's fascinating," Lexi said as she was inspecting the carvings.

#

Finally, on the third morning, they came upon an opening, and there, parked by a tree, was an ATV. As they came closer, they saw Isabella.

Running up to her, Lexi yelled, "Oh, my God. Isabella. Thank God!" as she hugged her.

"Lexi, how did you get here? What are all of you doing here?" Isabella was dirty, tired, and hungry, as her food supply had run out the night before.

"It is a long story, but it was Susannah. She told me that Hans was in trouble," Lexi clarified.

Just as Edward and Tamara were coming up to Isabella, the shaman pointed to the path that brought Isabella to the location they were all standing in.

Lexi turned in the direction he was pointing as Tamara said, "Oh good, the cavalry has arrived."

Out from the treed path came a troupe of security guards, actors, and the director of Isabella's film. Yelling from the edge of the trees, the director said, "Isabella, thank God you are alright. You had me frightened to death with your disappearance."

Lexi, Edward, and Tamara backed up as these people came swarming around Isabella, making sure she was alright.

Lexi yelled over the commotion, "Isabella, we need a translator!"

"A what?"

"We need someone who can talk to the shaman for us. I think he has something to do with Hans's rescue."

Isabella started pushing people aside, trying to get to Lexi. As she did, she screamed, "Dale! Get me a translator. NOW!"

Lexi looked over and noticed the shaman was gone and yelled, "Oh, my God. We need to find the shaman."

Frantically looking around for the shaman, Isabella yelled to her filming crew and co-actors, "Spread out, find that shaman!"

Chapter 47

"Isabella, we can't keep looking. It's getting dark," Dale said as he started to shiver. "We need to get you back to your RV."

"He's right, Isabella. We are going to have to call off the search," Edward said.

Looking at Edward with a discouraging look, she whimpered, "Fine," and started to cry.

Lexi put her arm around Isabella, walked her back to the quad, and guided her into one of the back seats. Edward jumped into the driver's seat as Tamara hopped in beside him.

Edward followed the others like a caravan back to where they were filming.

Once they were safely back at camp and inside Isabella's RV, Tamara said, "It's going to be alright. We are going to get Hans back."

"How do you know that?" Isabella asked in disbelief. "The shaman has him. He said he wasn't giving him back."

"The shaman has him?" Lexi said, surprised.
Isabella nodded.

Edward couldn't believe his luck. He was with the shaman, and that meant he was with Hans and didn't know it. *What good is this intuitive stuff if you don't know when it is working?* Looking over to Tamara, he said, "You couldn't tell that Hans was with the shaman?"

Tamara looked over and said, "Edward, that is not how it works. Unless I have a specific focus, question, or intent, I will not get the information I did not ask for. I trusted my guides and angels to bring me to Isabella, and that is what they did. I didn't think to ask if Hans was with the shaman."

"Edward, be nice. It is not Tamara's fault we are in this mess. It's mine. If you want to be mad at someone, it is me. You should be mad at me."

"Sorry, Tamara. I am just frustrated, tired, and hungry," Edward said apologetically.

Isabella picked up her walkie-talkie and said, "Dale, please bring some food and wine for my friends."

"Thanks, Iss, that is very kind of you," Edward said as he sat down on a chair.

Lexi sat down next to Edward and said, "What are we going to do?"

"Good question," Tamara said. "We need to create a list of questions to ask. Isabella, do you have some paper and a pen?"

Isabella picked up her walkie-talkie again and said, "Dale, please bring me some blank paper and a pen."

A few moments later, someone knocked on the RV door and said, "Miss Jackson, the food and supplies that you asked for are here."

Isabella opened the door and let the young man in. He put everything on the small table in the kitchen area and then quickly left.

Lexi picked up a grape and popped it into her mouth as she moved the paper and pen closer to her. Adjusting the pen, she said, "Alright, first question?"

Tamara said, "The first thing to write down is the word 'Hans.' He is the reason why we are all here because Susannah said he was in trouble."

"Good point. Yes, that is why we are here," Lexi agreed as she wrote down the word "Hans."

"We need very specific questions," Tamara said. "Lexi, write down, 'Where is Hans?,' 'Does the shaman have Hans?,' 'Will the shaman give Hans to us?' Let's start with that. I am going to go into a semi-trance state, and then, Lexi, I want you to ask me those questions and write down the answer to each one that I give you."

"Yep, got it," Lexi replied excitedly.

Tamara took a few deep breaths. *I ask my angels in Heaven to help me. To please let my ego get out of the way and allow for honesty and integrity of the answers to the questions that we will be asking.* Tamara subtly nodded and said, "I'm ready."

Lexi asked the first question, "Where is Hans?"

Tamara took a deep breath and let her mind accept the first answer that came, and without letting her ego in and judging the answer, she said, "I see a jungle. He is not where we were held captive."

Lexi wrote that down, word for word. Then she asked, "Will the shaman give Hans to us?"

Tamara took another breath, then said, "No."

"Oops, I forgot to ask if the shaman has Hans," Lexi said, a bit frustrated for making a mistake.

"No. Well, I guess that's why he can't give him back," Tamara said factually. "Next question."

"Umm, I don't have any more written down," Lexi looked at Edward and Isabella.

Isabella asked, "Can Susannah help us get Hans back?"

"Oh, ya, good question," Lexi said as she wrote it down.

"Yes," Tamara said as she nodded subtly.

"Are we going to get Hans back before we leave Peru?" Edward asked, clueing into how this worked.

"Yes."

"In two days?" he asked next while Lexi was writing everything down.

"No."

"Within the week?"

"Yes."

"Ah, well, that is good. Can we find out the exact day, Tamara?" Edward asked, not sure if a specific answer would come.

"Yes."

"Oh, good. Do we leave in three days?"

"No."

"Four days?"

"No."

"Five days?" he said, worried about the answer. *I don't want to be here for five more days.*

"Yes."

Edward wasn't sure what answer was now correct. He asked one but thought another. "Um, Tamara, is yes to finding Hans in five days or being here for five more days?"

"Yes, to being here for five more days."

"I hate to ask, but are we going to be here for more than five days?"

"Maybe."

"Great, just great. I'm done asking questions. Next," Edward said, not happy at all that he was going to be in Peru for possibly more than five days. *I have a business to run, and I need to find a phone that works.*

"Tamara, you said yes to Susannah helping. Is that how we get Hans back?" Lexi asked.

"Yes."

"Okay, what are some more good questions to ask Tamara?" Lexi said as she looked at Isabella and Edward.

Edward just put up his hands as if to say, "Hell if I know."

Isabella thought quickly and said, "Tamara, go ahead and ask Susannah some questions that you can think of, and tell us out loud what you are asking."

Tamara nodded and said, "Good idea." Taking a breath to shift her intent to Susannah, she said out loud, "Susannah are you there?"

"Yes."

"She said yes."

Lexi wrote it down.

"Susannah, can you go where Hans is?"

Susannah answered Tamara, and Tamara repeated her answers, *"Yes."*

"Can you get Hans for us?"

"No."

"Can you take us to Hans?"

"No."

"Can you take me to Hans?"

"Yes."

"Right now?"

"No."

"When?"

"In two days."

"Why do we have to wait for two days?"

"You need to be blessed first."

"What does that mean?"

"You need the blessing of a shaman."

"Can you set up a meeting with the shaman for me to receive his blessing?"

"Yes."

"Thank you, Susannah. Please, contact me with the details as soon as you have them." Tamara took a breath, wiggled her toes, and opened her eyes. *Thank you, angels, for helping me get the answers I needed,* then said to the others, "Well, that went well."

"So, we know that you get Hans back, and you will be blessed before that. But we have to wait for more than five days to go home," Edward recapped.

"Looks that way," Tamara said as she sat up from her meditative state.

Chapter 48

The three of them watched the dailies as they were being filmed. It was intriguing watching Isabella in action. She was a natural chameleon, shifting her persona into the character that she was playing. Even though the footage was raw and unedited, Isabella led you to believe you were back in the fifteenth century.

Edward leaned over to Lexi and whispered, "Amazing. She's just amazing. You would never have believed that just a few weeks ago, she tried to commit suicide."

Someone turned around and hushed Edward.

Lexi put a hand on Edward's hand and gave a little squeeze in response.

"Cut!" yelled the director. "That's a wrap. Great job, everyone. Don't forget that tomorrow we start at 5 AM. We need that early morning light!"

Edward looked at Lexi and said, "5 AM, what the heck. They have Isabella working from dawn to dusk already. How does she maintain her stamina with that much work?"

Tamara interrupted them by saying, "Susannah says she has the details."

"Oh, that's terrific," Lexi answered back.

Without continuing their conversation, they stood up and followed Tamara into the RV that the three of them were staying in.

Once inside, Tamara said, "Lexi, get ready to write down what I am about to say," as she sat down in a chair, shut her eyes, and took a breath.

Lexi grabbed the pad of paper and the pen she used the other day.

A moment later, Tamara said, "Susannah's telling me that an angel said it's tonight. We need to meet the shaman in the clearing where we found Isabella the other day. Susannah's saying to bring warm clothes, and unfortunately, to leave Isabella here. Her energy will only interfere with what we are about to do."

Tamara took another breath then said, "Wait, I think Archangel Gabriel is here. I think it's him.

"His energy is so magnificent, I can't quite tell.

"No matter who is speaking, they are talking about being a teacher of prophets.

"I am not sure what that means. Oh, he's gone now. Wow, he left as quickly as he came."

Tamara took a breath, wiggled her toes, and opened her eyes. "Weird. I am not sure what that has to do with anything, teacher of prophets."

"Maybe it has to do with Hans?" Lexi said, guessing.

"I don't think so. Susannah was the one telling me about Hans. No, I really don't think so. The angel left before I could ask anything else."

Edward remarked by saying, "Sure, leave it to the spirit world to give us riddles."

Tamara looked over to Edward, saying, "True, it does seem like a riddle sometimes, yet it always has an important meaning. When the time is right, we get to understand what it all means. Unfortunately, it's usually after the event."

Lexi looked at the paper and said, "Okay, here is what we do know. Tonight, we are to dress warm and meet the shaman in the clearing where we found Isabella."

"It hasn't been two days. Are you sure, Tamara, that it is tonight?"

"That is what she said. I have found in my experience that the spirit world's timetable and ours are a bit wonky. You can't always set a clock to it."

Edward looked down at his watch, saying, "Did Susannah mean after dark or at sunset? I would hate to miss the shaman by being late."

"Ah, he has a good point," Lexi agreed, turning to Tamara.

Tamara looked at the clock on the wall of the RV and said, "It's almost five-thirty. That gives us about an hour before dark. Edward, I think you're right. We better leave now."

Chapter 49

After driving the quad for about twenty minutes, Edward stopped abruptly because the road had ended.

Getting out of the vehicle, Lexi looked around and asked, "Should we make a fire?" Before anyone could answer, a man seemed to materialize out of thin air and waved at them to follow him.

Quickly running so they didn't lose him in the trees, Lexi, Edward, and Tamara ran single file on the path, soon catching up with him.

The path turned into a clearing, and sitting in front of a building resembling an ancient temple, were many natives dressed in tribal clothing. Just in front of the temple and standing behind a large stone altar was an older man wearing a large, feathered headdress. Lexi assumed he was the high shaman.

The man that they had been following motioned for them to have a seat on the ground.

As they watched with inquisitive eyes, the man behind the altar touched the ground with one hand and shook a rattle with the other, all the while speaking in his indigenous tongue.

On top of the altar was a multicolored woven mat with many of the items similar to those the shaman in the forest had used.

Lexi was fascinated by who she assumed was an apprentice, passing the high shaman a bowl with smoke coming out of it. She intuitively knew the bowl would contain crushed herbs, incense, and flowers. She also knew the high shaman was performing an offering.

As he was chanting, someone started to make a low and deep throat sound that carried throughout the clearing. Lexi could feel the vibration deep within the core of her body. A moment later, someone started to beat a drum. Her heartbeat shifted to match the rhythm, and she could feel her body go into a trance-like state as she relaxed into the energy of the ritual.

A man dressed in bright colors of the Inca people was sitting beside Lexi and quietly started translating what the shaman was saying and doing, "He calls out to *Pachamama,* 'Mother Earth,' and all the nature kingdoms, to join in this ceremony. Our people always honor our brothers and sisters, the stone people, the plant people, and all the animals, birds, fish, and insects, each time a group of us gathers within a sacred space."

Lexi watched as the high shaman reached up to the sky.

The man started to translate again, "The shaman is calling out to father sun, grandmother moon, the great spirit, and our star brothers and sisters."

Someone softly blew a whistle as the high shaman started to speak again. Lexi was intrigued by the sound of a small percussion instrument called a castanet, which she could hear occasionally being rung as he spoke.

The man beside her continued to translate, "What he is talking about now is the levels of becoming a shaman. He is saying that the first level is called *Ayni Karpay*. This is where the student develops a relationship with nature but is not yet considered a shaman. The path of the shaman is an incredible exploratory journey, one that you cannot master by studying and taking an exam. No, to become a shaman, you must live it! It is a path of empowerment, wisdom, and connection with the divine, a true journey of awakening and remembering how to listen, both to your intuition and the voice of nature.

"The second level is called *Pampamesayok*. At this level, the student becomes an apprentice and a mesa carrier. A mesa is a bundle of ' medicine stones' that restore balance to one's environment. Once the student has assembled his or her collection of medicine objects and has committed his duty of becoming an earth steward, the student graduates into level three.

"The third level is called *Altomesayok*. There are three degrees within this level. The student's responsibility is to the mountain spirits called the *apus*, the sacred mountains, and the teachings of medicine. Once the student learns and masters this level, he or she gains the title of shaman.

"The fourth level is called *Kurak Akuyek*. The word *kurak* means ' elder,' and *akuyek* means ' to chew' or ' to masticate.' At this level, the shaman ' chews' the knowledge so the others can ' digest' it. It can take a lifetime to reach this level, where your duty is to the stars. These first four levels are attainable, but very few shamans graduate from this level.

"The fifth and last levelhas been known by a few different names: *Inka Mailku, Sapha Inka,* and *Taitanchis Ranti*—one who shines with the God-light within. When we attain this level, we awaken the divine-light within us and become in charge of the care of all creation, from the smallest grain of sand to the largest conglomeration of galaxies."

As the man beside her stopped talking, Lexi was surprised as the head shaman pointed to Tamara and said something in his native tongue. Instantly the man who had been translating got up, took Tamara's hand, and guided her to the altar.

Lexi became uneasy as she heard him tell Tamara to climb up onto the altar and lie down, face up. At the same time, Lexi saw Edward make the sign of the cross and mouth what she knew would be a silent prayer. Lexi sat there transfixed by the fear of the unknown.

A moment later, two people came forward. One presented a bowl and knife, and the other a guinea pig. Lexi screamed out as the shaman slit the guinea pig's throat and drained all of its blood into the bowl. Lexi almost fainted. Thankfully, Edward had put an arm around her so she would not fall over.

Not sure now if she was hallucinating, Lexi watched as the shaman said something else and held the bowl high above his head with both hands. Bringing it back down, he placed his thumb into the bowl, and with his thumb dripping blood, he touched Tamara's forehead.

The man who had been translating came back and sat down beside Lexi. As he sat down, he calmly touched Lexi on the shoulder and said quietly, "Don't worry, your friend's soul is being cleansed by the Qero shaman. He is doing a ritual to bring all her lost soul pieces back and remove any that are not supposed to be with her. You have nothing to fear. She is more than alright."

Edward leaned over Lexi and asked, "Back from where?"

The man answered, "From the ether, floating in the upper regions of space. As a person has traumatic experiences in his or her life, fragments of their soul are scattered and attach to the element of ether."

Lexi watched as the Qero shaman closed his eyes and moved his hands in thin air as if he were retrieving something. A moment later, he opened his hand and then proceeded to blow at Tamara what he had found.

The man then said, "He is now returning her missing fragments, and in a moment, he will do the ritual of shamanic extraction, which involves the removal of misplaced energy that does not belong to Tamara. This negative energy can cause her illness and lower her vibration."

As the cleansing ritual bewitched Lexi, the man continued to explain, "Misplaced energy can come from emotional debris, a physical injury, or an organ transplant. Once the shaman locates the misplaced energy, he will communicate and merge fully with his guardian spirits or power animals to increase his power. This merge allows him to remove the energy from her body and protects him from taking on any of the extracted energy."

Just as the Qero shaman finished speaking, Lexi's eyes went as big as saucers as Tamara's body arched up as if something had hold of her torso. Not being in control of her emotions, Lexi let out another scream as Tamara's body fell flat and went limp.

The man sitting beside Lexi put his hand on hers and said, "Do not worry, your friend will be alright."

Lexi sat there in disbelief.

The man translated again as the shaman finished the ritual by blessing all four directions: north, south, east, and west. "What he is doing now is closing the sacred space. As each direction is faced, gratitude and thanks are given to the invisible forces that were called upon by the Qero shaman. He is also releasing the archetypal animals back to the natural world and honoring Heaven and Earth."

Barely hearing what the man beside her was saying, Lexi watched as the same two men returned to Tamara. One man took hold of her upper body as the other held her lower, removing her gently from the altar and carrying her into the temple.

Lexi stood up quickly. "Where are they taking her?"

Calmly, the man beside her stood up, took hold of her hand again, and said, "She has been taken inside the temple, where a couple of ladies from our tribe will bathe her and clothe her in a tribal ceremonial outfit. She is one of us now. From now on, the Gods will communicate with her as they do the Qero shaman."

Edward stood up beside Lexi and said, "Really? I'm pretty sure she could do that before she came."

"No, nothing like what she will be able to do now. She has been chosen for a very special task. It is part of her destiny."

"Her destiny?" Edward was surprised that Tamara's destiny needed any adding to.

Chapter 50

Inside the temple, the two men laid Tamara on a bed made of stone, which was covered with a thick wool blanket.

As a woman dressed in bright, colorful clothing came over and waved something of a unique smell under Tamara's nose, she awoke instantly.

Another woman dressed similar to the first came to help undress Tamara, then guided her into a pool full of warm scented water, motioning her to wash.

Tamara did as she was instructed.

After bathing, Tamara came out of the water and was dried by the women. They gave her clothing to put on that was similar to what the Qero shaman was wearing.

Once Tamara was dressed, the ladies guided her into another room and placed a smaller version of the shaman's headdress onto her head, and left her there by herself.

A few moments later, the man who had been translating for Lexi and Edward came in. "Hello, Tamara, I am Don Adolfo. I am an *altomesayoq* shaman, mentor, and teacher. *Altomesayoq* is pronounced *Al-to-me-sa-yok*. *Alto* means 'high,' and *mesayoq* means 'one who has power.'"

Tamara politely answered, "Hi, it is a privilege to meet you. I am very honored to be in your presence."

Don Adolfo continued in his Spanish accent, "The Gods, or as you call them Spirits or Angels, have informed the Qero that you are to learn some of our beliefs so that you can bring the knowledge back to your people. The cleansing ritual was to grant you the vibration needed to continue your journey."

Tamara was astounded that she was receiving knowledge that only shamans of the highest potential attained. *Thank you, angels, for this gift.*

"As you already have vast knowledge in how to journey—shifting into an otherworld state of consciousness to retrieve information—this will be quite simple for you to follow," he said matter-of-factly.

Tamara nodded, indicating that she understood.

"You are aware that in the Indian scriptures, written thousands of years before Jesus Christ, it is inscribed, 'One who can change his breathing can change his thoughts and feelings.'"

Not letting Tamara respond, he continued, "If one changes how one breathes, one can change his or her body. As a breath is taken, over eighty-thousand kilometers of blood vessels are shifted. Each breath we take wakes up our brain and our consciousness. As you already know, breath is the secret to the power of the universe."

Tamara understood this concept, knowing that she used the power of the breath in all of her spiritual communications and practices. Tamara listened very closely to every word as he spoke.

"As you know, consciousness creates our reality, and we are constantly being programmed by the environment around us and the experiences that we live. The subconscious mind becomes a filter of what we know. Our subconscious negative beliefs, emotional attachments, and intellect of information control our conscious actions."

Tamara nodded, agreeing with his beliefs.

"Tamara, your body and mind no longer have conflict. You have mastered supernatural willpower and have been able to release your inner conflicts, allowing you to align all your abilities with your conscious intention. Your light body, your soul, which is the blueprint or hologram of the universal energy you call God, and I call Spirit of the Universe, is ready for you to receive your next spiritual level."

Now that she consciously knew that there was another level that she could attain, Tamara's subconscious mind shifted ever so slightly for her soul to intuitively receive what she needed.

Tamara watched as he laid out the items needed for this part of the shaman ritual of atonement. She could see one of the items was a *mona*, a herb that brings clarity and vision.

Tamara listened wholeheartedly as Don Adolfo said, "Your luminous energy field that surrounds your physical body holds a record of all your personal and ancestral memories. Everything you have learned up to this moment, including your former lifetimes, has been preparing you to align your past with your present and bring forth a new chapter in your life."

As he touched the *mona* to Tamara's lips, he said, "Tamara, as you already know, balance is the second key and secret to life. And knowing that you have been able to balance your body, mind, and soul throughout your life's journey, Spirit has already granted you the power of removal. Today, Spirit is granting you something new: the power of transformation and evaluation. You now have the power without the permission of others to release Hans from the spiritual cage that bonds him. Please, do so now."

Tamara was a bit surprised at his request. Not exactly sure she understood how she could release Hans without Isabella's permission since

Isabella was the one that created his hold. Tamara took a breath and asked Archangel Gabriel for help, permission, and to guide her through the process.

Instantly, Susannah was there to help her. *"Hi, Tamara. Congratulations on your advancement. What an honor it is to have you as an Earth angel."*

"Hi, Susannah, so kind of you to come and help me. I appreciate that we can communicate now and so easily. I can hear you as if you are here with me in person."

"I am only in spirit."

"If I understand Don Adolfo correctly, I am to release Hans, but I do not know where he is."

"Take a breath, Tamara. His energy is waiting for you."

Tamara took a breath and set her intent on Hans. Instantly, she could sense his energy.

"Hans, it is me, Tamara, Isabella's teacher and friend."

"Hi, Tamara, I remember you," Hans answered.

"Hans, I am here with a shaman and Susannah. I am being told to release you from your location. Are you ready to be released into the light?"

"No."

"Oh," Tamara said, surprised. "What is holding you back from being released?"

"My beliefs."

"I see. You do not believe in the light?"

"It's not that. I have grown up loving the belief of elves and fairies. I want to go to the level of the Elementals, Alfheim in particular."

"I'm sure I can arrange that for you. Just give me a moment to make sure the path is cleared."

Tamara closed her eyes and took a breath, and asked Susannah, "Can you please ask Archangel Gabriel if Hans is allowed to go to the level of the Elementals, to Alfheim instead of into the love-light energy of Heaven?"

A moment passed, and then Susannah said, *"He says Hans's wish will be granted. Hans will be taken there as soon as you release him."*

Tamara took a breath and said, "Hans, I can release you now to the level of the Elementals." Before her last word was even spoken, Tamara could feel that Hans had instantly teleported to Alfheim. Knowing that Hans was released from the painting and her request was fulfilled, Tamara thanked Susannah and Archangel Gabriel for communicating with the spirit world and helping her release Hans.

Tamara opened her eyes as Don Adolfo said, "Your journey had *yanai*, clear vision, and you successfully communicated with *Hanaq Pacha*, the spirit world."

Just as he finished his sentence, the two ladies came in and retrieved Tamara, guiding her back out of the temple.

"Wow, look at you in that outfit, Tamara. You look just like the Qero shaman. Hey, what happened in that temple?"

Chapter 51

It was very early in the morning. Isabella, carrying three freshly made coffees, walked into their RV, saying, "Rise and shine, sleepyheads. Sorry that I have been so busy filming the last three days."

Lexi dizzily sat up from a deep sleep as she looked at Isabella. Rubbing her head, she asked, "What do you mean three days?"

Hearing loud voices, Edward and Tamara also woke up.

"You're funny, Lexi," Isabella said.

"No, really," Lexi said, shaking her head. Starting to freak out, she looked over at Tamara and Edward. "How is that possible? I remember getting back from the clearing just last night."

"You weren't anywhere last night. I came to check in on you, and all three of you were lying here sleeping. I even had the medic come in and make sure you guys were still breathing. Hey, wait a minute. What do you mean, clearing?"

Ignoring Isabella, Edward said, "They really don't trust anyone, do they?" and took a sip of his hot coffee.

"Who are they? Who are you guys talking about?" Isabella asked.

Lexi decided to explain. "Last night, well, the other night…" Lexi wasn't sure now what day it was. "Tamara went through a cleansing ritual performed by the high shaman, oh right, Qero shaman. What day is it, Isabella?"

"It's Thursday."

"Wow, we found you on Sunday and went to the clearing on Monday, and it's now Thursday." Looking at the other two, Lexi said, "How did the days go by without us knowing? Why did the shaman need us to be out cold again? A better question is, how did he put us under without us noticing?"

"What are you guys talking about? What shaman?"

"Susannah had told Tamara that the shaman wanted to see her. That Tamara was going to go through a cleansing ceremony. It was incredible but very scary to watch," Lexi said with a bit of added excitement in her voice.

"What, Tamara was in a real cleansing ritual, and I wasn't invited?" Isabella said as she now felt left out and hurt.

Tamara bluntly said, "Isabella, Spirit works in weird ways, you know that. Right now, your energy is too tied to Hans. You are not able to have unconditional thoughts. Your only intent is to get Hans back. The shaman would not have been able to do what he needed to do if you had been there. Unfortunately, your energy would have interfered with the sacred energy needed for the ritual."

"Oh, I see. I'm impure now," Isabella said a bit snarkily.

"I am not going to lie to you, Isabella, in a way that is true," Tamara said. "You are acting out of passion and not of a clear mind. Your love for Hans has clouded your thinking… and you did try to commit suicide. A piece of your soul has fragmented and has been missing since that day. Not to mention the negative energy you created when you stole the painting from Lexi's apartment."

"I paid for it."

"Yes, but that doesn't make up for taking it without asking," Tamara said.

Lexi noticed that Tamara was different somehow. She wasn't talking quite like she used to. She was factually blunt.

Tamara continued and said with tough love, "Isabella, we are here to help Hans. That is why we came to Peru. Not to get him back for you, but to free him."

Shocked, Isabella stormed out of the RV.

Chapter 52

"Tamara, does that mean Susannah is not able to get Hans for us?" Lexi asked, still trying to focus after sleeping for three days.

"Ah, about that." Tamara thought back to her time in the temple.

"Tamara, are you listening? I said, what do we do now?" Lexi asked again.

"I was with your sister when I was in the temple."

"You were talking to my sister? What did she say?" Lexi hadn't thought to ask Susannah for help.

Looking at Edward, Tamara said, "She helped me release Hans to the fairies."

"That is great, just great. I have heard everything now. Fairies. Tamara, if you think I am going to ride a night mare again, you've got another think coming," Edward said.

"Edward, don't you mean 'thing coming?'" Lexi asked.

"No, the saying is 'think.' I said it right."

"We have better things to do than argue about the saying," Tamara said.

Edward couldn't handle the belief in fairies and stormed out of the RV.

Lexi looked at Tamara. "Did I really hear you right? Hans is with the fairies? Tamara, you can't tell me you believe in fairies, do you?" Lexi said, sitting there in disbelief and almost as much shock as Edward was.

"Who would I be if I said I believed in ghosts but not fairies?"

"Fairies, really, Tamara, come on. I wished for them when I was a child, but as an adult, how do you expect me to believe in fairies?"

"Lexi, I can't make you believe in anything. It is up to you to decide what you want to believe or not, but I do have a question for you."

"Okay, I am listening," Lexi said, wondering what Tamara could say to convince her that fairies were real.

"Lexi, when you walk to work down 5th Avenue, do you touch every person that passes by you?"

"Of course not." Lexi was surprised at Tamara's question. *It's NYC. I would be pepper-sprayed.*

"Then how do you know for a fact that every person walking past you is human?"

"Oh, my God. Really, Tamara? I can see them."

"Are you sure, Lexi?"

"Of course, I'm sure."

"How can you be one hundred percent positive if you did not touch them?"

"I can hear them."

"So, just because you can see and hear something, that means that what you are walking past is a living human being?"

"Come on, Tamara. This is silly. What's your point?" Lexi asked, getting a bit frustrated.

"My point is that you could be passing by ghosts or an illusion. You may be hallucinating that you are seeing all those people passing you by. What if I told you that you might be passing fairies impersonating humans?"

"Oh, come on, Tamara. This sounds crazy even for me." Lexi shook her head in disbelief.

"Lexi, do you know what fairies are?"

"Of course, everyone knows what a fairy is. They are little mythical beings with wings. Every little girl pretends to be a fairy princess. I was one for Halloween when I was six."

"Okay, that is the marketable version. Many businesses have made oodles of money from that version, but do you know what they really are?"

"Um, I guess not if you're asking me again. Okay, I'll play along, Tamara. What is a fairy?"

"A *faie* or *fee* was a woman skilled in magic and knew the power and virtue of words, of stones, and of herbs. Over the years, the word fairy was used adjectivally, meaning 'enchanted.' Really, she's not much different from a witch, just a lot better-looking, and usually portrayed with wings."

"So, what you're trying to tell me, is that Hans is with the fairies, who were real people at one time?"

"Yes. Fairies in the underworld are a type of angel and can be mischievous when a non-believer is around. You can always tell the difference between a fairy and an angel by the difference in their wings. A fairy has transparent wings, like a dragonfly, whereas an angel has wings more like a bird, with feathers."

"Oh my, I never thought about their difference before. That is fascinating. Who would have thought that fairies are real?" Lexi said as she heard the door of the RV open.

Edward came back, saying, "I need you two to get ready. We need to go and find Isabella. She's missing again."

"Of course she is," Lexi said, shaking her head as she got up, not sure what it would mean if she started to believe in fairies.

"I'll be right there," Tamara said, standing up to get something out of her luggage.

Chapter 53

"Tamara, what is the point of living? I don't see it anymore," Isabella said as Tamara found her standing on the edge of a cliff.

"Isabella, I have known you for a long time, and this is not you. Grief is a hard thing to get a handle on, but you are stronger than this. You already know that if you jump, you won't be with Hans, so why would you even think about it?"

Isabella started to cry and said between sobs, "I am an actress, and I make others happy, but all I asked for was to be happy with Hans. I didn't think that was too much to ask for. Why did God have to take my love away from me? I can't let go of this feeling, Tamara. It hurts so bad that I can barely handle waking up each morning."

Tamara put an arm around Isabella and slowly walked her backward away from the cliff. Sitting down on a boulder, Tamara said, "Iss, life can be difficult at times. Sometimes it seems too much to bear. You are a gift from God, and Hans would never want you to end your life this way. Not for him. Hey, I never told you he is not attached to the painting anymore."

That made Isabella lift her head. "When did that happen?" she asked as she tried to wipe away some tears.

"I guess it was a couple of days ago. The shaman gave me the power to release him from the painting."

"Oh, good. At least he is in Heaven now."

Shaking her head, Tamara confessed, "No. He never made it to Heaven."

"What, he went to Hell?"

"No. He is in the underworld."

"I don't understand. Where is he?"

"The fairies are with him in the level of the Elementals."

"Tamara, you're kidding, right?"

"No. That is where Susannah and I released him."

"Lexi's dead sister?"

"Yes."

"Wonderful. That is just peachy. So, what do I do now? I can't let him stay for eternity with the fairies," Isabella said.

"I was hoping you would say that. How much longer do you have on filming the movie here?"

"I think just over a month. Why?"

"I need you to come back to New York so that we can get Hans to Heaven."

"Tamara, I've messed up really good this time. I am not sure I can go back and face the producer and director. I am sure they think I am a crazy diva by now."

"Isabella, I am sure all they care about is finishing this movie. Nobody will care in a day or two. They probably won't even remember."

"Maybe you have some special magic that can help them forget?"

"At least your humor is coming back, Iss. That's a start. Here, take this." Tamara pulled a crystal from her sweater pocket and gave it to Isabella. She had picked it up from the ground near where the taxi had dropped them off and stored it in her luggage. "Come on, let's go back and have a drink to celebrate."

"What are we celebrating?" Isabella asked as she held the crystal.

"Life."

Isabella made a huffing sound and said, "Thanks for having my back, Tamara. I really appreciate you caring enough to come all the way to Peru to save Hans."

"It has been life-changing, that is for sure," Tamara replied as they walked arm in arm back to Isabella's RV.

Chapter 54

The chapel at Edward's funeral home held over two hundred people. He was about to share his experience and knowledge with the gathered guests. After his experience with the shamans in Peru, he decided to study up on communicating with angels.

"Welcome, everyone, and thank you for coming. I recently had an unexpected experience in the high mountain tops of the Andes in Peru. Imagine that you were expecting to be driven to a friend who was filming a movie. Instead of being taken directly there, you were dropped off in the middle of nowhere with a couple of ladies wearing high heels."

The audience laughed at his interpretation of this event.

"Holding up his hand, he said, "No. Honestly, that is what happened. But… what I can tell you is this. God has humor.

"At the time, I didn't think it was funny, but I am sure God was looking down and smiling at our predicament.

"Think about it. If I weren't the one stranded high above the Amazon jungle, I would have thought it a bit funny too."

The audience laughed.

"Now, why do you think God set this particular experience up? Why would I need to be stranded with two beautiful women? One you may know as my girlfriend, Alexandra. Alexandra, will you please stand up for everyone to see you?"

Lexi stood up, blushing, gave a little wave, and quickly sat back down.

"The other woman is a teacher of the mystics. I can't speak for their experiences, but mine was profound."

Edward stood silently for a moment behind his podium in front of the congregation.

"There are three significant places in the Bible that the angel Gabriel has come down to Earth to speak God's words. He spoke to the prophet Daniel about the vision he had and confirmed that it was true. He spoke to the priest, Zechariah, on the up and coming birth of his newborn son, John the Baptist. He spoke to the Virgin Mary about calling her unborn baby Jesus, which means savior.

"Tonight, I am here to tell you that God sends many angelic hosts to communicate with us.

God hears your prayers and answers them… but on his timing, not yours."

Edward could see many heads nodding in agreement.

"Gabriel is the angel of words. He is God's messenger and has many angels in his command to help answer your prayers."

Lexi smiled at Edward's shift of belief and how he could now talk freely about angels. *He has had enough crazy experiences to trust that angels exist.*

"You prayed… God heard. He doesn't want to hear any doubt from you! If you ask for help from God, you better not be wishy-washy about it.

"In my own situation, I was second-guessing myself, and God sent me all the way to Peru to solidify my belief. I spent a few days walking through the rough terrain of the Andes and reconnected with God. I found God in the trees, in the mountain lakes, and in the sky. I found God even though I couldn't speak or understand the language.

"During my unexpected adventure, I watched and listened as the shaman chanted his prayers. I was mesmerized by the commitment this man had for blessing everything he did. The shaman gave thanks in the morning at sunrise, he gave thanks at each meal, and he gave thanks each evening. He never doubted that food or water would be supplied. He never doubted that there would be warmth from a fire. He never doubted that he would not get a full night's rest under the stars. He never doubted where he was going.

"From my experience in Peru, I realized that I must give more thanks. Trust and have faith that my prayers are being heard and answered."

The audience was silent as they listened.

"When Gabriel speaks, you better listen. Never second-guess his words. If God has told him to tell you something, you better be ready for your prayers to be answered. No matter the timing. What I know is this: You can ask the angel Gabriel for inspiration, a boost of creativity, and the answers to your prayers.

"You will know when Gabriel has been in your presence because you will have profound words that just flow out of your mouth. Uttering brilliant words that you never thought were possible from your lips. Words that after you have spoken them, you say, 'Wow,' that was amazing even for me."

Edward looked at Lexi and said, "The moment you began praying, a command was given. Gabriel's name means, 'God is my strength.' If all you take home with you tonight is this, know that it is Archangel Gabriel who helps to answer your prayers."

Edward bowed his head and said, "Amen."

Looking up again, he said, "Thank you all for coming. I will be giving these little bursts of insight from the Bible on a regular basis from now on. Please fill out your name and email on the forms at the exit if you would like to be included on my email list.

"Good night, everyone. God bless."

Edward left the podium and went to stand by the exit doors, saying goodnight to the guests as they left.

When it was Lexi's turn to say goodnight to Edward, she gave him a little kiss on the cheek and whispered, "I'll wait for you back at your place."

Chapter 55

"That was awesome! I loved how you tied your experience in Peru to an angel from the Bible," Lexi said to Edward when he came into his kitchen. "Here you go. I made you tea."

"Thanks." Edward took the tea and had a sip. "Chamomile. Nice."

Lexi stared at Edward and asked, "Hey, do you miss being in Peru?"

"That's a funny question to ask. Why?"

"I don't know. I guess because I do."

"What do you miss about it? Being tied up, unconscious, or held hostage? Or maybe trekking through the mountain tops freezing your butt off? Or maybe you miss the drama of Isabella?"

Lexi smiled at Edward. "Even though all that is true, I miss the spiritual part—the part of the shamans and feeling so close to God.

"I know our time together isn't what most would say is normal, but I can't believe how much I have changed. No, grown, since Susannah's death."

"I'll say it again. It hasn't been boring with you around, Alexandra."

"No, really, Edward. I can't get the experience out of my mind. The drumming, incense, and chanting. It was transformational."

Edward looked deep into Lexi's eyes and said, "Miss Constantine, I love you."

Startled, Lexi was lost for words. *He said, "I love you."* Getting off the chair she was sitting on, Lexi went over to Edward and put her arms around his neck, and gave him the sweetest of kisses, saying, "I love you too, Mr. Hawthorne."

"Alexandra, will you marry me?"

"Are you proposing to me? Aren't you supposed to be down on one knee or something? Isn't there supposed to be a ring?"

Edward got down on one knee, and from his jacket pocket, he pulled out a small velvet box. Opening it, he said tenderly, "Alexandra, I love you, and I can't wait any longer. I have been dreaming of this day for months. This isn't exactly how I had planned to ask you, but love has its own timing."

"Yes. Yes. I will marry you!" Lexi was so excited that she started jumping up and down. "Oh, my God. I have to call my mom. She will be ecstatic."

Edward held on to Lexi so she couldn't get away. Tilting her head back, he kissed her neck and said, "You can tell your mom in the morning. I have other plans for you, Miss Constantine."

Lexi became nervous as they hadn't been that intimate yet. He had been such a gentleman.

Edward picked her up and carried her in the wrong direction… to the front door. Helping her put on her coat, he said, "Miss Constantine, we're going dancing. It is time to celebrate."

Lexi stared at Edward. Nodding, she replied, "Oh, a celebration. Good idea." *Silly me, what was I thinking? He is such a gentleman. I guess that thought will have to wait until the honeymoon.*

Chapter 56

*I*sabella's flight to New York City was very peaceful. She was thankful that she was able to catch up on her sleep. As she drowsily walked to retrieve her luggage, it took her a few moments to realize that she wasn't in the JFK Airport.

Where am I?

Looking around, she found herself in a very odd place. She was surrounded by lush trees, ferns, and beautiful flowers. Isabella twirled to look at the place from all directions. It was so beautiful. One could live here forever and find bliss. It was a magical place with its waterfalls, butterflies, and singing birds.

Walking a little further, Isabella wondered if she was still dreaming. She pinched herself to see if it hurt. It did.

"Miss Jackson, we have been expecting you. Welcome to Bjälbo," a cute and pixie-like girl said as she came up to Isabella. "Please, follow me."

Dumbfounded, Isabella reluctantly followed the petite girl through a small botanical indoor park.

"Where am I?" Isabella demanded.

The young lady turned her head to answer, "Your private jet landed in Sweden. You are at the private landing site of Erik Jarl. You may have heard of his ancestors, Ingrid Ylva and her son, Birger Jarl."

"No, and why would I?" Isabella asked bluntly.

Not answering her question, the young lady said, "Herr Jarl heard that you owned the painting, 'The Wild Hunt of Odin,' and would like to speak to you about it."

"How did he find out about that? And it is not the original, so why would he even care?"

"I do not know the answers to those questions. He will be here shortly, and you can ask him yourself."

The young lady led Isabella through the backyard of a grand mansion, with pillars guarding the entrance of an elaborate patio. She motioned for Isabella to have a seat at an extravagant outside dining room set. A servant waiting nearby instantly came over and served her a cup of coffee and a cream-filled sugar-coated cookie.

Thirstily, Isabella took a sip of her coffee. It was stronger than she expected. Having no choice but to wait, Isabella looked out onto the estate. She saw green grass as far as the eye could see, with a few trees scattered among the rolling hills in the distance. Surprisingly, she saw what looked like ruins throughout the acreage but instead were strategically placed boulders. It was beautiful in a historical way. One could easily imagine that they were living hundreds of years ago, wandering through these fields.

Just as Isabella was getting bored with the landscape, her abductor emerged. Walking out of the mansion was a man in his late thirties, built like a Viking warrior but wearing a modern-day business suit. His blond hair was pulled back and tied. He strolled over to where Isabella was sitting and bowed.

"Miss Jackson, *tack för att du träffade mig.* Pardon me. Miss Jackson, thank you for meeting with me," he said again in perfect English.

"I didn't have a choice now, did I? You tricked my pilot into bringing me here."

"My apologies for that, but you will find it most beneficial that you have come."

"I doubt that. From what I understand, you will be disappointed that I do not own the original painting for one. And for two, I do not have it anymore. So, you've wasted both of our time."

Looking at her for the first time, he marveled at her beauty. "Miss Jackson, that is not entirely why I have brought you here."

Surprised, Isabella said, "So, tell me why a man of your means would want anything from me if it were not for the painting?"

"You dated my cousin, Hans Jarl."

"I dated a Hans, yes, but his last name was not Jarl. It was Magnusson."

"True, I heard he was going by that last name. Did you know the name 'Jarl' means 'chieftain, nobleman,' or 'earl' in Old Norse? According to Norse legend, Jarl was the son of the god Ríg and the founder of the race of warriors."

"No. I didn't."

"Did Hans ever talk about his *farfar*, Grandfather Olof?"

"Yes," Isabella said, a bit curious and wanting to know more about what this man had to say.

"I used to sit on Hans's lap while our grandfather told old Norse stories."

Isabella looked around the estate and then looked back at Erik. "Are you telling me that I am at Hans's grandfather's estate?"

"Yes, one of his estates. Hans didn't have any heir, so I was next in line to have inherited this estate and its contents, including that painting, but many of the contents were mistakenly sold before I received the news. Many of my grandfather's items were auctioned off. I have traced the painting 'The Wild Hunt of Odin' back to you. It was hidden under another painting. I am not sure how it ended up in your hands, but I want it back."

"As I told your young associate, I do not possess the painting."

"Who does?"

"Why is the painting important to you?"

"That doesn't matter."

"It matters to me. If you want to know where the painting is, I suggest you tell me."

Looking at Isabella, Erik said, "I had a dream, and Hans was in it."

"He is not in the painting anymore."

Erik looked at Isabella strangely. "I meant the dream."

"Oh. Of course. Go on."

"Hans was talking with my *farfar* about the future. Do you know anything about Ingrid Ylva?"

"No. I have never heard of her until today."

"Hans and I are her descendants. She lived in the 13th century. She emerged as the head of the family and was thought to descend from King Sverker's son, Sune Sik. In many stories, she's called a white witch. Her offspring all assumed prominent positions as bishops and lawmakers."

It makes sense now, Isabella thought to herself. *Hans chose the painting to be bound to because of his heritage.*

"It is said that Ingrid had a dream that things would go very poorly for her descendants if her head should ever tilt. So, on her death, she was to be buried with her head upright, in the walls of a tower where she lived. You can still visit the home today."

"Her head must have slightly tilted."

"Why do you say that, Miss Jackson?"

"Well, Hans is not here to chat with you, and you said you had the misfortune of not inheriting everything from your grandfather."

"Hmm. Interesting perspective."

"Mr. Jarl, I would like to be released now," Isabella said as she got up to walk back to her plane.

Quickly grabbing Isabella's wrist, he said, "I am sorry, Miss Jackson. That is not possible."

Isabella turned and stared at him in disbelief. Looking down at her wrist, she said, "You are hurting me!"

Chapter 57

Lexi was so excited about her engagement that she ran up to Sherie when she arrived at work. "Oh, my God, look," Lexi squealed as she held out her hand for her co-worker to see.

"My golly, that diamond is prettier than a peach and shinier than a star," Sherie said in her Southern belle accent.

"What is all the commotion about?" Sebastian, Lexi's boss, said as he came over to see.

"Miss Constantine is getting married," Sherie beamed.

"Well, it's about time. I thought he was never going to ask you. If you ask me, you should have married that detective. What was his name?"

Batting her eyes, Sherie dreamily said, "Redington."

"Yes. That is who you should have married. Now, he was a catch."

"Thanks, but I am very happy with the 'catch' that I have," Lexi said, emphasizing the word catch. "Hey, Sebastian, since you are here, I have a design idea that I think you would like. Do you have a moment?"

"Sure. Come to my office in about an hour."

"Thanks. I can't wait to hear what you think."

Sherie waited until he was gone and then asked, "Lexi, how was your trip to Peru? I mean other than getting engaged."

Thinking back to her time in Peru, Lexi said, "It was… how should I say, transformational?"

"Well, I declare."

"Actually, that is what my new fashion designs are based on, Peruvian colors."

"Heavens to Betsy. You ain't serious!"

Lexi looked at Sherie and smiled at her bluntness.

"Can a gal have a peek?"

"After I show Sebastian. I want his opinion first."

"I see. You don't want anyone to spoil your surprise."

"Ya, something like that," Lexi said as she sat back down on her stool at her easel. "You'll be the second person I show. I promise, Sherie."

"I reckon your promise will have to do," she said as she batted her eyelids and walked back to her station.

Lexi quickly finished up what she was doing and gathered her drawings to bring over to Sebastian, knocking on his door as she entered.

Sebastian looked up and said, "Ah, yes. Come in, Lexi."

Lexi placed her portfolio on Sebastian's easel and opened it. The first drawing showed a young girl swirling around. The cotton summer dress she was wearing was a replica of one of the Peruvian woven designs. The skirt of the dress flared out as she was turning. She looked like a rainbow shining in the sun.

The next drawing was of a young woman riding a horse in early spring. Her jacket was made from wool with a beautiful Peruvian woven design. It was a western look with wool tassels hanging from the bottom edge. It was incredible.

As she showed him her other designs, he said, "Wow. Your trip to Peru was very inspirational. I think you have a winner here. We might even be able to squeeze it into our summer line, and that jacket would work great for our fall line. Good work, Lexi."

As Lexi left, she smiled at the memories of Peru. *It's funny how one's life can be turned upside down and, if one chooses, can be given the gift of unexpected inspiration.*

Chapter 58

Erik had one of his many servants show Isabella to a guest room on the second floor in the mansion's east end, where her luggage was already waiting for her.

"He can't keep me as a hostage. People will wonder about me," Isabella said to the servant.

The servant replied in Swedish, "*Jag är ledsen, jag förstår inte engelska.*" Which meant, "*I am sorry, I do not understand English,*" as he walked out of the room and shut the door.

"How rude," Isabella said, unsure of her situation or how she was going to get out of it but knew she wasn't staying with an arrogant man like Erik Jarl.

Taking out her cell phone, she dialed her pilot; the no-service signal came on. Leaving her room, she tried in several places throughout the house. Same—no signal.

Erik came into the study that she was standing in and said, "You will not find any cell signal on the grounds. My grandfather did not believe in modern gadgets and thought that a cell phone was like a microwave. It could cook your brain cells."

"Well, then I will have to venture out into the yard and find reception."

"You will have to walk for miles. We are quite far from civilization," Erik said as he laughed at the look on Isabella's face.

Isabella huffed and stormed out of the room.

"Dinner is at six. Be on time and wear proper attire."

"The nerve of that man. Who does he think he is, a king?"

"I heard that. No. Not a king, but one step below him," Erik yelled out so that she could hear him.

Angrily, Isabella walked back to her room. Not paying attention, she got lost. As she tried to retrace her footsteps, she happened upon a wall filled with the paintings of whom she assumed were Hans's family. As she walked down the hallway, there was a painting of Hans. He was about eighteen and standing tall.

Oh, how I miss you. If you can hear me, I need your help. For some reason, your cousin has kidnapped me and is holding me against my will.

As she finished her thought, a picture further down the wall tilted. It startled her. Walking over to where she noticed the movement, she found a photo that had fallen to the floor. *It must have been tucked behind the painting.* She picked it up.

Looking at the photo, it was of Hans and Erik when they were younger. Hans looked about fifteen and Erik about five. Behind them was a shed. As Isabella looked closer, she noticed there was a face hidden in the window of the shed. *What are you trying to show me, Hans?*

Tucking the photo into her pocket, she decided that there had to be a reason that she was coincidently in Hans's grandfather's home.

What does Tamara teach? That the question is more important than the answer. But what is the perfect question to ask?

As she turned a corner, she found herself back in the study. Erik was not there anymore. She decided to walk in the opposite direction from where she had come and soon found her accommodations.

Chapter 59

Isabella put on one of the most beautiful dresses that she had in her luggage. It was a cobalt-blue velvet gown. A little fancy for dinner, but what did she care. She was, after all, Isabella Jackson, a famous actress. She could bloody well wear whatever she pleased.

Just as she was finishing with her hair, a servant came to fetch her to bring her to the dining room.

It was a grand room, large enough to fit twenty people at the table. Many old paintings were hanging on the walls.

Isabella entered the room with her head held high. She walked in as if she was a noblewoman and the lady of the house.

Erik rose as she entered, breathless and speechless at the beauty and grace Isabella possessed.

The servant moved a chair to the left of Erik's chair and waited until Isabella was seated before leaving.

Erik sat down. Gaining his composure, raising his glass, he said, "*Skål*," and took a sip.

Isabella had played a small part in a Swedish film years ago and knew that word translated to "Cheers." Not taking a sip of her wine, she said instead, "Why do you have me here against my will?"

"Getting down to business even before we start the first course, I see."

Isabella looked down at her pea soup, and without taking a bite, she said, "What is it about that painting that you found so important that you needed to kidnap me?"

"It is not the painting that I care about. It is the frame."

"The frame! Why in God's name would you care about an old wooden frame?"

"It has a secret message carved into the design."

"What? I didn't see any words written on the frame. I am sure I would have noticed," Isabella said, thinking back to how many times she sat caressing the frame talking to Hans.

"There are no English or Swedish words carved into the frame."

"I thought you said there was a message."

"Yes, but not in a language you or I learned in school."

"What language is it, then?"

"It looks like symbols to an untrained eye, but the message is carved using the ancient writings of the runic alphabet."

"Runes, like in divination?"

"I guess you could say that, but the written language was used as far back as 150AD. The three best-known runic alphabets are the Elder Futhark, the Anglo-Saxon Futhorc, and the Younger Futhark. One of the most famous displays of the short-branch style is carved on the Rök runestone. You can still see the stone today beside the church in Rök, here in Östergötland."

"So, what you are telling me is that on the frame of the painting, is carved a message using the runic alphabet?"

"Yes."

"What does it say?" Isabella was curious now.

"I don't know. I need the frame back to be able to decipher it."

"I see. What do you think it says?"

Erik took a sip of his wine as a servant brought them the next course of the meal. It was a marvelous display of meatballs in brown sauce, mashed potatoes, pickled cucumbers, and what looked like cranberries.

Isabella played with her food.

Watching her toy with her food, he said, "What, you don't like reindeer? I thought you would like to taste a traditional Swedish meal. The berries are lingonberries."

"How thoughtful of you," Isabella said a bit sarcastically. "What makes you think there is a message on the frame, and why didn't you know about it when you were younger?"

Erik laughed. "You didn't know my grandfather. He believed in the old ways, and every chance he got, he instilled them in all his grandchildren.

"I found a letter addressed to Hans, hidden in one of my grandfather's old books in the library."

"What did it say?"

"As you know, Hans was the oldest male grandchild and heir to the estate. I don't know why it was given to him and not one of our parents. Maybe because of his age."

"Go on. What did the letter say?"

"It was written in an old-style runic poem."

"I had it translated, and it said,
> *By the sea lies a lake.*
> *Endorsed by a key.*
> *There lies the treasure.*
> *Look inside*
> *Deep inside*
> *and you will find*
> *the next scripture.*"

"What does that all mean?"

"It took me many months to figure it out. Eventually, it led me to the painting's frame."

"I see. So, you think I have the painting and have brought me here, why again?"

"I hired a private investigator, and his team heard about a painting hidden behind another. They traced it to a girl whom it was gifted to from her employer."

"Ah, you are talking about Susannah Constantine."

"Yes."

"Then it was traced to her sister, Alexandra Constantine. I was informed that it was no longer in her possession. Instead, it was in yours, and you took it to Peru with you."

"If you know all that, then you know that it was stolen from me."

"Yes, unfortunately, my man had gotten to your RV a few hours too late, and it was not there anymore. At the moment, I have lost track of it." Changing the subject, he said, "You really are a diva, aren't you, Miss Jackson? My sources tell me that you tried to commit suicide again."

Isabella stood up. She had heard enough. "Good night, Mr. Jarl," she said as she stormed away from the table.

Chapter 60

After work, instead of going back to Edward's, Lexi walked home to her apartment. It seemed like a lifetime ago that she had walked through the door. The last time she was home was before she went to Peru.

After putting her keys and purse onto the kitchen island, she flopped down on her couch, closed her eyes, and took a much-needed "me" moment.

With her next deep breath, she relaxed even further into the couch.

Her cell phone dinged to let her know a text message had arrived. The sound brought her back out of her meditative state. Getting up, she almost missed it.

The painting was back.

Stopping in her tracks and backing up a few steps, she stared at the painting of The Wild Hunt of Odin.

Her phone dinged again, breaking her astonishment.

Lexi glanced down to read it, but there was nothing there. Not even a sign that a message was sent to her.

As she stared at her phone, it dinged again. Nothing.

What the? "Susannah, is that you?"

"No."

"Who is it, then?"

Nothing. Susannah didn't answer Lexi's question.

"Susannah, who is trying to contact me?"

"Hans."

"What, why?"

Again, Susannah didn't answer.

"Susannah, can you please connect me to Hans?"

"Yes."

Lexi waited, but Susannah didn't answer.

"Susannah, are you there?"

"Yes."

"I asked if you could communicate with Hans for me."

"No, you didn't."

"Yes, that is what I meant."

"You said to connect you, and I did."

"Oh, my God! I forgot how literal spirits are. Sorry, Susannah. Can you please ask and then translate what Hans wants to say to me?"

"Yes. He says Isabella is in trouble again."

"You've got to be kidding me. Again? Did she try to commit suicide again?"

"No."

"What then?"

"Not a good enough question. Ask me a more specific question that I can answer."

"Where is Isabella?"

"Hans's grandfather's house."

"Right now?"

"Yes."

"Here in New York City?"

"No."

"Where is Hans's grandfather's house located?"

"Sweden."

Lexi took a moment and went over the answers Susannah had given in her mind. "What am I supposed to do with this knowledge about Isabella?"

"Go and help her."

Lexi, feeling like this was way too much to bear alone, texted Edward and Tamara.

Chapter 61

Lexi was waiting for Edward and Tamara to arrive at her place any minute.

The intercom buzzed.

"Hello."

"Good evening, Miss Constantine," the doorman said. "Both Mr. Hawthorne and Miss Reeve are here to see you."

"Thank you, let them in, please."

Lexi went to the kitchen and poured three glasses of wine.

A few moments later, she opened the door and greeted them each with a glass. "So glad you two could make it on such short notice."

Tamara took her glass of wine and said, "Wow, you two, congratulations! Nice ring, Lex." Smiling at Edward, she sat down on the couch in the living room. "Lex, is that what I think it is…? You have it back!" Tamara exclaimed, staring at the painting.

Edward walked in and looked at the wall where Tamara was staring. "Did you have to give the money back?"

Just like a man to ask about finances. "No. The painting and the key I had given Isabella to my apartment were here when I came in yesterday. Sam, the valet, told me that he had come up with the delivery man and let him in with the master key and then locked the place up after they left."

"Interesting!" Tamara said.

"I wonder why she gave it back to you?" Edward asked, not sure how one gives back something they'd paid two million dollars for.

Tamara answered, "Well, Hans isn't attached to it anymore, so I guess she didn't care about the actual painting, just Hans."

Looking at Tamara, Edward asked, "Hey, I thought Isabella was supposed to be back here by now. Have either of you heard from her yet?"

"No. I thought she would have contacted me yesterday, but nothing yet."

"Ah, about that," Lexi said. "Actually, you guys, that is why I asked you to come here."

"Don't tell me I need to ride a night mare again," Edward said jokingly.

Lexi looked at him and said, "I don't think so, but I need help understanding what Susannah said."

"What did she say?" Edward sat down on the couch beside Tamara, looking concerned.

"Well, she contacted me. Okay, I should correct that. Hans contacted me, but I needed Susannah to translate."

"Hans contacted you, and you didn't tell me?" Edward looked hurt.

"I thought about it, but I decided I needed Tamara here too. Guys, let me explain. Hans said Isabella needs our help again."

Edward put his glass down on the living-room table, bending his head in disbelief as he shook it, saying, "What now?"

"Lexi, where is Isabella?" Tamara said before Lexi could answer Edward.

"Sweden."

Edward stood up and said, "My faith is being tested. I know it."

"Where in Sweden?" Tamara asked.

"Susannah said Hans's grandfather's house. I looked it up. It is somewhere in a small village called Bjälbo, in the province of Östergötland."

"Lexi, I can't go with you. I have too many funerals booked for the next couple of weeks," Edward blurted out.

Lexi looked at him and then at Tamara. "Can you come with me?"

"When are you thinking of going?"

"I was thinking about going this weekend."

"Hmm. I'm not sure," Tamara answered, just as a message from her angels came in.

"You must go."

Listening to the message from Spirit, Tamara said, "I guess I can change my plans. I finished my workshop, and I can switch a few clients around or work with them by Zoom."

"Oh, good. I didn't want to go by myself."

"Alexandra, I think you should call your detective friend," Edward said, a bit jealously.

"Why?"

"Hans said Isabella is in trouble, right? And she should have contacted us by now. I think it would be wise to get the police involved this time."

Chapter 62

"Detective Redington, thank you for getting back to me so quickly. I know you must be busy, but this should be quick," Lexi said, remembering back to their crazy adventure together.

"Miss Constantine, how can I help you this time? Don't tell me you have another demon chasing after you."

"Funny. Oh, my God, I never thought about that. Thanks, now I have to worry about the dark side being after me again," Lexi said, now scared that something evil was at work here.

"Alexandra, I was kidding. Why have you called me? I know. You missed me, right?" Redington said a bit flirtatiously.

"You're an arrogant one, aren't you? Of course, you would think that every woman is a damsel in distress and would fall madly in love with you."

"Well, as it turns out, not all women," he said, thinking specifically about Lexi. "Seriously, Alexandra, why have you called?"

"Right. Do you know who Isabella Jackson is?"

"Of course, doesn't everybody?"

"Well, I have it on good authority that she is in trouble."

"Good authority," Redington said sarcastically.

"Mr. Redington…"

"That's Detective Redington."

"Detective, I'm serious. Isabella is in trouble."

"Pray tell, how did you come to this knowledge?"

"Well, Susannah, but it was Hans who told her."

"Your belated sister, Susannah? Who is Hans?"

"Detective. I know you don't believe in ghosts, spirits, or demons, but I am telling you the truth. Isabella is in trouble."

Redington thought about their time together, and after what they had gone through, he wasn't sure what he believed anymore. "Okay, start from the beginning, Alexandra. I'm listening."

After Lexi had told him everything she knew, he asked, "Why are you telling me this and not the police?"

"You are the police."

"Well, yes, but I do not usually return calls unless I am on the case."

"I see. So, you can't help me, then?"

"I didn't say that. Let me look into this a bit further, and I will get back to you."

"Redington, I only have two days, and then I am flying to Sweden to find Isabella. I've already booked the flights."

"Alexandra, do you think that is wise? What flight are you on?"

Lexi told him and then said, "Susannah said Isabella needs my help. I am going to trust that my sister knows what is best."

"Alexandra, did you ask her if you should be going?" Without hearing her answer, Detective Redington said, "Sorry, Lexi, I'll have to call you back. Duty calls," and hung up.

Chapter 63

"Call me as soon as you all arrive," Edward said as he kissed Lexi goodbye. Pointing at Lexi, he said to Tamara, "You look after this one, will you? And have a safe trip."

Lexi and Tamara said goodbye to Edward as they entered security at the JFK Airport.

Boarding the plane and storing her carry-on, Lexi said to Tamara as she sat down, "I love first-class, don't you?"

"I could get used to this lifestyle," Tamara said as the flight attendant came by, checking their seatbelts.

After they were safely in the air and the seatbelt warning had gone off, the flight attendant came by and said, "Miss Constantine, there is a gentleman in the back that would like to have a word with you."

Lexi looked at Tamara and then back at the stewardess. "That is weird. Who is asking for me?"

"He said his name is Detective Redington."

"What the?" Lexi got up and moved past Tamara, following the flight attendant.

Seeing him standing there by the entrance to the economy section, Lexi said, almost whispering, "What are you doing here?"

"Nice to see you too, Miss Constantine."

"Seriously, what are you doing here?" Lexi pulled him into a more private place, not that there was one.

"I followed up on Miss Jackson, and you are right. She is missing."

"I told you that she was in trouble."

"Yes. Well, I couldn't let you go find her on your own."

"I'm not alone. Tamara is with me."

"Uh, huh. As I said, I couldn't let you go and save Isabella by yourself. I had some holiday time owed to me anyway, so I am using it to escort you to Sweden."

"Really? You decided to escort me to Sweden?"

"Hey, it could be fun!"

Lexi thought about it for a moment. *Well, I could use some professional help.*

Lexi signaled for the flight attendant. "I would like to upgrade Detective Redington's ticket to first-class, please."

"Right away, Miss Constantine. Please follow me, Detective Redington."

Sitting in a seat opposite Tamara, Redington said, "You didn't have to do that, Alexandra. I was comfortable where I was."

Tamara stared at the man talking to Lexi and moved a bit as Lexi got back into her seat. "What's going on, Lexi?"

"Aren't you supposed to be the psychic? Shouldn't you know already?" Redington said to Tamara.

"Have we met before? I don't believe I know your name," Tamara said, a bit confused.

Redington looked at Alexandra and said, "I thought you said she was intuitive?"

"Pardon me, but it doesn't work like that!" Tamara said, getting defensive. "Lexi, who is this clown?"

"Tamara, please meet Detective Redington. I know I didn't tell you the truth about what happened to me or where I disappeared for a couple of weeks before Christmas, but Detective Redington helped me clear Susannah's name."

Tamara looked at the man and then back at Lexi. "What is he doing here now?"

"He says he is escorting us to Sweden."

Looking at Redington, Tamara said, "Really?"

"Again, are you sure she is a psychic because she doesn't sound like one to me?"

Tamara glared at Redington.

"Enough, you two. We have bigger problems than this."

Tamara turned away from Redington and stared straight ahead. Taking a deep breath, she closed her eyes.

"Tell him the truth."

"What is the point?" She thought back to the angel, talking to her.

"He needs to know."

"Detective Redington, I am being informed to explain to you how psychic energy works."

"That's okay. I don't need to understand. I probably wouldn't believe it anyway."

"Don't interrupt me when I am talking, Detective," Tamara said bluntly. "A person who is granted the gift or ability of intuitive energy cannot see, hear, feel, or know about something unless they have asked. Most of my day, I am just like everyone else, blind to the future."

"Why?" Redington asked.

"Why? That is an interesting question. Well, it takes a lot of energy or concentration to focus on the answer. Imagine a baseball player concentrating on the ball. Most of his energy is focused when it is his turn to bat, catch, or run. The rest of the time, during the game, he is watching and learning what is needed of him next. When he goes home and has had some rest, he doesn't use the same intense energy as he did during the game. He goes about his day, as any other normal person would."

"I guess that makes sense. I never thought about it like that." Redington put out his hand and said, "Hi, I am Detective Redington, but my friends call me Red."

Tamara took his hand and shook it.

"Good," Lexi said. "Now that you two are over that, let's get down to how we are going to help Isabella."

Chapter 64

$\mathcal{L}$anding in Linköping, Sweden, Lexi, Tamara, and Detective Redington searched for transportation to Bjälbo, Östergötland.

They found out they had to take a train to get to Mjolby first, then to Vadstena.

They were exhausted with the six-hour time difference and decided to spend the night in Vadstena before carrying on to their destination. The next morning, Redington rented a car.

Lexi read the map and said, "Oh my, Edward would have loved to see this."

"What?" Tamara asked.

"The monastery that Saint Bridget of Sweden founded. Hey, Tamara, you'd like this part about her. It refers to Saint Bridget being a mystic."

"Alexandra, we don't have time to waste on sightseeing. We need to get to the estate and find

Isabella," Redington said, taking control of the situation.

"I guess that means the castle is off the sightseeing agenda as well," Lexi said disappointedly.

Looking at the map, Lexi said, "Detective, did you know that we could have gotten to Bjälbo from Mjolby? We didn't have to come to Vadstena."

"What? Let me see that map. Well, I'll be. Would you look at that?"

"Some detective you are," Lexi teased.

"Did you call him yet, Lexi?" Tamara asked.

Taking her mind off the unseen splendid sights in Vadstena, Lexi answered, "No. With the time difference, he would be sleeping."

"You better call him. He'll be worried sick," Tamara said urgently.

Lexi took out her cell phone and dialed his number. It went to his voice mail. "He is not answering." The beep sounded, and she left a message. "Hi, Edward. We are all safe in Sweden and making our way to the estate. I will call you later when I have more information. Love you."

Redington twinged as he heard her say, "love you." *What, did I expect her to be single forever?*

Redington didn't have to drive far, only twelve kilometers to the small village of Bjälbo.

Lexi googled Bjälbo on her cell phone. "Did you guys know that there is only a population of about sixty-five people here? It shouldn't be too hard to find Hans's grandfather's house."

#

"How could you get lost?" Lexi yelled. "If you had listened to me and turned when I told you to, we would have been there by now. You can't even blame it on driving on the wrong side of the road because Sweden's been driving on the right for over fifty years."

Pulling over, Redington got out of the car and said, "You drive."

"Red, get back in the car, big baby," Lexi said, annoyed with his theatrics.

Redington walked to the back of the car and leaned against the trunk, taking a moment to gain his composure. As he stared at the Nordic countryside, a bizarre thought came into his head, *Get into the car and turn right at the next dirt road.* Getting back into the car, he started to drive very slowly.

"What are you doing now?" Lexi asked.

"You would be happy to know that I have a hunch."

"Really? You are going to listen to your intuition?"

Interrupting Lexi, Tamara asked, "What did it say, Detective?"

"It said to turn right at the next dirt road. Hey, how did you know it was a voice?"

"Just my intuition," Tamara chuckled.

"Wait!" Redington said as he stopped the car and backed it up a bit. "Does that look like a dirt road to you?"

Both Tamara and Lexi looked out the window.

There, just beyond the tall grass, was a path wide enough for a vehicle.

Redington stopped the car and got out to see if it was safe to drive on. It was.

Getting back in, he slowly turned right and proceeded to travel on the dirt road. They drove the dirt road for about fifteen minutes before a grand and beautiful-looking mansion appeared.

Redington's hunch paid off.

"Now, what do we do?" Lexi asked as she stared at the impressive castle-looking house.

Chapter 65

Redington drove up to the house, then followed a paved driveway to the front. As he got out, he said, "You two wait here. I'll check it out and see if Isabella is inside." He walked to the front door and knocked using the massive metal door knocker.

A few moments later, a servant opened one of the two huge wooden doors. Lexi could see them talking and the servant shaking his head as he shut the door on the detective.

Redington came back into the car. "He said no one by that name was staying at the manor."

"You believed him?" Lexi asked, amazed that he wasn't going to do anything.

"What would you like me to do, call him a liar?"

"Maybe," Lexi said as she looked around, desperately searching for Isabella.

Redington pulled away and continued slowly down the driveway, away from Isabella.

"Stop the car!" Lexi screamed as she opened the door and got out while it was still moving.

"What in carnation is she doing?" Redington said as he stopped the car.

"Detective, I think you mean what in tarnation," Tamara said with a smile on his mix-up on the saying.

"What? Ah, whatever. What is she doing?"

As Redington got out of the car, he heard Lexi screaming out Isabella's name.

"Isabella! It's me, Lexi. We are here to save you! Isabella!"

"Alexandra, get back in the car. Don't be foolish!"

"Isabella!" Lexi kept screaming as she ran closer to the back of the house.

Redington ran after her.

Tamara got out and started yelling her name as well, "Isabella, it's me, Tamara. Where are you?"

Redington looked back at the car. "Great, now I have two crazies on the loose."

"Isabella!"

"Detective, this way. She is banging on that window. Look!" Tamara said, pointing. "Isabella, don't worry. We'll get you out."

At that moment, Erik came out of the house with a pump-action shotgun and yelled, "Get off my property!" He fired a shot into the air.

Everyone froze.

Redington said slowly, "Sir, I am with the New York City police and am following up on a missing person's report."

"You are a far distance from your jurisdiction. You have no authority here."

"Sir, it would be in your best interest to let Isabella go. If you shoot us, you will go to jail for a very long time."

At that moment, the windowpane broke. With her head framed by the broken glass, Isabella screamed, "Help me! He is holding me hostage."

Lexi had pulled out her cell phone and was recording it all.

Erik motioned for the three of them to get into his house. No one moved. He fired another warning shot.

Redington knew he had anywhere from two to seven more rounds left. He couldn't take a chance. He put his hands onto his head and walked toward the house, saying, "Girls, do as he says."

Tamara and Lexi followed Redington into the house.

"I don't understand. Why are you holding Isabella against her will? Are you looking for ransom?" Lexi asked, even though she was scared out of her mind.

Erik ignored her question, thinking to himself, *Now, what do I do?* A moment later, Erik called something out in Swedish. A few moments later,

Isabella was led into the parlor where Lexi, Tamara, and Redington were being held.

Running over to Tamara, hugging her, Isabella said, "Thank God you guys are alright. How did you find me?"

Tamara dropped her hands and hugged Isabella. "Hans contacted Lexi."

"You talked to Hans?" Isabella turned to Lexi.

Erik was confused. "Hans is dead. What are you talking about?"

Isabella turned to Erik. "His ghost communicates with us."

"That is crazy. Everyone knows ghosts aren't real."

"Then how do you explain how they found me?" Isabella asked Erik.

Redington said to Isabella, "Are you alright, ma'am?"

"He has not hurt me if that is what you mean."

Lexi blurted out, "I don't understand. Why do you have her here?"

Erik was staring at them all, not sure what to do next.

"He wants the painting," Isabella told them the truth.

"What painting?" Redington asked.

"The Wild Hunt of Odin," Lexi said, knowing that it could only be that painting.

Redington was confused. "He kidnapped you for a painting?" Redington looked at Erik.

"Dude, you don't look like you need the money, so why would you kidnap a famous star? That is ludicrous. Everyone and their dog will be out looking for her."

"He actually doesn't want the painting. He wants the frame," Isabella added.

"Why?" Redington asked.

"He says there is a message written on it in the old-style runic alphabet," Isabella clarified.

Lexi sat down.

Erik's gun followed her.

Redington stepped in front of Lexi and said, "Hey, cool it. She is just sitting down. No harm was done."

Lexi looked up in horror as the shotgun was pointing at her through Redington. "Oh, my God. This is crazy. We are in the twenty-first century. This can't be happening."

Tamara calmly said, "Erik, can we all please sit down and figure out a solution to this problem? Maybe if you explain what is really going on here, we can help."

Chapter 66

"Fine. Everyone, sit down," Erik said, moving his rifle as he said it. "The painting is mine. It was supposed to be mine, but there was a mix-up when my grandfather died, and the will was missing. Many items were sold to an auction house in the United States of America."

"Susannah's," Lexi said, knowing how her sister came to acquire the painting.

"*Ja*. How did you know that? Wait, I get it. You are Alexandra, Susannah's sister. Of course, I should have known," Erik said, surprised that the other owner of the painting was now sitting in his parlor. "So, where is the painting now? Somebody here knows where it is?"

Lexi looked at Isabella, and Isabella shook her head.

Erik caught the motion and pointed the gun at Lexi again. "Tell me what you know."

Lexi took a deep breath. *God. Angels, if you are there, I could really use your help right now.* Not knowing what to say, Lexi said, "The last time I saw the painting was in Peru."

"Nice try. My investigators found the shaman who took it, and he does not have it anymore. He said he gave it back." Erik moved the rifle to Isabella. "The truth. I want the truth!"

"What if I said I could get it for you? Would you let my friends go?" Isabella said, trying to negotiate, knowing that she had given it back to Lexi.

"I knew you had it," Erik said.

"I don't, but I know where it is," Isabella said honestly. "I will have to make a call to get it here.

"Where is it?" Erik moved closer to Isabella and placed the barrel of the gun to her head.

"Dude, that is not going to get your painting back. Shooting the person who knows where it is, is not the answer," Redington said, trying to get Erik's attention off Isabella.

Backing up, Erik said, "You better not be messing with me. If you are lying, I will kill all of you and bury you in the backfield. No one would ever know."

Redington had seen that facial expression many times before. Erik was desperate and serious.

Erik called out in Swedish again. A servant came to the door of the parlor. "Sir, give me the key to the car you were driving."

Redington sat there, not moving. *What should I do? If I give it to him, I am stuck here, miles from town.*

Erik pointed the rifle in front of Lexi.

He's quick. Pick the person I care about most. Redington thought as he pulled out the keys and gave them to Erik.

Erik gave them to the servant and said something in Swedish. A moment later, the sound of the car leaving could be heard. "Your vehicle is being taken back to a rental company. Don't worry. Your bags are being taken up to your rooms. You are my guests until the painting arrives, and then I will release you."

Redington knew the chances of being released were almost nil. The charges Erik would face would be too extreme.

Erik had a servant lead the way to the guest bedrooms, which were close to Isabella's. Erik followed behind with the rifle still held up. "You will behave yourselves. I will call you down shortly for supper." He watched as each one entered their room and locked each door, knowing there was no way out.

Chapter 67

At supper, Erik had each guest brought down separately. Once everyone was seated, he said, "I have learned much about you, Mr. Redington. I find it, how do you say… fascinating that you are here. I think I have missed something. I am not sure why a detective would be with Susannah's sister. And you, Miss Reeve, it is fascinating having you here, a psychic."

Erik took a bite of the first course, a freshly made cabbage salad. "I believe there is more than meets the eye here. I have been thinking to myself how the three of you found Isabella. I did hear you say that Hans told you, Miss Constantine, even if I don't believe in ghosts. I am going to tell you all the truth." Turning slightly to Redington, Erik said, "Detective, please don't think about using the knife on the table. I have a pistol under the table pointing at Lexi."

Lexi couldn't help herself. She looked under the table, and sure enough, there was a pistol pointing right at her. "He is telling the truth," she said, looking at Redington.

"As I was saying, I am going to tell you the truth. My grandfather, pardon me, Hans and my grandfather came from a Viking background. He used to tell us stories, many stories. His favorite was, in a mythological sense, about the first king of Sweden, Odin, who was said to have been the founder of the house of Yngling.

"There are many runestones scattered all over Sweden, telling many historic Norse tales and legends of the old ways and how the Vikings pirated, raided, and traded across Europe. My grandfather was obsessed with Viking history.

"From a very young age, I learned about the difference between theft and raiding. In my grandfather's mind, the Norse people believed that theft was repulsive. Thieving was one of the few acts that would condemn a man to a place of torment after his death. On the other hand, raiding was an honorable challenge to a fight, with the victor retaining all the treasure.

"The Vikings believed for those who died in battle, their souls would be carried away by the Valkyries, 'women warriors,' to Valhalla, 'the hall of the slain.' There they lived a good life, fighting battles during the day and finishing each evening in merriment and feasting.

"There was a price for this everlasting bliss. It was known that the slain fighter would join Odin's army and help the gods in the last great battle of Ragnarok. They would fight this doomed battle against the giants and fearsome creatures of darkness for the sake of saving Earth and the world of the Gods."

Lexi was fascinated by the tale. "What happened to the people who were not warriors?"

"The people who lived ordinary lives went on to a shadowy existence after death," Erik said with no remorse.

Erik continued, "My grandfather believed in retaining the family's wealth, but not in banks. *Ja*, he kept much of his riches in banks, but us grandchildren always knew that the most valuable of all his possessions were hidden somewhere on this property.

"I recently found an old journal of my grandfather's that had Hans's name on it. He wrote that the location of the treasure was carved on the frame of the painting using the old runic alphabet."

"What? I've never seen anything written on the frame," Lexi said.

"It's very small and would have looked like part of the design," Erik answered.

"So, what you are telling me, is that you brought Miss Jackson here to tell you where the painting is? Don't you think you could have just asked her?" Redington asked.

"You don't understand. I must get that painting back. My grandfather taught me the basics of reading the runes. I believe I can decipher the message." Erik was desperately trying to make these people understand his situation. "Did you know that runes are associated with the god Odin? He was the first to discover them from the Well of Destiny at the foot of Yggdrasil, the tree of life. My grandfather taught us that the runes were part of a deeper truth."

Erik pulled out an old cloth bag from his pocket. Moving his plate to the side, he poured out its contents. "These are called Elder Futhark and are a set of twenty-four runes. This is a type of Viking lore that you use to speak with the Gods."

"I have heard about these," Tamara said. "But I thought there were only sixteen pieces?"

"Those are called the Younger Futhork. They are an easier set to use. However, I believe in using the full set as my grandfather taught me."

He continued, "The word *runa*, from Gothic, translates more closely to 'secret whisper,' while *rhin* in Old English translates to 'secret writing.'

"There are many ways you can ask for an answer. First, you have to have a question or intent in mind, and then you can choose a rune, randomly picking one out of the bag. Or gently toss all the runes from the bag onto a soft surface, then the rune that stands out the most to you is your answer. Or you can lay the runes out in a row and let your opposite hand to your dominant hand pass over the runes slowly while concentrating on an answer, then choose the rune that you feel the most attracted to."

"Interesting," Lexi said, forgetting that there was a gun pointing at her.

Redington thought he heard everything now and said, "Let me get this straight. You're telling me that you speak with the 'Gods' with these pieces of old wood?"

Tamara looked at the detective and asked, "Detective, are you telling me that it is okay for you to have hunches but not a Swedish Viking?"

"I don't believe in superstitions."

"Really? Are you telling me that you don't believe that Friday the 13th is a day notoriously linked with ill fortune, bad calls, and bad karma? Or that dead bodies always happen in 3s or 6s? Or that the full moon brings out the aluminum foil brigade?" Tamara added, "Don't get me started on superstitions. Everyone believes in something supernatural that wards off evil."

Erik ignored both of them and continued, "In Norse lore, Odin impaled his heart with his own spear and hung himself on the world tree, Yggdrasil, for nine days and nights, to gain the meaning of the runes.

"The runes are why I brought Isabella here to my grandfather's home."

"What, why didn't you tell me? I might have been a better guest if I knew you were into metaphysics," Isabella said.

"I'm not into metaphysics," Erik corrected her.

"Hey, if you are talking to the 'Old Gods,' then you are into metaphysics. Tell him, Tamara," Isabella said.

"Enough, don't get me off track. The runes told me to bring you here, that you are the key to finding the treasure my grandfather has hidden away somewhere on this property."

"So, you are telling me that if I help you find the treasure, you will let us all go?" Isabella asked.

Erik closed his eyes and touched a rune. Picking it up, he replied, "*Ja.*"

#

After supper, Erik had the guests return to their bedrooms.

Sitting in the den, at his grandfather's old desk, he thought as he tossed the runestones, *What am I to do about the guests in this house?*

The first rune was ᚺ, which translates to havoc. Next was ᛕ, which means hidden game. The next rune was ᛜ, which translates to estate. The next one he read was ᚠ and it means wealth. The next two were ᚾ and ᛗ, meaning need and man. All the other runes were face down and showed no symbol.

Erik translated the symbols on the runes to mean, "havoc hidden game estate wealth need man."

The message of the runes was the same as before, except for this time, "need man" was added.

Chapter 68

The next morning, Lexi and the rest of the gang sat down to what looked like crepes filled with fruit and cream. *At least we are not being starved,* Lexi thought to herself.

"It comes to my attention that there is a man that we need to complete this task of finding my grandfather's treasure," Erik said matter-of-factly.

"A man?" Lexi said, wondering what he meant.

"Yes. You are not telling me something. I need to know now. Where is the painting?" Erik stood up from the dining room table and banged his hands down hard on the wood surface. "I am done being the nice guy. I demand you tell me now, or I will be forced to do something drastic."

"Calm down, dude. No need to get your panties in a bunch," Redington said, trying to lighten up Erik's mood.

Erik pulled the pistol out from behind his jacket and pointed it at Lexi. "You. Tell me now. Where is the painting!"

Lexi dropped her fork, put her hands up, and swallowed the bite in her mouth. "Okay, Yes, I know where the painting is."

"Lexi, no," Isabella said.

Erik pointed the gun at Isabella and said, "Shut up."

Bringing the gun back to Lexi, Erik demanded, "Where?"

"I have it in my apartment."

"Liar, your apartment was checked yesterday. You do not have it."

"Yes. Yes, I do. Isabella gave it back."

"No. My men have checked all of your homes, and the painting is not there. Where is it?"

Lexi looked at the others, then said, "I don't know. When I left to come to Sweden, it was in my apartment. If it isn't there, then it has been stolen again. What is it with that painting?"

Lexi closed her eyes and prayed to God for help.

"Hey, Lexi, the Reverend has the painting," Susannah answered the prayer.

"Oh, my God," Lexi mistakenly blurted out loud.

"What?" Erik said. "What do you know?"

Erik went over to Lexi and pulled her out of her chair.

Redington didn't know what to do. He didn't have his gun and felt powerless. He couldn't do anything reckless for fear that one of the girls would get hurt.

As Erik pulled Lexi out of the room, he had to pass Redington.

Just as Erik moved past him, Redington pushed his chair backward, knocking Erik sideways. Scrambling for the gun, Redington used his size and strength to grab the gun out of Erik's hand.

Lexi screamed.

Before Erik had time to regain his power, Redington had him on the floor, face down, with the gun now pointing at Erik's head. "I believe, Mr. Jarl, that you are under arrest."

Acting out of instinct, Isabella grabbed the cord, which was holding back a drape, and gave it to Redington to use in place of handcuffs.

"Thank you, quick thinking. How did you know to do that?" Redington asked.

"I played a part once that required me to do the exact thing. It seemed appropriate," Isabella said.

Lexi and Tamara ran over to Redington. "What can we do, Detective?" Tamara asked.

"Go find a phone and call for the police."

"No! Do not call the police. I beg you! If you call the police, I will never find the treasure," Erik pleaded.

"Go call the police now!" Redington ordered.

The village wasn't very big, and within a few minutes, you could hear a siren getting closer to the house.

"Get up," Redington ordered Erik, pulling him up. "Girls, go let the police in. Show them my badge." Redington passed his badge to Lexi.

Lexi ran to the police officer and showed him the recording.

Within moments a very heavy accented Swedish police authority ordered, "Detective Redington, I have the situation under control. Please, move aside."

Redington did as he was ordered.

The older policeman removed the corded handcuffs from Erik's wrists. "Erik, I warned you that one day you were going to get yourself into trouble over your grandfather's treasure hunt. What were you thinking, keeping these people here like this?"

Erik rubbed his wrists and said something in Swedish.

The policeman escorted Erik into the back of his patrol car.

Redington went with them. Then turning to the girls, he said, "I need to call into my commander and tell him that I will be staying here a few more days. I will be back in a bit."

"What should we do?" Lexi asked.

Erik yelled out from inside the car, "Find my treasure!"

Chapter 69

Lexi called Edward. "Hi, sorry to be calling you at this hour. I just have to tell you what has been going on."

"Alexandra, are you okay? I have been worried sick!" Edward said, waking from his sleep.

"I am now. You wouldn't believe what you missed. We have been held captive at Hans's grandfather's house."

Edward made the sign of the cross as he sat up in bed. "Dear God. It's that darn painting, isn't it?"

"How did you know that?" Lexi said, surprised that he guessed it dead on. "Why do you have my painting?"

"How did you know that? Don't tell me. Susannah told you, right?"

"Yep. You guessed it, she did. How come you have it?"

"It's a bit of an embarrassing story."

"Come on, Edward, I am dying to hear all about it," Lexi said in a sexy voice. She leaned back into the chair in Hans's grandfather's den as she moved the phone to a more comfortable position. She had forgotten how the sound of his voice made her feel.

"Well, I missed you. So, I went to sleep at your place."

"You what? Really?"

"I know, kind of sappy, right?'

"No, it is really sweet."

"Well, while I was sleeping on your couch—"

"You slept on my couch and not in my bed?"

"I'm old school. Yes, I slept on your couch. Stop interrupting me. Let me tell you the story."

"Okay, okay. Go on," Lexi said as she smiled at the thought of him sleeping on her couch.

"It was late, and I awoke to the painting vibrating on the wall."

"Oh, my God. That must have freaked you out."

"Alexandra, let me finish. Okay, fine. It freaked me out a little. This painting has a mind of its own, and well, anything seems possible nowadays since I have had to ride a night mare.

"Instead of running out of your place, I decided to close my eyes and ask the painting what it wanted to tell me."

"What did it tell you?" Lexi asked, sitting on the edge of her seat.

"That I was to leave the apartment right that moment and take the painting with me."

"Holy cow, you heard a spirit talking to you?"

"Not exactly speaking to me, but the message was clear. I got up, grabbed the painting, and hightailed it out of your place."

"What did the night security say?"

"Nothing, nobody was there when I went by the desk."

"Weird. I'll have to complain when I get home." Lexi laughed, knowing that the spirit world worked in mysterious ways and can coincidently create synchronicity.

"So, where is the painting now?"

"In the morgue. I didn't think anyone would go looking for it there."

"Of course, you would think of that."

"Alexandra, what is so important about this painting?"

"From what I have gathered so far, Hans's grandfather carved a runic message in the frame."

"What is the message supposed to say?" Edward was now curious as he loved a good mystery.

"Erik, Hans's younger cousin, he is the one who held us captive, says it tells where Hans's grandfather's treasure is hidden."

"Why do you sound like you care, Alexandra? It is not your treasure."

"You're right. I guess I got caught up in Erik's quest. I don't know for sure why, but all I can tell you is that I need you to bring us the painting."

"What? You want me to come to Sweden and bring the painting? That is absurd. I love a good mystery as well as the next guy, but come on, Alexandra, you sound a little crazy."

"Edward, if you cherish our relationship, then you will bring yourself and the painting to Sweden. I will text you your travel arrangements."

Chapter 70

Lexi was in the library with Tamara and Isabella, looking at Hans's grandfather's massive collection of books on Viking lore and mythology, when she found one that piqued her interest. "Hey, you guys, you know how Erik talked about Yggdrasil, the 'Tree of Life?' Well, listen to this… this book explains how the Tree of Life in Norse mythology connects Heaven, the underworld, and all living creatures."

Tamara and Isabella both put down what they were reading to listen.

"It goes on to explain that this Tree of Life connects to nine celestial worlds via its roots and branches. Two of the worlds consist of gods. The first is Asgard, the world of the Aesir tribe of gods and goddesses. This is the world where Odin and Thor live. The other world is called Vanaheim, which is the world of the Vanir tribe of gods and goddesses, known for their wisdom, fertility, and the ability to see the future. Earth is called Midgard, which is the world of humanity. Niflheim is a world of ice and mist and where rivers are created. Muspelheim is a world of fire, and Hel is a world of the dead. Hey, Tamara, I think this world is where Edward went, Alfheim. It is the world of the dark and light elves. Nidavellir, or sometimes called Svartalfheim, is the world of the dwarves, and lastly, Jotunheim is the world of the giants."

Tamara commented by saying, "Many movies today are based on these worlds. Not only that, but many religions also preach about the Tree of Life."

"Interesting how folklore and religion find common ground through a tree," Isabella added as she took part in the conversation.

Reading more, Lexi said excitedly, "Yggdrasil translates to 'Odin's horse.' This interpretation comes about because *drasil* means horse, and *Ygg(r)* is one of Odin's many names. This book also refers to how Odin rode a magical eight-legged horse, known as Sleipnir, to each of these worlds. Hey, Tamara, didn't you say that the shamans also used an eight-legged horse to travel spiritually?"

"I did. They do."

Cutting into the conversation before Lexi went on, Isabella asked, "Tamara, I never took those classes from you. Is that how a person travels through the spirit world, using a horse?"

Tamara looked at both the girls and replied, "Other than riding a horse between the worlds of the Tree of Life, there are many ways one can travel through the spirit world, but there is one thing they all have in common."

"What's that?" Lexi asked.

"As a human, you can only have access to the spirit world through your subconscious. To do that, you need to be in a meditative state or dream state, also known as an alpha state."

"Why does that matter?" Lexi asked.

"When you are awake or in a beta state, your mind is too conscious and does not want to miss out on anything that might happen, so it will not let your 'soul' hear, know, see, feel, or travel."

Getting hooked on the word soul, Lexi asked, "Tamara, when you say soul, do you also mean spirit?"

"No."

"No. Then what is the difference between a soul and a spirit?"

"Okay. Let's start with one of the oldest records that a soul and spirit are different. In the Bible, 1 Thessalonians 5:23, it is written, 'Now may the God of peace make you perfect and holy; and may your **spirit**, life—meaning **soul**, and **body** be kept blameless for the coming of our Lord Jesus Christ.' There is another mention of them being different in Hebrews 4:12."

"So, if a soul and a spirit are different, how can you tell them apart?" Lexi asked.

"Now, that is an interesting question. In many religious, philosophical, and mythological traditions, it is believed that a soul comprises your mind, will, emotions, and consciousness. It is your soul that connects both ways, to the human world via your body and to the celestial world via your Spirit."

"I still don't understand how to tell them apart."

"Lexi, I believe that the soul is a spark of life that is downloaded into a baby. **It is the part of you that contains your intellect, emotions, and will.** It is the part of you that seeks knowledge and truth. It is the emotional part of you that seeks love, be that of a person, place, or thing. It is the part of you that has made a contract for this lifetime's experiences and purpose. It is the part of you that can advance and be reborn, accomplishing all the requirements to be granted access into Nirvana. The best part of Heaven.

"Your Spirit, on the other hand, **is the part of you that connects you to God and all that is spiritual**. Some believe it is your aura that surrounds your body and collects the life-force energy it requires to feed your soul. It is the part of you that can shift and change as needed. It can extend far out into the distance or be drawn in so close to you that you can't tell where your spirit and body tissue starts and ends. It is called your vital body in quantum medicine. It is what keeps you connected to God."

"Okay. Then, do all celestial entities from any other world have a spirit and a soul?"

"First off, you should know that spirit with a small 's' refers to an attitude, and Spirit with a big 'S' are entities that have a consciousness of some type, supernatural being or essence, like the Holy Spirit.

"Many people believe that animals and mammals, including humans, have a soul. A philosopher believes that since humans are aware of their consciousness and can use reason to problem-solve, they must have a soul, whereas most scientists would say that an animal only lives off of basic survival instinct. Now, religion believes a Demon is also called a Spirit, but it is believed to be soulless and acts on basic survival instinct, searching for souls to devour. So, I am not sure if all spirits or entities have a soul, but I do know there are entities similar to both animals and mammals."

Another question popped into Lexi's head. "So, what part of us leaves the body? Are you saying that when I meditate, it is my Spirit that astral-travels or is it my soul?"

Tamara smiled at her inquisitive mind and answered by saying, "Think about astral-travel, which is a term used for an out-of-body experience, no matter if it is to travel in this world or to another. When a person meditates, their soul consciously chooses an intent of where they want to travel. Now, to astral-travel, the soul has to leave the body. It is usually from the crown chakra, found on top of the head. But at all times, all three body, soul, and Spirit are always connected. I guess you could say that the soul uses the body on Earth to physically travel and uses its Spirit body to astral-travel."

"I like that. Okay, but why do many of these stories like in Odin or the shamans talk about needing a horse to travel through the cosmos?"

"There are many ways to travel, Lexi. I have used a 'train' and a 'horse' method for you to travel throughout the cosmos during meditation."

"That's true."

"There are other stories that tell about a 'boat' bringing people to hell."

"I've heard that one in church," Lexi agreed.

"Way back in Odin's day, there was no such thing as a train. It hadn't been invented yet. Though, it was easy for people to imagine a horse. They could relate to that. To be honest, you don't need anything to astral-travel, but the mind likes to use something it can easily imagine as possible."

Lexi was about to ask how but changed her mind. "Tamara, where does the Spirit go when the body dies? I know that the soul can ascend to Heaven or one of the other celestial levels and that the body turns back into dust, but what happens to the Spirit?"

"Imagine your Spirit body is like a vehicle that any 'soul' can use or own, like a car. It is just waiting in the ethers for a baby to be born and need a ride. As in any car, whoever owns it has major control of it, but it can be stolen (possession) or granted use to another (walk-in), or it can stay parked and not be used at all (unconscious or comatose patient). It can also be demolished and used to create a newer model (ascension). It is just a mode of spiritual transportation, and there are millions of them."

"Wow, that is deep!" Lexi confessed. "Okay, I think I get it. My body is made up of flesh and bones and is the part of me that cares about my survival and has life experiences based on my soul's needs. My soul is the part of me that cares about my life's purpose and uses my Spirit body for travel between all aspects of the Tree of Life, especially my connection to God."

"Yes, that pretty much sums it up," Tamara confirmed.

Isabella said after listening to the girls, "Don't you find it fascinating that other cultures tell stories about the Tree of Life and its celestial world connections? To me, it is just another way of saying God in Heaven and the connection between all other souls. Hey, if modern religion uses the Tree of Life, I wonder why it covers up the truth about other realms and beings?"

"Now, that is a great question."

Chapter 71

Redington walked into the library with Edward tagging behind. "Look who I found."

At the same time, the girls all looked toward the doorway.

"Eek," Lexi squealed, running over to Edward throwing her arms around him. "Oh, my God, I've missed you," she said as she planted a big kiss on his lips.

"Okay, you guys, go get a room. Wait, I didn't notice that earlier. Lexi, let's see your finger. Wow, you guys, congratulations!" Isabella said. "I was actually going to say, with that kind of theatrics, you could have a job as an actress. One would believe you really missed him. Now I see why."

Removing her lips from Edward's, she smiled at Isabella and said, "Thank you." Then, looking at Edward, she asked, "How was your flight?"

"Ya, it was okay. Long, but it was good," Edward said, still dazed from Lexi's luscious lips.

Redington stood back. He hadn't noticed the ring until now but knew real love when he saw it, and Edward and Lexi had it. Changing the subject, he said, "Hey, look what he brought with him," Redington said, holding up the painting. "I am assuming this is the notorious painting?"

Everyone stared at the painting in Redington's hands. Slowly moving forward, as if time was moving in slow motion, they all walked over to the painting and stared at its frame.

It wasn't immediately apparent that there was something special about it. Lexi looked over, and sitting on a small table was a handheld magnifying glass. Picking it up, she brought it to the frame and said, "Well, I'll be. Will you look at that? Erik was telling the truth. Look, there are tiny symbols using the runic alphabet engraved into the design." Lexi passed the glass on, so the others could see.

After everyone looked, Edward asked, "How do you read it?"

Lexi looked at Tamara, and Tamara shrugged, saying, "Don't look at me. I've never learned the meaning of the symbols."

Lexi scrambled through the books in the library and pulled down a couple from the shelves, saying, "Here, you guys, start translating. Somebody go get a pen and paper."

"Where do we start? What symbol is the first one to read?" Redington asked.

#

They had been at it for hours, and so far, they only had a few words figured out. There seemed to be extra symbols that weren't shown in the books.

"What do we do now?" Isabella said out loud to anyone who would answer.

"I think it is time to eat supper, have a glass of wine, and rest up. We can start fresh in the morning," Redington said, taking control of the situation.

#

After dinner, while they were sitting in the parlor, Edward asked, "Hey, how are you able to stay here in Erik's house?"

Isabella looked over and said, "I guess the servants know who I am and that I dated Hans. They seem to have no problem listening to me. It seems that I pay better than Erik did."

The group laughed and said good night to each other.

Chapter 72

Isabella tossed and turned all night. She was dreaming that she was a young girl being chased through the fields by two wolves. They captured her and dragged her into a cave. Waiting for her there was Odin.

"So, you've met my wolves, Geri, which means 'Greedy,' and Freki, which means 'Ferocious,'" Odin said to her.

"I don't understand. Where am I?" Isabella said to the man standing in front of her.

He was tall, husky, and had a full white beard. He resembled a large Viking warrior, dressed in gray, and wore a patch because he had lost an eye. He had the energy of a king and the magic of a God. Perched on his shoulders were two ravens. Their names were Hugin, "thought" and Munin, "memory."

"Isabella, you have been brought to me because Hans asked that I help you."

"Hans is with you?"

"No, he is living out eternity in the level of the Elementals. My ravens fly all over the realms and report back to me what is needed for me to hear."

"How can you help me?

"I have brought you here so that you will take a ride with me."

"Where are we going?"

"To Hans."

Isabella perked up and asked, "When do we leave?"

Odin whistled, then called out, *"Sleipnir,"* and a magnificent eight-legged horse appeared. He was gray in color with his tail and mane a deeper dark gray. His teeth were engraved with runic symbols, and he possessed special strength, speed, and the ability to fly anywhere in any of the realms.

Isabella mounted Sleipnir with the help of Odin, pulling her up and behind him in one sweeping gesture.

Instantly, they were galloping through the field with the wolves chasing closely behind and the two ravens flying not too high above Odin's head.

Isabella blinked. They had left Earth and were heading toward the levels of the Gods. She blinked again, and they were flying over a countryside that she had never seen before. No book she had ever read described what she was seeing, worlds of fire, ice, dwarves, giants, and finally, elves. She blinked again, and Sleipnir was landing in a meadow with brilliant light. As the horse came to a halt, standing just in the near distance by a stream was the most magnificent man she had ever laid eyes upon.

Isabella slid off the horse and walked toward him. The wolves followed her, circling her as if to protect her from harm.

As she came closer, she could see the man was slender, with long golden blond hair tied behind, revealing pointy ears. He seemed to glow with a heavenly light.

"Hi, Isabella. Thank you for coming."

"Hans, is that you?"

"Yes, my love, it is I. They call me Erland now, which means 'outsider' or 'foreigner.'"

Isabella ran up to Hans and hugged him. Her head came up to his waist. In the vision, she was a small girl about the age of ten, whereas he was a very tall man. No matter their age difference, she loved him. "How come you are with the elves?"

"I have always loved the Norse stories told about the elves. My grandfather would tell us about how they helped animals and nature."

"I didn't know how to find you. I have missed you so," Isabella said as she hugged him again.

"Isabella, I do not have much time. Odin will not wait long. You need to find my grandfather's treasure."

"We are looking for it now."

"Isabella, you mustn't show it to anyone once you find it. They will not understand."

"Why?"

"Here, take this." He passed her a journal, whose pages looked like they had seen better days, then kissed her on the top of her head. *"I will see you again, my love."*

In a blink, she was back on Sleipnir, flying back through the realms.

Chapter 73

Isabella awoke from her dream. Wiping a few tears away, she hugged herself, remembering his embrace.

"Iss, are you awake?" Tamara asked as she lightly knocked before opening her door. Coming in, she sat on her bed and said, "Hey, why the tears?"

"Oh, nothing."

"Come on, Iss, you know it was something."

"I saw him last night."

"Who?"

"Hans."

"Really? How was he?"

"He is an elf named Erland. He seems happy."

Just as Tamara was about to ask Isabella something, Lexi knocked on the open door and came in. "Hey, you guys, I had the strangest dream last night. I think all those Viking books are getting to me."

"What was your dream about, Lexi?" Tamara asked.

"It was about Odin and Isabella riding on a horse through the realms. Crazy, right?"

Lexi sat down at the end of Isabella's bed but instantly stood up, saying, "Hey, what's this? Were you reading in bed, Isabella?" Lexi passed the book to her.

Isabella took the book and stared at it in disbelief.

"What? Why are you looking at it like that? As if it was possessed or something?" Lexi said, not understanding the look on Isabella's face.

"What is it, Iss?" Tamara asked.

"It is the journal Hans gave me last night… but how can that be? It was a dream."

"What does it say?" Lexi asked, trying to peek at it.

Isabella opened it and turned a few pages. "I don't know it's in Swedish, I think, but there are a couple of pages with those same runic symbols on them."

As she turned a couple more pages, a photo fell out and onto the bed. It was a shot taken in the backyard. Isabella looked at it more closely and said, "Hey, Lexi, can you go get that magnifying glass, please?"

"Sure thing."

"What? What is it that you're seeing?" Tamara asked, trying to see what Isabella was seeing.

Isabella got out of bed and put on a robe. Then she went over to her luggage, pulled something out of the inside panel, and brought it back to the bed where Tamara was sitting.

Lexi came in, a bit out of breath. "Here."

"Great. Thanks, Lex." Isabella looked at both pictures.

"What are you looking at?" Lexi asked, not seeing anything unusual. "All I see is Hans, and I think that is Erik, right?"

"Ya, but look at the shed." She passed the photos and the magnifying glass to Tamara and Lexi to see.

"Who is that?" Lexi asked as she sat back down on the bed. "It looks like a ghost."

"Okay, so you guys see her, too?" Isabella said, happy that she did not imagine it. Isabella stood up and said, "Follow me. You have to see this."

Both girls followed her down the hall.

"Here. Look. Do they look like the same person?"

Lexi and Tamara looked at the painting and then at the photos.

"Ya, but how could that be? The painting's date says it was painted in eighteen hundred and fifty-nine. That would make her at least one hundred and eighty if you added the date to her approximate age," Lexi said.

"Who is it?" Tamara asked.

"It must be Hans's great, great, great grandmother, Astreldi," Isabella said, reading the nameplate on the painting, knowing the name because Hans had mentioned her before.

"What is she doing in both photos?" Lexi said, creeping out that there was a ghost in not only one photo but two.

Chapter 74

Edward came around the corner saying,

"There you all are. I have been looking everywhere for you. Redington went into town to check on Erik. He said he would be back soon."

Lexi looked at him and gave him the photos. "What am I looking at?"

Lexi passed him the magnifying glass.

He looked closer and then looked at the painting the girls were staring at. "Is that who I think it is?"

Lexi nodded. "This family is creepy. First, it was Hans attached to a painting, and now we see that it runs in the family."

"Come on, you guys. Let's get some breakfast. I need a coffee," Isabella said as she took one last look at the painting.

"Where did you find these photos?" Edward asked.

"One fell out of a book," Lexi said.

"The other one fell out of a painting. Actually, I think it was that painting, now that I think about it," Isabella said as she recalled finding the other photo.

"Well," Tamara said, "I have taught you all that the spirit world talks in mysterious ways. Obviously, it is a message that we need to listen to." Continuing, she said, "What do we know so far?" Pausing for a moment, she then said, "Okay, we have to back it up."

"Back what up?" Lexi asked, not sure that she understood.

"Oh ya, you haven't learned that part yet. In an intuitive reading, the reader must back up all the information from the point of contact with a client."

"But this isn't a reading," Edward said.

"No, but intuitive energy all works the same way," Tamara said. "Let's see, Isabella, you are the common denominator. You came to me at that lecture I was giving on tongues, where I was speaking about the celestial language. That was the day you first asked for my help. Then you were also at the workshop, learning about the four celestial channels: Audio, Knower, Visual, and Feeler. You are also the connection to the notorious painting at Lexi's via Hans. Then there is your suicide attempt, and Edward having to ride a night mare to get you to come back into your body."

"Ya, what is it with horses anyway?" Edward said.

Tamara nodded but continued her train of thought. "Next, we followed you to Peru. Now that was the adventure of a lifetime," Tamara said, reminiscing about the temple and the shamans. "Lastly, here we are with you in Hans's grandfather's home in Sweden.

"What we know is this: Hans is trying to tell us something. He is giving us clues."

"Right, and Hans magically gave you the journal and the photos, Isabella," Lexi said excitedly.

"We know there is a treasure hidden here somewhere," Edward added.

"But the messages are in a language that we don't understand, Swedish and Runestone," Lexi said, just as Redington walked in.

"Looks like you guys have found something. You've translated the symbols on the painting's frame?" he asked.

Not answering him and furious at the thought of what Erik did to Lexi, Edward asked, "Is he going to prison?"

"Unless you drop the charges, he will get eight years," Redington said. *Erik's fate is up to the others now.*

No one seemed eager to drop the charges.

"So, what have you found out so far?" Redington asked again, excited to join in on the treasure hunt.

"No. We haven't been able to translate the symbols, but look at these," Lexi said as she passed the photos and the magnifying glass. "It freaks me out."

Disappointed that they hadn't figured it out yet, Redington looked at the photos. Being a detective for so many years, subtle details that others did not notice pop out at him. If he believed in ghosts, this ghost was in the shed and was not just revealing the clue; it was the clue. Chills went down his body as he figured out where the hidden treasure was buried. With added excitement, he said, "Well, who needs to translate runic symbols when you have two photos pointing you in the right direction? What are you all waiting for? Let's go find the treasure." He got up and started walking toward the backyard.

"Where's he going?" Lexi said as the others got up to follow him. "Don't we need to translate these symbols?"

"If I am right, then we won't need to translate them," Redington said as he went out the back door. Walking directly to the shed shown in both pictures, he tried the door. It had a padlock on it. He looked around and found a shovel that was leaning on one of its walls. Picking it up, he took it over to the door and banged at the lock. It only took a couple of blows, and the lock popped off.

"Remind me to get better locks when I get home," Lexi said, watching how easy it was for him to break into the shed.

Redington opened the door and went inside.

It had dust and cobwebs everywhere.

"What are we looking for? The ghost?" Lexi asked, waving her hand at a cobweb.

"This shed and your ghost are in both photos. It must mean something," Redington said as he investigated the shed.

"I don't see anything," Lexi said, trying to figure out how to get out of there without letting everyone know that she was scared.

Isabella asked Tamara, "Do you sense anything?"

"Not really. It is a little cold, but I don't see a ghost."

Redington moved some boxes out of the way. He bent down and moved some dirt aside from what looked like a hatch in the floor. Pulling on the metal handle, he opened the hatch, revealing stairs that went down.

"See if you can find a flashlight or a light switch," Redington ordered, forgetting that these were civilians and not his team.

Lexi turned on the flashlight on her phone and passed it to him.

Taking it from her, he started to descend the stairs. The others followed, turning on their phone flashlights.

There were about twenty steps, and at the bottom was a large room filled with many antiques and old relics.

"Oh, my God, you guys, a treasure chest," Lexi said as she opened the latch.

The chest was filled with gold, silver, gems, and old trinkets.

"Do you think this is what Erik was looking for?" Lexi asked.

Redington turned the light and looked in all directions and said, "It must be. There's stuff here from ancient Viking times. This room would be worth a few fortunes."

"It is definitely the hidden treasure…" Isabella said as she looked at an envelope with Hans's handwriting on it.

"What did you find?" Lexi asked, peeking over Isabella's shoulder. "How is that possible?"

Tamara, Edward, and Redington all went over to see.

"Isabella" was written on the front.

"Open it!" Lexi squealed.

With shaking hands, Isabella opened the letter.

My dear Isabella,
I love you to the moon and back.
You are my stars at night,
And my sun during the day.

If you are reading this, then I am dead.

Do not cry, sweetheart, for your love will be with me always.

In this envelope, you will find a business card. Call the name on the card.

Jag älskar dig. Hans

"What does *Jag älskar dig* mean?" Lexi asked.

"I love you," Isabella said as she started to cry.

Chapter 75

The next morning, Isabella came out of the bathroom, got dressed, and went downstairs to the dining room.

"Morning Iss, how are you feeling?" Tamara asked.

"Not good. I think I have caught something."

"Here. Have some breakfast," Lexi said as she passed her a plate of bacon and eggs.

Isabella got up and ran out of the room.

Edward moved out of the way as Isabella ran past him. Waking into the dining room, he said, "What is wrong with her?"

"I think all this drama has caught up to her," Lexi said.

Just then, Redington came in and said, "So, what has Isabella decided to do? Is she going to call the number on the card?"

"Hmm, good question. She ran out of here before I could ask her," Edward said.

Isabella came back into the room and said, "I think I need to go to the doctor. I really don't feel well."

Tamara got up and went over to Isabella. "Come on, let's go find you a doctor."

They borrowed the car Redington had been using and left to go into town.

Seeing Isabella coming out of the doctor's office, Tamara asked, "So, what did he say?"

"I'm pregnant."

"Funny, I had a dream about you the other night, and you were playing with a little girl."

"Tamara, I'm serious. What am I going to do?"

"I guess, have a baby," Tamara said as she came over and put an arm around Isabella. "Let's go tell the others, so they don't have to worry about catching anything from you."

#

"Your what!" Edward almost yelled. "How? When? Whose?"

"Thanks, Edward, for being so sensitive," Lexi said as she hit his arm.

"How far along are you?" Lexi asked.

"The doctor figures I'm about four months. What am I going to do now?"

"It is exciting. You are going to have Hans's baby. It is Hans's, right?" Lexi asked.

"Yes. It has to be. I haven't been with anyone else."

"But how did you not know before now?" Edward asked.

"I had a student once tell me that her sister had bad stomach cramps and went to the emergency room and delivered a baby. She didn't know right up until she gave birth," Tamara said.

"You're kidding. How could a woman not know she is getting fat?" Edward said bluntly.

"My sister didn't show until she was almost six months, and many ladies don't have regular menstruation or morning sickness," Tamara said.

"Crazy," Edward said, shaking his head.

"Congratulations, Isabella, that is wonderful news," Redington commented.

"Thank you. I am still trying to get used to the idea that I am going to be a mom."

"Hey, did you get a chance to call the number on the card?" Redington asked.

"No. Not yet, but I will soon. I promise," Isabella said, too excited about the baby to care about that right now.

"Isabella, I get the feeling that whoever is on the other end of that phone number is really important. If I were you, I would do it asap. Hans wouldn't have given you the card unless it was important," Lexi said, trying not to sound pushy.

"Ya, ya. Okay, you guys, I will go and call right now. Will that make you happy?"

They all answered at once, "Yes!"

Calling the number on the card, Isabella sat there, rubbing her tummy. *Hi little one, I'm your mama.*

A moment later a female voice came on the line. "*Hallå. Hur kan jag hjälpa dig?*"

"Ah, hello, I am Isabella Jackson, and I was to call this number. I am sorry I do not speak Swedish."

"Ah, *ja*. Miss Jackson, we are very sorry for your loss. We were wondering when we would get your call. One moment please, while I transfer you."

A man's voice came onto the line. "Miss Jackson, I am glad you called. Congratulations on finding the clues Hans left you. He said that if anything happened to him that you would be calling one day."

"Who am I speaking with?" Isabella asked.

"Ah, *ja*, sorry. I am Herr Svensson. I am Hans's lawyer."

"His lawyer? I wonder why I am supposed to talk to you. We weren't married?"

"No, but Miss Jackson, he has left you everything in his will. I was hoping you could come in and sign some documents. Is it possible to come in this afternoon?"

"Ah, I guess I could. What is the address?"

Hans's lawyer gave her the address and directions to his firm.

"Thank you. See you soon," Isabella said as she hung up.

Coming back into the dining room, Isabella said, "Detective, would you mind driving me to Hans's lawyer's firm?"

"Not at all. When do we have to leave?"

"In about an hour."

"No problem, I will have the car waiting for you." Redington got up from his chair and walked out of the room.

"So, the number on the card was for Hans's lawyer," Lexi asked.

"Yes. Hans left me something big," Isabella said in shock.

"What does that mean?" Edward asked.

"I don't know. I guess I will find out shortly."

Chapter 76

Isabella came back from the lawyers with Redington and walked into the library where everyone else was waiting.

"So?" Lexi said as Isabella walked in.

Isabella sat down on a chair and started to cry.

"Oh, my God. Is it bad news?" Lexi asked Isabella. When she didn't answer, Lexi looked at Redington.

Redington shrugged. "I don't know. She has been crying ever since she got into the car."

"Isabella, talk to us," Lexi said as she came over and kneeled by Isabella. "What did the lawyer say?"

Tamara broke her belief of letting a person cry and passed Isabella a tissue. This wasn't a counseling session.

Wiping her nose, Isabella said, "He knew."

Lexi looked at Isabella, then at Tamara, trying to figure out what that meant.

"Who knew?" Edward said, hating word games.

"Hans," Isabella said, crying again.

"For goodness' sake, Isabella, tell us what is going on," Edward said, louder than he had to.

Isabella looked up and wiped her eyes. "Well, at least now I know why I've been a basket case lately."

"What does that mean?" Edward said, getting tired of her not finishing her sentences.

"I'm pregnant!" Isabella said as if Edward should have gotten what she meant.

Lexi looked over to Edward and said, "Pregnant women have mood swings."

"Oh. Oh, that does make sense now that I think about the last few months," Edward said, thinking back to her suicide attempts. "What did he leave you?" Edward said, dying to know.

"He knew that I was pregnant."

"He did? How?" Lexi asked.

"He left me another letter with the lawyer. He said that his grandmother, Astreldi, came in a dream and told him."

"Wow, I didn't see that one coming," Edward said. "What did he leave you?"

"Actually, he left everything to his heir, not me. Though as guardian, I am in control of his estate until the child turns twenty-one."

"What did he leave his heir?" Edward couldn't help himself from asking again.

"All his properties around the world, his art collection, and the hidden treasure."

"Wow!"

"What are you going to do now, Isabella?" Lexi asked.

"Have a baby, I guess."

"Besides that," Lexi said.

"I will be staying here for a bit. I have hired some movers to help me place the treasure in a safe place, and then I will go to Switzerland and stay there until the baby is born. Hans asked if I could do that so that the baby has all three citizenships on the birth certificate: American, Swedish, and Swiss."

"Well, that is good. Good that all this mess has come to an end. Now we can all return to our boring humdrum lives," Edward said, half-jokingly.

Lexi came up to him, hugging him, and said, "Don't worry, I'll make sure your life is not humdrum."

"I was kidding. Since your sister died, my life has been anything but humdrum," Edward said as he kissed her.

Chapter 77

Lexi was back in her own bed in her own apartment, loving the feeling of not having any crazy stuff going on when her intercom buzzed.

"Miss Constantine, it's Sam. There is a parcel for you. Is it okay if I let the deliverymen up?"

"Who is it from, Sam?"

"It is from Miss Jackson."

"Thank you, Sam. Let them up.

Lexi popped out of bed and hurried to pull on a pair of sweatpants and a top and put her hair into a ponytail just as the doorbell rang.

Lexi ran to the door and opened it. "Wow, that is big."

"Sign here, please," said one of the men ignoring what she had just said. "Have a nice day, ma'am."

Lexi opened the box, and inside was a painting and a note.

> *Lexi, thank you so much for all that you have done for me. Words will never be able to express my gratitude.*
> *Enjoy the painting.*
> *Iss*

Well, sis, I guess the painting is back. Lexi carefully unwrapped the painting and turned it around. She was pleasantly surprised to see what Isabella had sent.

It was a magnificent masterpiece of an angel. He had long golden blond hair with a beautiful face. He was wearing metal armor and holding a copper feathered quill and a scroll. He had a horn hung over his shoulder. He was magnificent. The painting had a heavenly glow to it. On the nameplate, it said, "Archangel Gabriel."

"Wow, Isabella, you outdid yourself. Pretty impressive. Okay, Susannah, Isabella didn't give me back your painting, but I think I love this one even more. I hope you don't mind."

"Not at all. Whose idea do you think it was anyways?"

"That was nice of you, sis, thanks."

Lexi hung the painting in her living room, in place of the other. "Perfect! It looks as if it were made for me."

"It was. Isabella had it made specially for you. You are going to need it."

"Oh, my God. What does that mean?"

Before Susannah could answer, Lexi's phone rang.

"Hello?"

"Did you get it yet?"

"It just arrived. Thank you, Isabella, that was so thoughtful."

"Your welcome. I dreamed of you the other day and had this painted a few days later."

"Hey, Iss?"

"Yep?"

"Susannah said that I am going to need it. Do you know what that means?"

"She's your sister. Your guess is as good as mine. I am just the messenger of the dream, not the interpreter. Ask Tamara. She might know."

"Good idea. Hey, how have you been feeling?"

"Fat."

"Well, at least there is a good reason for the weight gain."

"True."

"Has it been kicking yet?"

"Like an alien is about to come out of my tummy."

"Great, that makes me want to have kids."

"You'll love the feeling, Lex. There is nothing like it. This sensation makes life worth living."

"Oops, my other line is ringing. Can you hold on a moment, Isabella?"

"No. Go ahead and get it. Love ya, Lex."

"You too, Iss."

Lexi answered the other line.

"Hi, Lexi, it's Tamara. Did you get the gift from Isabella yet? She told me the other day that she was sending it."

"Ya. It just arrived. It is incredible."

"I bet it is. I can't wait to see it."

"Hey, Tamara, any idea why Isabella sent me this particular painting?"

"When Archangel Gabriel wants to be heard, he doesn't mess around. I guess you are being initiated."

"Initiated for what?"

"Gabriel is the angel responsible for not only God's message but also creativity and inspiration. He is also the teacher of prophets."

"Teacher of prophets, what does that mean?"

'I am glad you asked. I am going to have the ladies come over Thursday night. Can you make it?"

"Thursday night, two days from now? I guess I could. What time?"

"Seven, at my place."

"Do I need to bring anything?"

"Just a pen and a journal to keep notes."

"Great, see you Thursday," Lexi said as she hung up and stared at her new painting.

Chapter 78

The next day, after work, Lexi had time to research everything she could about Archangel Gabriel.

Lexi was not sure what sex he or she was. The websites were very wishy-washy on Gabriel's gender. He was mostly known as God's communicator, delivering the divine messages through numerous channels: writing, art, music, verbal expression, emotional expression, and just about any type of communication.

Many websites said that if you keep hearing or seeing the name Gabriel, he is trying to pass on a message from God.

There were even a few websites that wrote about how Gabriel could come in any form, even as a raven or crow, to deliver his message.

Lexi thought back to the painting, "The Wild Hunt of Odin," and knew that Odin had two ravens that brought back important messages to him. She also remembered that the shamans in Peru honored birds for bringing them messages from the spirit world.

Looking up "raven" on the internet, Lexi found that the bird symbolizes a creature of metamorphosis, change, and transformation. The raven is the foreteller of messages from the cosmos and could help determine answers to our own "hidden" thoughts and was called upon in rituals to clarify one's visions.

It was believed that if you saw a raven who flew high toward the heavens, it would take your prayers to the spirit world, and as it returned to the earth, it would bring back messages from the spiritual realm.

Lexi sat back and thought about all she had been through the past few weeks.

God, why have you allowed all these weird yet wonderful things to happen to me? I sit here thinking back, believing that all these crazy things are too outlandish for anyone to believe. It is one thing talking to you, but another to have you answer.

And why is it that only a few people understand how to hear your messages?

Tamara says that I am a Visual and that I see things that many others cannot see. To hear you, I will see first, and that is how I will end up hearing you, by interpreting my visions.

Some days though, it is too hard, too hard to switch from reality to the unknown. Too hard to be different from others. My family would never understand. Heck, Edward doesn't understand, and he has experienced some of this weird stuff.

I can't tell my friends at work for fear that I would become an outcast. I can't tell my mom because she would have me go and get exorcized by the priest.

Thank God I have Tamara, who does not judge what I tell her and is far beyond me in her spiritual growth.

Again, why have you allowed me to have awakened to this knowledge if I cannot share it with others?

At that moment, Susannah said, *"Lexi, he hears your prayers, but unless you ask him a specific question, he will not answer you."*

"Susannah? Hi. Hey, thank you for being my big sister. I love you so much. Even though there are still days when I hear you talking in my head and think that I have gone insane, how is it possible that my dead sister could be talking to me? Others would think I have lost my mind."

"So, don't tell them."

"I don't understand what is happening to me. I don't understand why all these weird and crazy things are happening in my life. You, the spirit world, that demons are real, that shamans exist, that the Nordic lore is based on real experiences. Some days it is too much to bear."

"Lexi, God, will only give you what you can handle. Some days that may seem a lot, but your

soul has a purpose and will try any way and every way possible to achieve success."

"But what is my purpose?"

"Before you came down to Earth, your soul chose to advance and learn the nine spiritual gifts granted by spirit."

"How can I learn something that was from thousands of years ago, and many believe to be only gifts in that time, not gifts that we can achieve today?"

"Lexi, you don't have to worry about everyone else, just yourself. That is all you are responsible for, just you."

"But to believe, I need to see it, to experience it. Then I have the proof that it is real."

"And you will. What have you learned so far?"

"What do you mean?"

"Since I died, what have you learned?"

Lexi took a breath and thought about all she had learned so far. "Well, there are good and bad ghosts and spirits. When a person dies, they choose where and what they do in the afterlife. Um, what else have I learned?"

Lexi took another breath and said, "Recently, I learned that other cultures have spiritual beliefs that are very different from what I learned in catechism."

"Are you sure they are that different?"

"Yes. Catholics don't believe that ravens carry messages."

"No, but they do believe in God, the Holy Ghost, and angels."

"That is different."

"Is it?"

"Of course, it is."

"Why? Who cares if someone has created an image of a messenger as a bird instead of an angel? They both have wings. Maybe someone saw wings and decided it was obviously a bird that had sent the message."

"I never thought of it like that. I guess that makes sense."

"What else have you learned?"

"That there are levels or realms in the spirit world and a hierarchy to the occupants."

"Good. What else?"

"Susannah, this is hard. Um, what else have I learned?" Lexi thought a bit harder. "What else have I learned? I don't know."

"Take a breath and remember."

Lexi took a breath and asked herself, "What else have I learned?"

A few moments later, she answered, "How to distinguish spirits and how to tell them apart. Tamara taught me before Christmas how to test a spirit so that I am not possessed by a dark entity. Recently, Tamara has taught me how to communicate with the spirit world. Some people see spiritual information, some hear spiritual information, some feel spiritual information, and others just know the spiritual information. I learned how to communicate, how to speak, and how to interpret tongues."

"Yes, you have learned three of the nine spiritual gifts: how to distinguish spirits and both tongues—how to speak and how to interpret."

"What is left for me to learn?"

"The other gifts are wisdom, knowledge, faith, miracles, healing, and prophecy."

"Which one do I get to learn next?"

"Patience. You haven't practiced what you've learned so far."

"When do I get to learn the next one?"

There was no answer from Susannah.

"Susannah, are you there?"

Again, there was no answer from Susannah. Just then, Lexi's phone rang.

"Hello?"

Chapter 79

"Hey, Lexi, I was just thinking about you and thought I would call. How are you doing?" Detective Redington asked.

"Hi, I am doing okay, thanks. How about you? Are you recuperated yet from your jet lag?"

"Funny. I was wondering if you and Edward wanted to meet up for a coffee?"

"Oh, that would have been nice, but Edward is out of town for a couple of weeks on a business trip."

"Well, maybe Tamara could come with us? I wouldn't want you to think this was a date or anything."

"Now who's being funny? I don't need a chaperone. I am a big girl and can ward off evil when I need to," Lexi said, laughing. "When, where, and at what time, Detective?"

"Are you busy tonight?"

"Ah, no. I can meet you tonight. What time should I meet you?"

"I will come and pick you up at your place at eight."

"Where are we going?"

"It's a surprise. See you soon, Alexandra," Redington said, hanging up.

Lexi got off the phone and looked at the time. Where had the day gone? It was seven o'clock already. She had to hurry. Redington would be here to pick her up in an hour.

Lexi arrived downstairs just as Redington pulled up to her apartment.

"Good evening, Miss Constantine," Sam said as he held the door open for her. "I see you are in the company of the Detective again. I hope everything is all right."

"Yes, Sam. Thank you for your concern, but it is a friendly coffee we are going for," Lexi said, concerned that Sam thought it was police business, or worse yet, that she was cheating on Edward.

After getting into the car, Lexi said, "Great. Now Sam thinks there is a problem because you are here."

"Well, he has seen quite a few weird things happen around you."

"I guess you're right. Poor kid. I am going to have to get him something special for caring about me so much."

"Careful, he might think you are flirting with him. Better not give him a gift. You know young men love the thought of being with a cougar."

"A cougar? I'm not that old."

Redington looked her over and said, "Well, you're not getting any younger, and to him, you're a cougar."

Lexi made a huffing sound and crossed her arms. "Tell me again why I came out with you? Right, I remember. I forgot how funny you are."

Redington smiled at how easily he could get her riled up.

After driving in silence for a few miles, Lexi finally asked, "Where are you taking me?"

Redington just looked over and smiled.

Pulling up and parking, Redington got out of his car and went over to open Lexi's door. "Miss Constantine, we have arrived."

Lexi saw that they were walking into a cocktail bar in Brooklyn.

Redington had made reservations in the restaurant's vineyard-covered garden. He knew she would love the European ambiance of the outdoors while dining indoors. It was a little hidden gem tucked away in the Big Apple.

As they sat down, Redington said, "Friday, Saturday, and Sunday, they have live music here. Depending on which band is playing, you will hear jazz, swing, or New Orleans. They even have a gypsy guitarist who plays here. If you ever get a chance, you have to see their

Flamenco performers. Their dancing is phenomenal."

Lexi was impressed. She never thought of Redington as a romantic type.

Taking charge, Redington ordered them some appetizers and a bottle of wine.

"I thought you said we were going out for coffee to catch up, not on a date," Lexi said, looking around at all the people, who obviously were on dates.

"Hey, this isn't a date, Miss Constantine. It's a stakeout. I needed a cover, and you were my best choice."

Lexi was speechless. *A cover, what nerve.*

Redington saw his suspect and said, "Alexandra, I need you to talk to me as if we were good friends, or if it tickles your fancy, you could pretend that we are on a date."

"Redington, you have some nerve. Fine! What do you want me to do?"

"Just talk. I can listen and watch the guy at the same time."

Lexi went to turn to see who he was looking at.

Quietly but sternly, Redington said, "Don't turn around, Alexandra, you'll give me away."

Lexi straightened up and said, "Well, this is boring."

"Tell me what you think about Isabella being pregnant?"

Lexi looked at Redington. "Detective, how do we end up in these weird predicaments?"

"I guess I am a sucker for punishment," Redington said jokingly.

Just then, Redington's suspect got up to pay for his bill.

"Oh, it looks like the date is over." Redington pulled out a wad of money and said, "Please pay for our drinks and find yourself a cab to take you home."

Redington got up, kissed Lexi on the head, and quickly followed his suspect.

"What the?" Lexi said as she was shocked that Redington would have the nerve to use her like that.

Instead of getting up and leaving, she decided to move over to the bar and finish her glass of wine.

A cute young man came over and said, "May I buy you a drink?"

Lexi's first instinct was of surprise but quickly changed to flattery. "Thank you, but no, I was just leaving."

"Too bad. Maybe next time," he said as he smiled and walked away.

Miss Constantine, you still got it. Lexi thought to herself as she paid the bill and went to hail a cab.

Chapter 80

"Welcome ladies, I am very excited to be sharing tonight's information with you," Tamara said after everyone had arrived.

"Where is Edward?" Karla asked Lexi.

"He's working out of town for a couple of weeks."

"Oh, too bad. I would have liked to have seen him."

Lexi wasn't sure what Karla meant by that. *Should I be worried that she has a crush on him?*

"Tonight, you are all going to start practicing tongues, communicating using the frequency of the celestial world."

"Oh, this is so exciting!" Betty said, clapping her hands.

"Tonight, we are going to go over the basics, and then I am going to teach you a new way to receive messages."

Betty clapped her hands again.

"You have learned that celestial energy is a wavelength of energy that is similar but at the same time different from a cell phone or satellite transmission and receiver. Different because it is a frequency of energy that travels faster than light."

To clarify the idea in her mind, Jane asked, "We do have the ability to learn how to send, receive, and interpret this celestial information, right?"

"Yes, Jane, that is correct," Tamara said. "I want you to understand that science is quickly catching up to the celestial technology. Did you know that there is a machine called a femtosecond laser that writes using light energy on a crystal, nicknamed 'the Superman memory crystal?'"

"What? Like the crystals that Clark Kent used to receive messages stored at the Fortress of Solitude?" Kate asked.

"Kind of, yes. This new technology uses a memory crystal, which is the size of a nickel, that can store up to 360 terabytes worth of data, which is more than 10 million CDs' worth of data. The crystal can last for billions of years. My point is… that new science is being discovered all the time."

"Fascinating. What do they call this new technology?" Lexi asked.

"5D optical data storage," Tamara answered.

"Is that anything like 5G?" Betty asked, knowing that the new towers were being installed near her place of work.

"No, 5D is a five-dimensional concept with several different images that are lasered onto and into a silica disk about the size of a nickel.

"Whereas 5G is a technology standard for broadband cellular networks using radio waves. 5G is used for faster internet speed and the ability to send larger pieces of information.

"Meaning 5G is a frequency of energy used to teleport information from one place to another, and 5D is the storage of information," Tamara answered.

"I never did really understand what science meant by five- dimensional," Betty injected.

Tamara tried to explain 5D."Simply, dimensions are different facets of what we perceive to be our reality. Imagine that you were going to draw a box on a piece of paper. To start, you would draw the first line. A straight line is one-dimensional. It is like a ruler, showing length.

"Then you would continue to draw the other three sides, creating a square or rectangle shape. This flat plane figure or shape of the rectangle you drew now has two dimensions, length and width, or width and height, but there is no thickness. It is a flat drawing of a rectangle. A painting is considered two-dimensional.

"To make the box look 3D, three-dimensional, you would need to draw depth. In geometry, 3D can be defined as a solid figure or an object or shape with three dimensions: length, width, height, and depth, as in a box. If you have two eyes that you can see out of, then you perceive a three-dimensional world.

"Now, these next dimensions are where it gets tricky. They are not proven scientifically. They are more of a theory. The fourth dimension is another dimension in addition to length, width, height, and depth. Many scientists believe that the fourth dimension is time. If we keep it to the box analogy, you could imagine a box on top of a box, slightly pivoted, and you are above both boxes looking through them. In the fourth dimension, you can see through the objects.

"The fifth dimension is considered part of the string theory, which uses vibrational states and gravitational forces."

"Why do they call it 5D?" Lexi asked.

"If we use the crystal as an example, the nanostructures or images written on the crystal can change depending on how the light travels through the crystal. The fifth dimension uses the frequency of light energy.

"Now, this is where it really gets exciting and where you will be focusing your intuitive abilities—in the sixth dimension."

"I am scared to ask, what is the sixth dimension?" Lexi inquired.

"Science explains the sixth dimension as a godlike dimension and the highest plane of existence that exists beyond imagination and time. To communicate with the celestial world, you do have to use your imagination. Most of the time, it feels like a BS story, all make-believe."

Lexi nodded, remembering when she went into a meditative state to get her sister, Susannah, out of the Void. Any normal person would have thought she had lost her marbles if she'd told them what she had imagined doing. She still had problems believing any of this woo-woo stuff was real.

"It won't be long before science catches up and can scientifically explain the sixth dimension. Just wait to hear what they are going to do with the information Spirit, the Mars Exploration Rover, really found."

"I don't understand why everyone can't sense ghosts?" Kate said. "They would believe if they could see what I see."

Tamara patted Kate on the shoulder and said, "Don't worry, I believe you, Kate. I can see what you see, and it isn't make-believe."

Turning to the group, Tamara said, "Okay, everyone, let's take a break while I set up the aura machine."

Chapter 81

Once everyone was back in their seats, Tamara continued, "I know that most people consider me a psychic, but I like to refer to myself as a scientist of sorts. I love studying quantum physics, mostly metaphysics, and religion. Over the years, I have studied why I can do what most say is impossible. I found that in the Bible, written over two-thousand years ago that people could do what I can do. Science is changing so fast. What was science fiction in the past is now a reality.

"I love the fact that everything in this universe has its own vibrational frequency. It is our frequency of perception of electro-magnetic waves that defines what we can and cannot see within the visible spectrum of light. As the father of quantum physics, Max Planck, once said, 'All the physical matters are composed of vibration.'

"My particular interest is in light energy, as it happens to be one of the secrets to understanding how to communicate using the celestial language. The Visual channel in the celestial language uses the vibration and frequency of each color of light.

"I find it fascinating that if a frequency is vibrating fast enough, it's emitted as a sound, and if it is vibrating much faster, it is emitted as a color of light.

"Since we will be using the 'sixth dimension' to interpret tongues, it is essential that you understand how to use light energy. Tonight, we are going to start to learn how to communicate with the celestial world by learning how to sense energy and then how to interpret the energy."

Tamara asked the group, "Does anyone know the most famous proof of an aura?"

Everyone shook their heads.

"The halo on Mother Mary and baby Jesus's head," Tamara stated.

"Oh, my goodness, she is right. There are definitely halos of energy emanating around their heads," Lexi said, remembering back to the paintings of the holy family she had seen in church.

"I am going to teach you a method on how to sense energy by seeing it, feeling it, hearing it, and knowing it.

"How many of you have heard about Kirlian photography?"

Everyone in the group put a hand up.

"Did you know that Kirlian photography does not claim to show a person's aura?"

"What? That's not true. I had a photo taken at a psychic fair, and they called it Kirlian photography," Kate said.

Tamara nodded, saying, "I know, most people call it that, but Kirlian photography is showing a corona discharge due to ionizing fluid creating a region of plasma around the electrode.

"It is actually an aura camera that is usually used, and it measures the galvanic skin resistances from the subject's hand based on their stress level.

"No matter, what I am fascinated with is that in either case, a photograph of energy that our eye cannot detect will show up on the photo."

Tamara took a picture of each of the ladies using the aura camera.

Lexi was excited to learn about the aura colors that showed up around her. They were mostly orange and purple.

"Okay, now, I need to teach you the difference between an aura and a complementary color," Tamara said as she picked up some pieces of colored construction paper.

Tamara took one of the papers, a blue one, and placed it against the wall, and said, "Stare at this paper for thirty seconds, after which, I will take the paper away. Once I have removed the paper, tell me what color you see."

Tamara counted to thirty and then took the blue paper away from the wall and said, "What color do you see?"

"Orange," Lexi said instantly.

The others agreed.

"Great, now this one?" Tamara held up a red paper on the wall. "Stare at this one."

Removing the red paper, Tamara said, "What color do you see?"

"Green," Karla yelled out, excited that she could see the complementary color.

Tamara did the same action to the yellow, black, and green papers.

"Crazy, how is that possible?" Karla asked.

Tamara smiled. "What you are seeing is not an aura but a scientific explanation of what happens to your eyes when you stare at a color for long enough. What you are seeing is called a complementary color, the opposite color to the one you stared at. If staring at blue, you will see orange, red is green, yellow is purple, and white will be black. The opposite is true if you reverse the colored paper.

"If you stare at green, you will see red when it is removed. That is why operating rooms are painted in a specific light green. It is the opposite color of blood red. You wouldn't want a doctor to look up and get a blind spot, now would you? This way, as the doctor looks up to the green and down to red or vice versa, no blind spot will be created.

"Of course, different shades will give different shades of complementary colors."

"That is so cool!" Kate exclaimed.

"I wanted you to have this experience first so that you will know the difference when you see an aura. "Kate, if you think that was cool, wait until you see this."

Betty clapped her hands, even though Tamara directed the comment to Kate.

"Now, the first thing a person has to do to use tongues or any of the four celestial channels is to raise their vibratory rate."

"Is that by taking at least three deep breaths?" Betty asked, learning this in other classes.

"Yes, that is one of the best and quickest ways to raise your vibratory rate," Tamara affirmed. "Everyone, take notice of your surroundings. What do you hear, see, feel, smell, and taste? Take notice of what you are thinking.

"Now, take three deep breaths. Breathe in deeply and let it out slowly, imagining any unwanted or negative energy being released into a cosmic vacuum cleaner or garbage can.

"Again, breathing in, relaxing, and exhaling.

"One more time, breathe in and exhale.

"Great, now, take notice of your surroundings. What do you sense?"

"I can hear the clock on the wall tick louder," Jane said.

"It looks brighter in here," Lexi added.

"Me too. It looks brighter, Betty agreed.

"I feel colder," Tammy said.

"My thoughts are clearer," Karla declared.

"I agree with them all," Kate said, nodding.

"Wonderful. Now take three more deep breaths and supercharge your senses."

Tamara waited until everyone had taken the three extra deep breaths. "Perfect. Now you are ready to see the energy of an aura."

Karla was skeptical and said, "I'll believe it when I see it."

Tamara smiled, knowing that this exercise worked well even on the people who overthink things.

Tamara dimmed the lights and had everyone stand opposite a wall that she had removed a painting from. "Okay, I need one person to go and stand at the wall, please."

Lexi went and stood at the wall, facing the group.

"Okay, everyone, I want you to look about a hand width above Lexi's head." Tamara walked over to Lexi, put her hand flat above Lexi's head, and then pointed to a spot just above and said, "Stare right here. Try not to move your eyes from this spot, and let your eyes go out of focus, like an artist does when they draw, or like when you are staring at a 3D picture, let your eyes blur a bit."

The ladies all stared at Lexi, just above her head.

"I see a white glow forming around her," Betty said excitedly.

Tamara smiled, knowing that Visuals usually saw the aura first. "Yes, most people notice that part of the aura first. Betty, if you shift your intent a bit, you will notice that the white glow shifts from place to place and in size."
"Oh, ya, it is moving. Cool!" Betty said, amazed at the intensity of the white glow.

"Everyone, try not to move your eyes from that spot. Stay focused above her head. You will see the aura with your peripheral vision."

"I think I see some purple hovering around her head," Karla said, unsure of herself.

"I see it too," Betty said.

Tammy said joyfully, "Me too. Oh, it's gone. I think I see yellow now."

"You are right, it's purple, but as Lexi started to think about what you all were saying, it turned yellow." Tamara explained further, "When a person starts to think, their aura turns yellow. Okay, I need someone to switch places with Lexi."

Betty went up and stood where Lexi had been.

"So, you want me to stare above her head?" Lexi asked, a bit unsure of what she was doing.

"Yes," Tamara said as she went and pointed to the spot on the wall. "It takes a few seconds before your eyes will adjust to her aura. Remember, if someone is wearing a yellow shirt and you see purple around them, you are likely seeing the complementary color and not their aura. BUT, if you see blue or any other color than purple, then you are for sure seeing their aura."

"I see pink," Kate said.

"I still don't see anything. What am I doing wrong?" Jane asked with a frustrated tone.

"Jane, sometimes it takes looking at a few people before you see an aura. Just try to relax your eyes. Maybe take a couple more deep breaths and try shifting your energy again."

Tamara had all the ladies take a turn standing at the wall.

"I still didn't see anything," Jane said.

"Don't fret about it, Jane. I am teaching you many ways to sense energy. This is just one of the ways, and because you are an Audio, it takes practice to use the Visual channel. Not everyone has that channel open. Don't worry. You will be better at some of the other techniques."

Hearing that made Jane feel better.

"Okay, ladies, come and have a seat," Tamara said as she passed out a pack of colored construction paper. "Next, we are going to draw energy. Pick three colors, any color."

"You can draw energy? But energy is invisible," Karla said.

Tamara smiled at Karla and said, "It is invisible until you look for it. I haven't had a student yet, who couldn't draw energy. Now, out of the three pieces of paper you have, pick one and put the other two under your chair.

"Great.

"Now, in this container are some colored chalks. Pick one, and put it on the tissue I have given you.

"Excellent, now close your eyes. Feel where your paper and the chalk are.

"In a moment, I am going to play some music, and I want you to draw the music on your piece of paper. Don't worry about what you are drawing. Any markings will do. Just listen to the music and feel the beat, draw whatever comes into your mind." Tamara turned on the music. "Keep your eyes shut."

After about three minutes, Tamara turned off the music. "Okay, you can open your eyes."

There was laughter in the group as everyone looked at the drawings.

"Great. Now switch your paper to a new one. Now choose two more colored chalks and place them next to your other one. Close your eyes."

Tamara turned on a different piece of music. "When you are ready, with your eyes closed, draw anything you want on your paper with any or all of the three pieces of chalk."

After about three more minutes, Tamara turned off the music. "Okay, you can open your eyes."

"What are we accomplishing doing this, Tamara?" Jane asked.

"Good question. You are learning how to sense energy, and then you are interpreting what you are sensing by drawing it. Sound is a frequency of energy that your ears can hear and your body can feel. You are translating the sound waves into an aura of color," Tamara explained. "Most people can sense music, but most people do not know that their body receives the message of the music by the sound waves being played. That is why some people love some music while others hate it. Their body does not interpret the music the same way.

"Let's try another piece of paper. This time with your eyes open. You can also choose any piece of colored chalk to draw with. Go ahead, draw." Tamara turned the music on, playing a third melody.

After about five minutes, Tamara turned off the music.

"Wonderful. Notice that you have all drawn something on your paper. You now know how to turn soundwaves into something you can see. It doesn't matter that you all have a different interpretation. Tonight's class is about learning how to sense energy and translate it into something tangible."

"Tangible?" Jane asked. "What exactly does that mean?"

"Okay, Jane, tell me. Did you hear the music?"

"Yes."

"Did you pick up a piece of chalk and start to draw something?"

"Yes."

"Why?"

"What? Because you told me to."

"Yes, but I didn't tell you what to draw, just to draw. Your subconscious mind decided what to interpret the music into. That is tangible proof that you can interpret soundwaves, energy."

"Is there more to this exercise?" Jane asked.

"Yes, later, in another class, I will teach you how to read a person's energy by using this technique of aura art," Tamara said, answering Jane's question.

"Oh, I can't wait for that class," Betty said.

"This is aura art?" Jane asked.

"It is the first step on developing the technique of aura art. We must start with baby steps, Jane," Tamara said with a smile. "Okay, class, tell me what you have learned tonight. Let's start with you first, Betty."

"I learned that I could see the white halo of an aura and what the difference is between a real aura color and a complementary color."

"Great, and you, Tammy? What did you learn?"

"I learned to feel the music and then draw what I was feeling."

"Perfect. And how about you, Jane? What did you learn?"

"That I need more practice."

"Awesome! The more someone practices, the better they get. How about you, Karla?"

"I am not sure what I have learned. I need time to think about it. Please, ask me later."

"No problem. How about you, Kate? What did you learn?"

"I learned that people have amazing energy pulsating around them, and as they change their thoughts, the colors change. Your auras are amazing. I can see them right now."

"That is wonderful, Kate. Oh ya, and to turn off seeing an aura, all you have to do is take a breath and imagine a light switch being turned off. I only see auras when I want to. They are not visible to me 24 / 7. How about you, Lexi? What did you learn?"

"That I am going to love this technique of coloring auras. Can I draw a plant's aura or an animal?"

"Yes, every living thing produces an aura of some type," Tamara said.

Karla asked, "Tamara, when did you see your first aura?"

"It was a long time ago when I was at a weekend women's retreat. I wasn't into this stuff yet. It was Saturday night, and we had been taking in lectures all day. I was tired since it was past my usual bedtime. We were gathered into one room listening to a singer. She had an amazing voice, so soothing and calm.

"As I listened, I was mesmerized by this beautiful pink fire that danced around her like a silhouette. It was as if pink flames radiated around her whole body.

"I knew I was hallucinating because I was so tired, but I didn't care because it was so beautiful to watch.

"When she was done singing, and I had stood up to leave, someone in the front row called out, 'You have the most beautiful pink aura.' Shocked that someone had seen what I had, I ran after the lady who said it. When I caught up to her, I said, 'You saw the pink light around her?' She answered yes. Still in shock, I asked her what it was. She said an 'aura' and walked away, looking at me like I was crazy.

"I still remember how shocked I was seeing my first aura."

"What an amazing story, Tamara. Do you still see auras like that one?" Lexi asked.

"No, I haven't seen one like the singer's again. Now, a lot of the time, the aura colors are in my head where I can imagine them, not see them for real. Either way, though, I am still sensing an aura but using a different channel to interpret the energy. When it is in my head, I am using the Knower channel instead of Visual."

"Good to know," Lexi said.

"Night, everyone. I have two more classes I would like to teach you on sensing energy. Does next Thursday work for everyone?"

It did.

"See you all next week. Practice seeing auras."

Chapter 82

A week went by fast, and Lexi was excited about learning more about sensing energy. She was just wondering what they would learn in class tonight when Edward called.

"Hi, Alexandra, I've missed you. How are you doing?

"Good, thanks, it is nice to hear your voice. I've missed you too."

"I'm sorry that I haven't been able to call much. They have us so busy learning these new cadaver techniques."

"Oh, how nice," Lexi said sarcastically. "That's okay, I understand."

"Do you have time to talk right now?"

"Actually, no. I am just pulling up to Tamara's. She is teaching us techniques on how to sense energy and interpret it."

"Man, I wish I could be there. That sounds interesting."

"Don't worry. I'll show you everything I've learned when you get home. When are you coming home?"

"Actually, that is part of why I'm calling. I have to stay for another week."

"What, why?"

"One of the ministers is going to be teaching about angels, and I really want to hear what he has to say."

"That does sound interesting. I can't wait until you get home to tell me all about it. I love you."

"You too, Alexandra. Night," Edward said as he made a kissing sound.

"Night, Edward," Lexi said as she ended the call and got out of her car.

As she walked up to Tamara's, Susannah said, *"Hey, Lexi, you are going to love tonight's class."*

"Oh, my God, you scared me. Don't sneak up on me like that," Lexi said out loud.

"Sorry, but tonight, you are going to learn how to really communicate with spirits."

"Oh, that does sound exciting."

"Who are you talking to?" Jane asked as she was now behind Lexi, walking up to Tamara's.

"Oh, my. Now you scared me. Ah, I was talking to my..."

"She was talking to her sister. Can't you see her? She is right there," Kate said as she caught up to them.

"You can see her sister?" Tammy asked as she started to walk up the stairs to the front door. She had come with Jane.

"Wow, Kate, I wish I could see her. I only hear her in my head," Lexi said.

The ladies went into Tamara's house together.

"Hi, everyone, have a seat. Tonight, we have a lot to learn. Hi, Susannah. Nice of you to join us."

"You can see her too?" Lexi asked Tamara.

"No. Tonight, I can feel her here. Okay, everyone, now that you are comfy, stand up and shake the day's energy off into a cosmic garbage can. I want you to walk around the room and notice what it feels like."

Everyone did as Tamara had asked and walked around the living room.

"Great, now as you take your next step, I want you to imagine that your feet have thick roots that go deep into the ground. Now, walk around the room."

Lexi started to laugh as her feet were heavy as bricks, and she was having a hard time picking up her feet to walk.

"Great, now shake that off and imagine that you are as light as a feather. Now, walk."

Again, the ladies did as they were instructed.

"Wow, that is cool," Kate said as she walked like she was lighter than air, making her arms raise.

Lexi said, "I feel like I could be blown away in the wind."

"Me too," Jane agreed.

"Great, now shake that feeling off, and then partner up."

The six ladies partnered up. Lexi was with Jane, Tammy with Betty, and Karla with Kate.

"Shake yourselves back to normal. Now pick who is going to be the 'A' partner and who is going to be the 'B' partner."

Lexi was the "B" partner, and Jane was the "A" partner.

"Now the 'A' partners, I want you to push your partner on their right shoulder. Not too hard. Feel how they move."

Jane pushed Lexi's shoulder, and it moved backward, but her body stayed where it was.

"Good. Now, Bs, I want you to think that your feet have roots again going deep into the ground." Tamara waited a moment, then said, "Okay. As, push on their right shoulder now."

This time when Jane pushed, Lexi didn't even flinch. She was solid as a rock. Jane tried again, and still, Lexi didn't budge.

"Great. Now, Bs, shake that off, and this time I want you to think that you are light as a feather." Tamara waited another moment, then said, "Okay. As, very lightly push on their right shoulder. BUT make sure they don't fall over."

Jane pushed on Lexi's shoulder and had to catch her quickly as she almost fell backward.

"Holy cow, I barely touched her, and she went flying," Jane said to the group. "Crazy."

"Okay, B ladies, now shake that off and switch. Bs will do the touching this time." Tamara repeated the exercise.

"Wow! That is amazing," Lexi said as she touched Jane's shoulder a couple of times to test each motion. "Now I know why they say, careful what you think. Who knew it was true?"

"So, true," Tamara said. "Okay, ladies, have a seat at the table."

"That was really fascinating, Tamara," Kate said. "I liked this example of what we think we create."

Tamara nodded, acknowledging what Kate had said, and passed out a blank piece of paper and a pen to each of the girls. "Okay, in this exercise, I would like you to draw your hand."

Tamara demonstrated on her own piece of paper. "Start at one side of your wrist and go around all the fingers and back down to the other side of your wrist."

It reminded Lexi of drawing a turkey when she was in elementary school.

"Now, I want you to draw a plus sign above the middle finger, a minus sign above the pointer finger, and lastly, put a circle with a line through it above the thumb.

"The middle finger is positive energy, the pointer is negative energy, and the thumb represents neutral energy." Tamara waited until they all had written the symbols on their drawings.

"Great, now on the piece of paper, write 'yes' above your middle finger, 'no' above the pointer finger, and 'maybe' above your thumb." Again, she waited. "Good."

Next, Tamara passed out a pendulum to each of the ladies.

Lexi looked at the rose quartz crystal that was dangling from a ten-inch chain. As she looked at the other ladies' pendulums, she noticed theirs were different, some had a wooden design hanging from their chain, and others had metal.

"Does it matter what is hanging from the chain?" Lexi asked.

"Not usually, as long as there is some kind of a weighted object hanging from the chain, it wouldn't matter if it was plastic. For tonight's demonstration, it doesn't matter. I am going to teach you how to get an answer using the pendulum."

Betty clapped her hands, and her pendulum bounced around crazily.

Tamara smiled at Betty's enthusiasm. "Hold your pendulum between your thumb, pointer, and middle finger. I want you always to have these three fingers holding the pendulum. That way, you are never controlling the positive or negative energy."

"But I can hold it with two fingers," Lexi said, demonstrating.

"Yes, but depending on which two fingers you are holding the pendulum with, you are contributing energy to a 'yes' or 'no' answer. If you hold all three, you will always have a neutral charge."

Karla asked, "Why does that matter?"

"You always want to be neutral, so the answer comes out honestly and without you influencing it."

"Makes sense."

"Next, put your elbow on the table and let the pendulum hang. Make sure you are holding the chain so that the pendulum isn't touching the table or holding it too high. The pendulum should swing easily. Also, make sure you have the excess chain out of the way. I ball it up in my hand, holding it with my remaining two fingers."

The ladies practiced what Tamara had instructed.

"Great, now hold your hand back down over your drawing, and have the pendulum hang above your middle finger, not touching it. Adjust the chain if need be. The pendulum should swing freely."

Tamara watched as everyone placed the pendulum into position. "Okay, now say to yourself, show me a 'yes' answer. Allow the pendulum to move in any direction it wants.

"Great, now hold it over the pointer finger and say, show me a 'no' answer. Then over the thumb saying, show me a 'maybe' answer." Tamara kept watching.

Tamara demonstrated the moves that happened when she used a pendulum. "I get a straight line over the middle finger, a circle over my pointer, and the pendulum stops dead over my thumb. You are programming a 'yes,' 'no,' or 'maybe' motion into your subconscious mind. Now, practice over each of the three digits until the same motions are consistent."

"I am getting a straight line for both of my fingers," Lexi said.

Tamara watched. "Yes, but notice that over your pointer, it is moving sideways, and over your middle, it is moving forward and back. That counts as two different actions."

Tamara looked up to the group and said, "Some of you might have a clockwise movement and the others a counter-clockwise movement. That is also okay. Now, practice a bit more."

Tamara waited a few minutes until everyone looked like they had definite movements to each finger.

"You are now ready to ask your first question. Move your paper aside and hold the pendulum with your elbow down on the table. This gives you support and less movement. We wouldn't want someone to think that you are cheating by moving it intentionally.

"Let's start with your name. Say, is my name, say your name. Take a breath and allow the pendulum to move." Tamara watched everyone.

"Mine is saying no to my name," Lexi said.

"Try using your full first name, Alexandra."

"Oh, my God, it's moving on its own."

"Lexi, it is not moving on its own. Your subconscious mind is moving it." Speaking now to the group, Tamara said, "Your subconscious mind controls your breathing, your heartbeat, and the manufacturing of your cells. You do not get a heads-up when your body tells it to function, so you are not going to get a heads-up when your subconscious mind moves your pendulum."

"No matter what is moving it, it's weird," Lexi said, amazed at the movement of the pendulum.

"Hey, Tamara, mine is also not working, and I don't have another first name," Kate said.

"Say in this lifetime."

"Yep, that works."

"Now, everyone, try a man's name. Ask, is my name Ted?"

"Mine said yes," Betty said.

"Say in this lifetime."

"Weird, now it is 'no,'" Betty confirmed.

"My pendulum is not moving," Tammy complained.

"Tammy, try this." Tamara held up her hands to her own chest and said, "Rub these two spots just below your collar bone. You should feel two little indentations. These points are actually real points on the kidney meridian, point twenty-seven, also called K27. Tammy, if that doesn't work, get a drink of water, and if that doesn't work, go pee. Actually, I think it is a good time for a bathroom break."

Lexi kept practicing with the pendulum. *Amazing, just amazing.*

Once everyone was back, Tamara said, "A pendulum is an incredible tool to use to get answers. Now, you have a couple of ways in which to receive an answer from Spirit. A pendulum is great for a 'yes' or 'no' answer for those of you who use the Feeler channel. You can also trust your gut to give you an answer, depending on whether it feels good or bad. For those of you who are Visual channels, seeing a person's aura or getting answers in your dreams works as well as the pendulum."

"What about us, Audios?" Jane asked. "How can we get answers?"

"Or us, Knowers?" Karla asked.

"We are going to practice those channels next week. Is it okay for everyone to meet here again next Thursday?"

Everyone could.

"Perfect. Now let's practice what we have learned so far. Remember, be specific and literal in your questions. A pendulum can only answer 'yes,' 'no,' and 'maybe.'"

"Next week, please bring a piece of jewelry and a photo with one adult in it where you can see their eyes. Night everyone, see you next week."

Chapter 83

Lexi was sitting down on the couch at Tamara's, thinking how fast that week had gone by when Kate came up and said, "Susannah sure likes following you around."

A little surprised that her sister was with her since she couldn't sense Susannah herself, Lexi said, "Hi, Kate. Well, I guess as one of my guardian angels, it must be part of her job to be with me always."

"Don't you ever get tired of having spirits following you around?"

"That's a funny question. I never thought about it. Usually, I never even notice that she is there until she says something."

"It must be nice to be able to turn it off. I can tell that there are always spirits following me around. I never seem to get any privacy."

"Have you asked Tamara about that? Maybe she has a solution."

"Hmm, I guess it has crossed my mind to ask her, but I am afraid that they might go away and never come back, and I don't want that either."

"I am sure you will figure something out," Lexi said just as Tamara was ready to talk.

"Tonight, we are going to learn how to do automatic writing. Jane, you will be happy to know that this technique is using the Audio channel."

"Yeah," Jane said enthusiastically and clapped her hands as Betty had in the past.

"Take three deep breaths and try to clear your mind. Shake the day's energy off and rub your K27 points. Doing any of these actions will tell your subconscious mind that you are switching into the intuitive energy."

Everyone did as Tamara had instructed.

Tamara passed out a few pieces of blank paper and a pen to each of the ladies. "Automatic writing is a method to get an answer or message that is more than just a 'yes' or 'no.' With this technique, you can receive full sentences and many times paragraphs of information."

Jane was ecstatic that she was going to learn how to communicate her way.

"Before we think of a question that you want to have answered, we are going to try an easy question. At the top of your page, write down, 'What makes the sky blue?'

"After you write out the question, take a deep breath while you are thinking about what makes the sky blue…"

Betty interrupted by saying, "We sure have to take a lot of breaths."

Tamara answered by saying, "Yes, your breath is what shifts your subconscious mind to use the part of your brain that controls your sixth sense, your intuitive ability." She then continued with what she was saying prior, "Once you have written out the question, take a deep breath to switch your intent, and rewrite the question. After that, it is time just to let your hand continue writing whatever information comes to you. Don't judge your spelling or what the sentence structure is like. Just write."

Tamara gave the ladies about five minutes to complete the exercise.

Lexi read to herself what she had written. *It is made up of blue light and laughed.* It made sense but only to a kindergartener. Lexi tried a couple more of the questions that Tamara asked them to try.

After a bit of laughter from the ladies reading their answers, Tamara said, "Now, try a question that you want to know the answer to."

Lexi had fun practicing this method of receiving answers. Some made sense. Many seemed encrypted or above her comprehension. She couldn't get a straight answer to her question.

"Great, put that aside. Next, I am going to teach psychometry. It is another way to receive answers. There are three ways to sense the energy, using a piece of jewelry—great for the Feelers, a photo—great for the Visuals, and a written name—great for the Audios. Knowers, you all have a second channel that you use, and it will be one of these three. Or you might get information that you do not see, feel, or hear, but you just know the answer.

"Okay, everyone, without showing each other, I want you to bring out the piece of jewelry and the photo you brought and secretly give them to me."

Tamara brought a bowl around, holding it higher than eye level, and had everyone put their items into it. She then separated the jewelry from the photos.

"We are going to start with the jewelry. What I want you to do is this… after you have randomly chosen a piece of jewelry that you didn't bring, I want you to hold onto it without looking at it. Then, I want you to write on a piece of paper whatever comes to your mind. No matter how silly or stupid it may seem. After that, I will be asking you some questions to answer."

Tamara held out the bowl to each lady to choose a piece of jewelry without looking at it.

Lexi chose a piece, shut her eyes for a second, then instantly started to write.

After everyone stopped writing, Tamara asked these new questions, "The person whom this piece of jewelry belongs to, are they a male or female?" She let them write down the answer, then asked, "What age are they, approximately?

"What color of hair do they have? Trust the first thing you sense and write it down. Don't second-guess yourself.

"How tall are they?

"What is their favorite color?

"How many children do they have?

"What do they do, or what did they do for a living?

"Are they married?

"Are they alive?

"Where do or did they live?"

Lexi kept writing down the first answer that popped into her head, trying not to judge what was coming.

After everyone had written down their answers, Tamara asked each lady to show what piece of jewelry they had and repeated the questions to hear each of their answers.

Lexi found out that she had a ring that belonged to Betty's grandmother and was happy that her answers were mostly correct.

"Ladies, what you want to do is practice until you are receiving above ninety-five percent accuracy," Tamara said. "One hundred percent is the real goal, though."

Lexi figured out that her average had only an eighty-five percent accuracy. *I guess I need more practice.*

To make sure the ladies couldn't see who was in the photo, Tamara passed them out face down. "Okay, close your eyes. This time, sense the energy coming from the photo for the answers. Keep the photo face down. When you want to write, open your eyes and write the first answer that comes to your mind." Tamara asked everyone the same questions as she had with the jewelry.

"Now, turn the photo over and show us who you have."

Lexi had Karla's sister and was disappointed that her accuracy went down to fifty percent.

Seeing the disappointed faces, Tamara said, "At this point of the game, don't worry about your accuracy. Chances are you are over-analyzing your answers before writing them down.

"Give the photo and your info to the owner of the photo. Your accuracy may be as simple as asking these questions to the person in the photo and see how correct you really were."

Tamara passed out a small piece of paper to each of the ladies and said, "Sign your name and fold the paper in half."

Taking all the papers back, Tamara folded them one more time and then passed one back to each lady, saying, "Don't look, and yes, it might be your own."

Tamara had the ladies hold the folded piece of paper in one hand while writing their answers with the other. She asked all the same questions as she had before.

When they were allowed to look, Lexi was surprised that she had Tamara's. Her accuracy went down to twenty percent.

When Tamara found out, she said, "Lexi, you are overthinking this. You didn't know that I threw my signature into the mix. You were counting on guessing between the six of you. It is important to clear your mind and not care what answer you get, even if that means being wrong. You must let go and let the person's energy come through. That is the only way you will have a hundred percent accuracy. You have to pretend, pardon my French, that it is all a 'bullshit' story that you are making up. The harder you try, the less accurate you will be."

Tamara took the signatures back and had them try again.

This time Lexi was ninety percent accurate.

The rest of the evening, they practiced what they had learned so far in the last three classes.

Tamara ended the class with, "See y'all next week."

Chapter 84

Lexi was excited that Edward had come back home. She had explained to him everything that Tamara had taught. She loved teaching what she learned; it helped her to solidify her knowledge.

Together they went to Tamara's last class.

Everyone said hi and gave hugs to Edward as they came in. Lexi felt a little left out. She never got hugs like that.

"Jealous much, Alexandra?" Edward whispered.

"Yes. You would be too if it happened to you," Lexi said as she tried not to be jealous.

"Welcome back Edward. It is nice to see you," Tamara said, smiling at Lexi. *I wonder if she knows how deeply in love she really is with him.* "Okay, class, tonight you are going to learn how to astral-travel to receive answers."

Edward started to wonder if he should have shown up tonight. *Now, what am I getting myself into?*

"Get yourselves comfy, and take a few deep breaths. In a moment, I am going to ask you to imagine an animal, any animal anywhere in the world."

Ah, well, even I can do that, Edward thought to himself as he closed his eyes and took a few deep breaths.

Lexi took three deep breaths and shut her eyes, imagining a black panther. She couldn't remember where they came from in the world, so she imagined one in the Bronx Zoo. She had seen it last year when she went on a tour with Susannah.

"Nod if you all have an animal that you are thinking about," Tamara said as she was waiting to see the nods.

Everyone nodded.

"Great, now imagine that you are the size of a pea in the center of your head. You are going to teleport out of your body using your crown chakra, the baby soft spot. You are going to teleport into the animal's crown chakra. Make sure you go into the animal backward, so you are able to look out of his or her eyes."

Tamara waited a few moments then said, "Now, imagine what it feels like to be your animal. How do they walk?

"How do they eat?

"How do they sleep?

"What are they thinking?

"Add any other interesting questions that you want answered about them. When you are finished asking your questions, write them down on the piece of paper that I have sitting beside you."

Tamara had handed out blank paper and a pen to everyone while she had been talking. She waited for everyone to stop talking before asking each person what they were and their answers. She loved this part, hearing all their experiences.

Lexi had shared her dream of being a black panther and told everyone, "I had this weird thought that as the black panther, I escaped the zoo, and was leaping from chestnut tree to chestnut tree. I even imagined that I was eating people's lunches. And then I had wandered into a garden and then splashed into the Bronx River. I remember that I shook myself off and went into the trees, never to be seen again."

"Lexi, that really happened," Edward said matter-of-factly.

"What, no. It was my crazy imagination," Lexi said, trying not to create too much of a fuss.

"No, really. Tamara, it happened, but back in the early 1900s at the Bronx Zoo," Edward said, amazed that Lexi described the exact details.

"You must have read about it, Lexi," Jane said.

"No, I don't remember ever knowing that story," Lexi said, trying to defend herself.

"This happens all the time. When a person astral-travels, time does not matter. Unless you specify a time in history, you could end up anywhere on the timeline. Lexi, when you went into the meditation, did you say today or have any reference that you meant today?"

"No. You didn't say I had to."

"Fascinating. Class, it just proves to you that astral-travel can happen."

Edward patted Lexi's leg and said, "Good job."

Lexi smiled back, not believing what just happened. *I am going to have to google if this story is real.*

Tamara continued with the class by saying, "This time, you are going to astral-travel to a monastery in Tibet, the Potala Palace. Take a deep breath and just say to yourself, Potala Palace in Tibet, and let yourself teleport there. Write down whatever you sense."

Lexi was scared to astral-travel again, but she wrote down the word "fortress" anyway. Then she wrote down that she saw people praying, but they were wearing normal clothes. She didn't see it high up in a mountain but on top of a large hill. Starting to analyze her answers and not wanting to be wrong, nothing else came. Her mind went blank.

After everyone had stopped writing, Lexi found out that she was actually quite accurate.

The Potala Palace was a thirteen-story building, built approximately nine-hundred and eighty feet above sea level. It was the winter palace used by the Dalai Lamas and is now a museum.

That makes sense why I saw people wearing normal clothes, Lexi thought to herself.

Next, Tamara said, "This time, teleport yourself to Russia, to Yekaterinburg. What makes this place important? Then write down whatever comes to your mind."

Lexi had trouble with this one. She didn't know how to spell the name and wasn't sure she had gotten to the right place.

Tamara noticed that Lexi wasn't writing anything down and said," Lexi, is there a problem?"

"I don't know how to spell it."

Tamara gave a bit of a chuckle. "I see, well, ask your spirit guides to help you teleport to Yekaterinburg. They don't need to know the spelling."

"Good idea. I will try that." Lexi closed her eyes again and asked Susannah, *"Hey, sis, do you know where Yekaterinburg is? I need to teleport there, and I need some help."*

"Take a breath, Lexi, and I will get you a ride with someone who knows the way."

A second went by, and then Susannah said, *"Lex, here is your ride. You remember Phantachus?"*

How could Lexi forget Archangel Michael's winged horse? *"Hi, oh my, I am so sorry to have bothered you, I didn't mean..."*

"Lexi, just get on. You are wasting time," Susannah said.

Instantly, Lexi was flying above what seemed to be a city. An industrial city in the Ural Mountains. *"Phantachus, I am supposed to find out what makes this place important. Can you please show me what Tamara is thinking?"*

A moment later, Phantachus was flying above a scene of a man and his family being executed.

"Thank you," Lexi thought to Phantachus. *"That should be enough. You can take me back to where you found me."* The next thing she knew, she was opening her eyes, in Tamara's house.

"Oh, my God, now that was cool!" Lexi said after she saw that everyone had finished writing.

"What did you see, Lexi?" Tamara asked.

"Phantachus came and helped me with this one. I saw a man and his family being executed."

"Hey, that's cheating, getting help," Karla said.

"No. There is no such thing as cheating in the spiritual world. Just other ideas," Tamara said.

Lexi asked, "So, did I see anything of importance?"

"You will have to google and see," Tamara said.

"Really? That is your answer? I have to google it?" Lexi said, disappointed.

"If I tell you, then you won't learn the real lesson."

"What is the lesson?" Edward asked.

"To use your skills and practice using the Knower channel and traits."

"I don't get it," Edward said, confused.

Karla piped up and said, "I do. One of the traits of a Knower is to do research."

"Yep, Karla, you are absolutely right. A Knower needs to know the truth about something, and even if I told you the answer, a Knower would go and look up what I told them."

"Interesting, so, what you are trying to tell me, is that to develop each of the channels, I must mimic the traits of each channel?"

"Yes, exactly. An Audio reads and listens, a Visual dreams and sees things, a Feeler feels and trusts their gut instinct, and a Knower needs time and the ability to research the facts."

The rest of the night, the group practiced what they had learned.

#

That night when Lexi got home, she googled "Yekaterinburg in Russia" and found out that was where Tsar Nicholas, the last tsar of Russia, and his family were executed in 1918 during the Russian Revolution.

Chapter 85

The following Thursday was Lexi's birthday, May twenty-eighth. Her mom had invited her and Edward to come and celebrate at her house in Dyker Heights, Brooklyn.

As Edward drove up to the house, Lexi felt overwhelmed by Susannah's death. Lexi was now the same age as when Susannah died. "I can't imagine dying at the age of thirty-five. There is so much more I want to see, do, feel, and learn."

As Edward pulled into the driveway, he asked," Wow, what brought that on?"

"I was just thinking about Susannah."

"Miss Constantine, you have a lifetime of experiences to enjoy with me, so don't worry about dying, worry about living."

"He is right, you know. If you have to worry about something, worry about what the spirit

world has in store for you next," Susannah said to Lexi.

"Great! Now my sister has me worrying about what the spirit world has in store for me," Lexi said to Edward just before she knocked on the door and let them in. "I wonder what she meant."

"I'm in the kitchen!" Olivia, Lexi's mom, yelled.

Not knowing what to say to Lexi, as Edward entered the kitchen, he said, "Oh, that smells good, Mrs. Constantine."

"It does, mom," Lexi said as she came over and gave her a hug.

"Well, it wouldn't be a birthday without your favorites," Olivia said as she leaned her head against Lexi's since her hands were dirty from cooking.

"How have you been, mom?"

"Pretty good. You remember Mrs. Peterson?"

"Ya, the lady who lived next door and died about ten years ago."

"Well, Mr. Peterson has been coming over quite a lot lately. I'm not sure if he is hitting on me."

"Well, you are a catch, Mrs. C. I think any man would be crazy not to want you," Edward said endearingly.

"Oh, Edward, you always know what to say to make a girl's heart flutter," Olivia said, as her face went a shade redder.

"Edward, you are making my mom blush."

Edward winked at Olivia.

"Here, you two love birds, help me set the table."

Once Olivia had everything on the table, she sat down and asked Edward to say grace.

Dinner was all of Lexi's favorites: chicken, ribs, cob salad, mashed potatoes, and an angel food cake for dessert.

After supper, when Lexi had blown out her candles and made a wish, her mom then asked, "So, when is the big day?"

Lexi looked at Edward and explained, "Sorry, my mom is a little blunt and excited for us to get married, so she can start bugging us about babies."

"Babies, wow, I never thought that far in the future," Edward said. *Hmm, babies.*

"Well, what date have you two picked?"

"Mom. We haven't discussed it yet."

"What? Why not?"

Looking at Edward, Lexi said, "We've been busy, I guess." Lexi thought back to the last couple of months: Peru, Sweden, and Tamara's classes. *Yep, busy.*

"Well, pick a date tonight, so I can start preparing. I'm not getting any younger, you know," Olivia said honestly.

Olivia went and got her calendar. "It should be about a year from when you got engaged. That will make it sometime in… Well, June is a beautiful time of the year. What date in June do you two want?"

Lexi looked at Edward and shrugged.

Edward looked at the calendar and said, "How about June twenty-sixth? That was my parents' anniversary."

"No. I don't want our anniversary to be on the same day as someone else's."

"Well, it will be on somebody's," Edward said sarcastically. "How about July tenth?"

"Why that date?"

"Well, I don't know anyone with a birthday or any other celebration on that day. Do either of you?"

Both ladies answered no.

"Perfect. July tenth it is," Edward said as he kissed Lexi on the cheek and winked at Olivia.

Olivia started to cry.

"What? Why are you crying, mom? I thought you would be happy that we picked a date," Lexi said.

"I am happy. I just wish your father and Susannah could be here to see you two get married, that's all."

"Don't worry, mom. They will be."

Olivia looked at her daughter strangely and changed the subject.

Chapter 86

*T*amara had been getting some headaches, which was unusual for her. *All I need is to get away and go on a little vacation with Greg. I must be working too hard.* She decided the best medicine would be to go somewhere where she could get pampered.

The following weekend, they headed about two hours south to Sea Girt, New Jersey. She had booked them into a grand Victorian seaside inn that dated back to the late 1800s.

As they drove up, there were two spacious guest houses. Both were framed by wrap-around verandas on the first level, and their windows were dressed in handsome green and white awnings. Tamara instantly noticed the wicker chairs and rockers for the guests to enjoy.

Upon registering, the innkeeper said, "The ocean is just a block in that direction, but the pool is open from 9 AM to 10 PM. Make sure that you don't miss our gourmet breakfast. It is scrumptious. It is served in our elegant dining room, between eight and ten each morning."

Tamara and Greg were given their keys to a quaint room on the second floor of the main house. Entering, Tamara went directly out onto the private balcony where she had seen the rocking chairs. Looking at the panoramic view—east to the Atlantic, north toward Spring Lake, and west for what Tamara saw would make gloriously romantic sunsets. She knew she had made the right decision to come here.

After settling in, Tamara and Greg went out to explore the area. Walking down the Jersey Shore boardwalk, Tamara noticed a person doing tarot-card readings and pulled Greg over to see.

"Hey, Tamara, knock yourself out and indulge in a reading," Greg teased her.

The sign on the purple velvet tablecloth read, "Gypsy Readings $10". *What the heck,* Tamara thought to herself and sat down. Before taking Tamara's money, the young lady directed in a thick dialect of Romani, "Give me your hand."

The young lady proceeded to look at Tamara's palm, and suddenly she let go. Startled, the young lady said, "Leave, I can't read you. You are cursed."

Looking at her own hand, Tamara said, "What do you mean? I am cursed?"

The young lady looked at her and said something in Romani, gathered her tablecloth and everything it was holding, and ran away. Looking back at Tamara, she kissed a pendant hanging from her neck.

Greg had quickly come over from where he was watching and said, "What was all that about?" as he was looking at the young lady running through the sand toward town.

"I don't know. She took one look at my hand and let go. She let it go as if it was diseased. She said I was cursed."

Tamara looked at her hand again.

"How weird, you of all people would know if you were cursed. Wouldn't you?" Greg asked, now not sure.

"Let's go. I am sure it is nothing." Tamara got up and put her arm through Greg's, and walked back along the boardwalk. Tamara quickly looked back to where the gypsy had been sitting and thought to herself, *Weird.* Trying to lighten up the mood, she said, "At least she didn't charge me."

Greg patted her arm and gave her a kiss on the cheek. "I am sure she is an amateur, and your power just scared her."

Deciding not to think any more of it, Tamara had a marvelous time the rest of the weekend by being pampered in the B&B's spa with a relaxing massage, followed by a pedicure, and two romantic evenings, being wined and dined by Greg.

On the drive home, Tamara couldn't help but think back to the gypsy.

Chapter 87

Tamara's headache turned into a migraine, which put her in bed with the lights off for two days.

Lexi happened to stop by just as Greg was leaving Tamara's. "Hi, Greg. Is Tamara home?"

"She is, but she has a killer headache, which is odd because she never gets headaches."

"Oh, that sounds horrible. Can I go in and see her?"

"I guess, but be warned. She might kick you out."

"Okay, I'll take my chances," Lexi said as she moved past Greg and went inside.

Lexi quietly went into the bedroom and whispered, "Tamara, it's me, Lex. I'm going to get you a cool cloth to put on the back of your neck."

Lexi didn't wait for an answer. She just went into the bathroom and got a cloth. Coming back, she lightly turned Tamara's head and started to massage the back of her neck. Instead of her neck, she applied the cool cloth to her forehead.

Tamara could see the most vivid yet bizarre aura around Lexi and thought she was hallucinating. "Lexi, I don't know what is going on with me. I was fine just a week ago, but now this headache is pounding, and everything is so bright and loud."

Lexi didn't know how to help. In desperation, she called down Susannah and asked for help.

"Lexi, I can't help without her permission."

"Tamara, do I have your permission to ask Susannah for help?"

At this point, she felt desperate to have the pain stop. Barely a whisper, but Tamara said, "Sure, I give you and her my permission."

"Lexi, she is cursed. Somehow, somewhere, she was cursed."

"Susannah says that you have a curse on you," Lexi said, not believing that anyone would curse Tamara.

Tamara tried sitting up in bed. "What the?" That is the second time I have been told that."

"Really? Who else told you?"

"A gypsy, in Sea Girt."

"Oh, my. So, what do I do? How can I help?"

"Good question." Tamara lay back down. "Lex, can you please go and make me a chamomile tea?"

"Sure thing."

Lexi got up and went into the kitchen.

"She needs an amulet to protect her and a reversal spell."

"A what?"

"Did you say something, Lex?" Tamara called out from the bedroom.

"Sorry, no. I was just talking to Susannah. I'll be quieter."

Lexi placed the steamy tea on the bedside table. "Tamara, Susannah said you need an amulet and a reversal spell. Do you know what she is talking about?"

"Lex, I have some crystals in a wooden box sitting on a shelf in my office. You'll see it. It is beside the sparkling box that I brought to Edward's."

Lexi got up and walked into Tamara's office, turning on the light as she went in. Just as Tamara had said, sitting on the shelf was a plain wooden box beside the beautifully jeweled box that Tamara had brought when they had rescued Susannah. As Lexi lifted the wooden box off the shelf, a feather fell onto the floor. Lexi picked it up and brought it with her. Once back in the bedroom, Lexi gave the box to Tamara.

Instead of taking it, Tamara said, "Lexi, open the box and set your intent on an item that can protect and help me, and then put your hand in and pull something out."

Lexi opened the box, and inside were all kinds of crystals, stones, feathers, sage, and odd-looking pieces of jewelry. Intuitively, Lexi knew that the feather she found had something to do with this curse. Thinking it could help, Lexi passed it to Tamara, saying, "Tamara, this wasn't in the box but fell out when I took it off the shelf."

Tamara shrieked and dropped it.

"What, what is it?"

"Lexi, look under my bed!"

Lexi looked under Tamara's bed and pulled out a piece of rope tied with many knots. Inserted into the knots were similar black feathers to the one she had found. "What is this?"

"It is a witch's garland, or some people call it a witch ladder."

"A witch's what? Why is it here?"

"That is a good question. Well, at least we found the curse."

"How could this thing be a curse?"

"The feathers are plucked from a live black hen, and one by one, the feathers are inserted into each knot. As each knot is tied in the cord, the maker of the witch ladder utters a malediction, more commonly known as a curse. Once the item is completed, it is placed under the victim's bed to cause ill fortune."

Lexi was mortified. "Who would want to do this to you, and how did they get it under your bed?"

"Those are both good questions. I hate to say it, but my guess is that one of the ladies from the class you were taking."

"Oh, my God. No. Who? No, I can't believe any of those women would want to hurt you."

"How do you know it was a woman?"

"What? Well, we both know it couldn't have been Edward. There is no way he would ever do something so sinful."

Tamara laughed. "Dang it, that hurts. Don't make me laugh, Lexi."

"Who do you suspect?" Lexi couldn't believe that any of them would do something so nasty.

"I don't know. I have a hard time believing it could be one of them as well, but I haven't had anyone else here."

"Okay, but now that you know that this was under your bed, is it enough to reverse the curse?" Lexi asked.

"It will help, but no, I will need to figure out who placed it under my bed. Lexi, please help me up. We need to go over to the fireplace."

Lexi helped Tamara over to the fireplace in her living room.

"Place the cursed rope into the fireplace, please, and sprinkle some of this on top." Tamara passed a glass container from on top of the fireplace to Lexi.

Lexi pulled the cork out of the top and sprinkled the water-looking substance onto the witch's ladder. "What is this?'

"Holy water."

"Oh."

"Now, light the paper under the rope in the fireplace and step back."

Lexi did as Tamara had instructed.

"I ask my angels and guides to remove the negative energy from me and my home and take it to a safer place."

Lexi watched the flames as the witch's ladder burned and turned into ash.

"What now?" Lexi asked.

"I will sweep the ashes up, but I will need to bury them in a graveyard. Maybe Edward won't mind burying them at his place."

Lexi took a deep breath in and said, "This should be interesting."

"Lexi, can you please go back into my bedroom and get the box?"

"Sure thing." Lexi quickly brought back the wooden box.

Tamara pulled out a necklace with what looked like an orange stone hanging from it.

"What kind of crystal is that?" Lexi asked.

"It isn't even a rock. It's actually petrified amber from the sap of a tree and is known by shamans to ward off demonic and negative energy. Until I can figure out who has a reason to put a curse on me, I will need to wear this."

Looking at the time, Lexi had to go but asked, "Anything else I can get for you?"

"No, you've been a huge help. I wouldn't have found the witch's ladder for months. I don't usually look under my bed. Hey, Lex, I think it would be a good idea to look under your bed. The ladies were at your place, too."

Chapter 88

"Hey, I've been thinking all night about who could have put the witch's garland under your bed."

"Hi, Lexi, that is sweet of you. I hope you haven't been worrying too much."

"Well, you know me. I love a good mystery."

"Right," Tamara said sarcastically but laughed.

"You must be feeling a bit better. I didn't hear you wince when you laughed," Lexi said.

"I am, thanks to you, but I am still wearing the amber to be on the safe side."

"Hey, Tamara, I know this may seem odd, but Edward and I would like you to come over to his place for two reasons. One, to bury the witch's garland, and two, to do a curse reversal. I know I don't know much, but I have been researching the subject, and I think I can do it."

Tamara smiled to herself. "Lex, that is very sweet of you. I would love to. What day are you thinking of doing the ritual?"

"Is tonight okay?"

Checking her schedule, Tamara said, "I could make it after seven if that works for you."

"Perfect, see you tonight at Edward's," Lexi said as she hung up.

Calling Edward, she left a message on his cell. "Tamara said that tonight would work. She will meet us at your place at seven. Love you. See you soon."

Lexi went back on the computer and looked up more information on curses. *Who knew the power of a word could have such an impact?*

#

Tamara showed up at Edward's with her beautiful box filled with goodies that Lexi might need, like incense, candles, sage for smudging, crystals, and feathers.

Opening the front door before Tamara was even on the first step, Lexi said, "Oh, my God, I can't believe how excited I am. Who would have guessed that all this weird woo-woo stuff excites me now?" Lexi met Tamara partway down the steps and slipped her arm into Tamara's as they walked back up together.

Once inside, they walked to the left and into the counseling room. The same room they had used a few times in the past for other spiritual rituals.

"Oh, by the way, I looked under my bed, and nothing was there. I guess my apartment is too small, and we would have noticed someone going into my bedroom," Lexi said, thinking back to the class held at her place.

"Good to know. So, what have you two come up with?" Tamara asked, curious what Lexi might have found.

"We have been thinking this over, and Edward and I have come up with a few ideas. First, you said that you had to know who cursed you. We were wondering why that matters."

"Sure, the words used in a curse are for a specific intention of malicious misfortune aimed at a person by the person speaking the words. Depending on which culture performed the curse, there will be a different reversal to the curse needed. The most common cultures that are typically known for curses are hoodoo, voodoo, Wicca, and any superstition used from a Pennsylvania Dutch, Mediterranean, or Middle Eastern person.

"If witchcraft was used as in Wicca, the curse would be created as a specific misfortune caused by a supernatural method like a spell or prayer.

"In the African American hoodoo practice of curses, they usually present using a jinx, crossed condition, or as a form of foot track magic, whereby cursed objects are laid in the paths of victims and activated when walked over.

"Now, in African voodoo, they use a doll and some of your hair to make the curse personal. That is why many people believe in never leaving discarded hair lying around freely.

"In the Middle Eastern and Mediterranean cultures, they believe in the evil eye. In order to protect you from the evil eye, a protection item can be made from dark blue glass cut in a circle, and drawn in the middle is a black dot with a circle of white around it, resembling a human eye.

"In the German culture, including the Pennsylvania Dutch, people spoke in terms of hexing. Years ago, a very common hex, usually said by a stable-witch, was causing milk cows to go dry and horses to go lame."

Edward said, "Well, none of the students in our class were African, Middle Eastern, or Mediterranean, so we can probably rule that kind of curse out."

"Hmm, let's see," Lexi said out loud as she was thinking about her classmates. "What nationality do you guys think everyone is?"

"I really don't want to believe that it could be any of them," Tamara said.

"Well, it was somebody," Edward said. "Are you sure that no one else was at your place?"

"No one else has been at my place. I've been too busy with teaching to see any clients."

Lexi started going through the ladies by saying, "Betty seems nice, but she isn't from one of the cultures you listed. She has a slight English accent. Tamara, it could be her. I was reading that the first witch's ladder was found in Somerset, England."

"No, it can't be her. I've known Betty for years."

"What about Kate? She might be into Wicca at her age?" Edward said.

"Her age? Edward, anyone can be Wiccan. No matter their age. Not to mention the fact that she hates sensing ghosts, so I don't think she would mess around with spells."

"Why would that matter?" Lexi asked.

"Spells used in black magic have a price, and Kate would have been able to sense the dark entities helping to create the spell. No, I don't think it was her."

"What about Karla? She was quite stand-offish?" Edward said.

"There is a difference between being rude and stand-offish. No, she is a Knower, and they tend to be stand-offish."

"Well, we know it wasn't Edward or me, that's for sure," Lexi said, defending her honor.

"Don't worry, Lex. I don't suspect either of you. We have been through too much together, and it couldn't be Isabella, because she was in Switzerland. Her alibi is tight, and she says hi to everyone."

Lexi laughed at the thought of Isabella cursing a piece of rope. Absolutely hilarious.

"That only leaves Jane and Tammy?" Lexi said. "I can't believe a person who lost her son and was grieving so badly could ever do something so horrible as curse someone. Why? What reason would she have to curse you? Tamara, you were only trying to help her," Lexi said, trying to defend Tammy. Thinking a moment longer, Lexi said, "Then that only leaves Jane. What do we know about her?"

"We know that Lancaster is an English name," Edward said, thinking about Somerset, England.

Frustrated with trying to figure out who did it, Lexi said, "Whatever, and no matter who did it, this is what I found on the internet that might help you, Tamara." Pulling out some papers, Lexi continued, "At dusk on a new moon, a person could draw themselves a bath with a cup or two of salt mixed in the water. They will need to submerge themselves at least once completely, and the bath should last at least ten minutes. During which you have to say this prayer, three times, 'In the names of my ancestors, past, present, and future, and my angels, I call upon thee, elementals of the Earth and Water, to come forth, and cleanse me of all evil and black magic. Restore my body, mind, and soul to optimum balance and health. By our wills combined, make it be. Amen.' Then immediately after the bath, you have to make sure to shower and wash every grain of salt off, carrying away with it any residue of the black magic."

"That could actually work," Tamara said. "I like that one. I will try it when I get home. What else do you have?"

Lexi looked down at the notes she had brought. "I was also studying Irish curses and folklore. Man, they were a wicked bunch, cursing anyone, even when there was no justification. As an example…" Lexi flipped through her papers and read what she had written. "A farmer from Limerick, Ireland cursed his landlord for evicting him by saying, 'May the curse of God alight on you and your family throughout their generations… may the curse of God's thunder and lightning fall heavily.' Crazy to know that someone can say something and cause misfortune, even when the person didn't deserve it."

"Words are powerful," Tamara said.

"I remember reading something years ago about Ireland's politicians and senior churchmen trying to suppress the foul habit of verbal cursing," Edward said.

"Well, we know it wasn't an Irish curse because we found the witch's garland under my bed, and the Irish didn't curse that way," Tamara said.

"Enough," Edward said. "Tonight, we are going to try it the religious way. Follow me and bring the garland."

Tamara took the bag of ashes and followed Lexi and Edward into the cemetery.

Edward had dug a small grave close to the statue of Archangel Michael in hopes that the saint knew what to do with the negative energy.

"This seems appropriate," Tamara said as she put the bag and all of its contents into the small grave.

Edward said a type of prayer, "In the name of the Father, the Son, and the Holy Ghost, I now break and release Tamara and any of her family or friends from this curse, or any and all evil words or prayers, idols, charms, vexes, hexes, psychic cords, witchcraft, enchantments, spells, jinxes, or potions that have ever been put upon any of them, as far back as fifty generations on both sides of their families. Through the power invested in me, I ask You, Heavenly Father, to allow Archangel Michael to remove them now and do with them as needed. Amen."

Edward made the sign of the cross, then poured holy water onto the bag and covered the bag and ashes with dirt.

"That was nice of you, Edward. Not allowing the energy of the curse to be received back by the person who cast it upon me."

"That would be unholy."

"Well, most reversal spells send it back to the original caster."

"Fascinating," Lexi said, listening to their conversation.

Going back inside, Tamara said, "Thanks to you, I feel so much lighter."

Chapter 89

Following her hunch, Lexi was in Edward's office researching the last name "Lancaster." As Edward passed by and saw Lexi working on his computer, he went in. Teasingly, he said, "Whatever you found must be good because I have been standing here for five minutes, and you haven't even noticed me."

The sound of his voice broke her focus. Lexi looked up and said, "What? Hey, no, you haven't, you just got here."

Edward came over and kissed her lightly on the forehead and laughed. "Seriously though, what are you researching?"

"I couldn't get Jane's last name out of my head after you said it was an English name. Listen to this." Lexi looked back at the computer and said, "There is a place in Pennsylvania called Lancaster County. Didn't Tamara say something about the Pennsylvania Dutch using curses?"

"Ya."

"Well, get this, all kinds of weird things have happened in Lancaster County. People claim that there are all kinds of buildings and houses that are haunted, even a brewery."

"Really?" Edward said as he sat down in one of the winged back chairs.

"This one is fascinating. It says that back in the late 1800s, three sisters lived in a small house atop Chiques Hill, which people in the town usually referred to as 'The Rock.' It was a common belief of the town's people that these three women practiced the black arts."

"What does this have to do with Jane?"

"I'm getting to that. There was a plan for the railroad company to build an amusement park on the west end of the ridge, atop 'The Rock,' overlooking the Susquehanna River. Their problem was that the sisters wouldn't sell.

"When the sisters were forced out of their home, they turned to the black arts for revenge and made a suicide pact. They cast a spell from 'The Sixth and Seventh Book of Moses. The curse was an affirmation that greed on the part of the new owners would certainly bring death on the said land.' It says that all kinds of misfortunes happened, and the trolley line was finally abandoned on April 25, 1932. It's believed that the sisters' black magic spell still curses the ground today."

"Again, what does that have to do with Jane?" Edward asked.

"Do you remember at Tamara's when we helped to release Jane's mom?"

"Of course, she was the spirit attached to the park chair."

"Yes. Well, I looked up her name, Teresa Jane Lancaster, and found that she was born in Lancaster County, Pennsylvania. Her mom was Dutch, and her dad was English."

"Really?"

"I know, right? So, it has to be Jane. She never married and goes by her maiden name."

"Why do you think it is Jane?"

"Because she was upset about having to let her mom go. I think she only did it because Kate said how rude it was holding onto her mom like that."

"Good point. Kate was pretty blunt about it. But why Tamara? Why not Kate?"

"My guess is because it was Tamara who made her mom go away, not Kate."

"But her mom was begging Tamara to let her go."

"I know that, and you know that, but tell that to a grieving daughter."

"I see your point. We'll have to tell Tamara what you found," Edward said, picking up the landline phone, dialing Tamara's number, putting it on speaker. He waited for Tamara.

Seeing the call display, Tamara said, "Hey, what did you find now?"

"If modern technology wasn't so advanced, I would have thought you were psychic," Edward called out, laughing.

"Funny, Edward."

"Hey, we know who did the curse!" Lexi said excitedly. "It was Jane. I did my research, and her mom was Pennsylvania Dutch. Her dad was English, and her motive was you making her mom leave."

"I had my suspicions. Thanks, Lex, for letting me know what you found. I can lay this curse thing to rest now."

Curious, Lexi asked, "What are you going to do about it?"

"To be honest, I don't have to do anything. The angels will look after this matter. All I need to do is break all connections with her and never have any contact with her ever again."

"That's it?" Edward questioned, not believing it could be that easy.

"Hey, don't sell yourself short. Edward, your reversal spell would put any demonic curse at bay. Thanks again. You were both such a big help. Who knew you two would become ghostbusters? Have a good night, you two."

"You too." Hanging up the phone, Lexi thought to herself, *Ghostbusters!*

Chapter 90

"Lexi, are you awake?" Susannah asked.

Edward had gone out of town again, and Lexi was sleeping in her own bedroom.

"Hey, Lexi, wake up. This is important."

Lexi lay in a deep sleep.

"Lexi?"

Nothing but snoring came out of Lexi's mouth.

Susannah switched from talking to making Lexi's phone ring.

That got Lexi's attention.

Fighting waking up from a beautiful dream about her and Edward lying on a beach in Hawaii, soaking up the sun while drinking a Mai Tai, Lexi looked at her phone. Nothing.

"Oh good, you're awake."

"Susannah, that is rude. I was having a marvelous dream about Edward and me enjoying our honeymoon. It was just getting to the good stuff. Really, Susannah, this better be important."

"It is."

Making a huffing sound, Lexi said, "So, what is so important that you had to wake me up?"

"Archangel Gabriel needs your help."

Still sleepy, Lexi said, "Is that all? You could have told me that in the morning. What? Who?" Lexi sat up. "Is this some kind of joke?"

"No, really, he needs you right now. Phantachus is here to take you."

Shaking her head in disbelief, Lexi said, "Why?"

"He has a message that you need to hear."

"Tamara's not here. I don't know how to ride Phantachus without her."

"Yes, you do. Lie back down and close your eyes and take three deep breaths."

"What happens if I can't?"

"Let me worry about that."

Lexi lay back down and covered up. She closed her eyes and asked God to help her. Taking three deep breaths, she thought of Phantachus.

Instantly he was there in her mind.

She imagined that she was on top of him, and instantly she was. *"Phantachus, you know where to take me. Please, take me to Archangel Gabriel."*

Within the blink of an eye, Lexi was sliding off Phantachus and walking up to a man. Saying a silent prayer hoping that he was Archangel Gabriel. Lexi bowed and said, "Your majesty."

"My angelic disciple, welcome and please have a seat. Thank you for your loyalty and trust in us. We grant you many thanks for helping us."

Lexi couldn't believe what she was hearing. Taking a seat, she continued to listen.

"Lexi, you will become a prophet."

"I think you have me mistaken with someone else. That is impossible. Only the holiest are true prophets, and the last one was Jesus."

"Nothing is impossible with God."

To be continued.

Book 3: Prophecy of a Soul...

The Author

Constance Santego is an author, artist, and retired holistic health and healing teacher. She is known for bridging the body, mind, and soul consciousness to help turn your dreams into reality.

Her passion is teaching self-empowerment through the many ways of improving yourself: emotionally, spiritually, mentally and physically.

MY GOAL
To provide information that motivates, inspires, and transforms enlightened souls. Doing this through the development of the nine spiritual gifts you were born with: Knowledge, Wisdom, Faith, Healing, Miracles, Prophecy, Distinguishing Spirits, and Tongues.

Also Available

Play the "Ikona" game and test
your Virtues and Sins.
For additional information on
Constance Santego's wide range of
Motivational Products, Spiritual Retreats,
Live Events and Educational Programs
Go to
www.ConstanceSantego.ca

Follow me on:
Instagram – Constance_Santego &
Facebook – constancesantegoo
YouTube – Constance Santego

Subscribe and receive free information &
meditations.

www.ingramcontent.com/pod-product-compliance
Lightning Source LLC
Chambersburg PA
CBHW050603170726

48283CB00001B/86